"PROPERTY OF FOLCROFT SANITARIUM"
HAD BEEN STAMPED ON THE SIDE OF THE
CHEAP MUG

"I can't tell you who runs it from the top,"
MacCleary said. "But I'm your boss. I promise
you terror for breakfast, pressure for lunch,
tension for supper and aggravation for sleep.
Your vacations are the two minutes you're not
looking over your shoulder for some hood to put
one in the back of your head. Your bonuses are
five minutes when you're not figuring out how
to kill someone or keep from getting killed.

"If you live six months, it'll be amazing. If you
live a year, it'll be a miracle. That's what we
have to offer you." MacCleary stopped dead,
resting his gleaming hook on the base of Remo's
bed. "What do you say?"

"You frame me?" Remo asked.

"Yeah," MacCleary answered without emotion.

"Good job," Remo said.

Created by Murphy & Sapir

THE DESTROYER™

THE END OF THE BEGINNING

MASTER'S LINE BOOK

A GOLD EAGLE BOOK FROM
WORLDWIDE®

TORONTO • NEW YORK • LONDON
AMSTERDAM • PARIS • SYDNEY • HAMBURG
STOCKHOLM • ATHENS • TOKYO • MILAN
MADRID • WARSAW • BUDAPEST • AUCKLAND

First edition July 2002

ISBN 0-373-63243-6

Special thanks and acknowledgment to
James Mullaney for his contribution to this work.

THE END OF THE BEGINNING

Excerpts from *Created, The Destroyer* used by permission.

Printed in U.S.A.

For the Sinanju Archives of Texas,
for the loan of a trashable copy of #1.
And for head archivist Dale Barkman,
for not wasting all our time trying to collect late fees
he knew he'd never see anyway.

Also for Pam, Sarah & Jake.

And for the Glorious House of Sinanju,
e-mail: housinan@aol.com

("Chiun's boards"—there, they made it in)

AUTHOR'S NOTE

This is not a retelling, reimagining, or re-anything of the first Destroyer adventure. Rather, this story takes place *around* the events of The Destroyer #1, *Created, The Destroyer* and the novella *The Day Remo Died*. Great pains were taken to not contradict already established Destroyer continuity. Even so, a few things were unavoidable, a few circles had to be squared (for instance, the author knows when state executions stopped in New Jersey, so no "gotchas," please).

This two-book miniseries can hopefully stand as bookends to the entire Destroyer series thus far. To see where you're going, it's sometimes good to take a look at where you've been.

—Jim Mullaney

I Will Give Them "Great Pains"
—a note from Chiun

Where am I going? I am going to be sick. I have never read such drivel.

Where have I been? More on that later.

When that first Destroyer abomination was foisted on an unsuspecting reading public 950 years ago (Was it less than that? Let me check my shame. No.) I made arrangements to be left nearly entirely out of the first volumes. I did not trust that the paper-wadders at that time would capture the me-ness of me, and what with movable type being only a few centuries old in the West, I assumed reading was just a passing fad to you people and that in no time you would be back to worshiping trees and trying to divine the future by pawing through animal entrails. But enough of those first two Destroyer books sold that I reconsidered my original decision. Better, I thought, to have a glimpse of wonderful me than to have none of me at all.

There is not the space here to get into how big a mistake *that* was. However, part of the agreement to include me in later books was that certain aspects of my original meeting with my dim pupil Remo Williams were not to become public. This was for one simple reason: They were none of your business.

Now, after all these years and a hundred solemn promises, they are in print for all the world to see. I blame the current scribbler; I blame the Destroyer creators; I blame the publisher, Gold Pigeon; and I blame Canadia—a country that I have yet to find on any real maps and which I am beginning to doubt exists at all.

So where have I been, you are still wondering? I will tell you where. To my lawyers, that is where. To force Tin Pigeon to recall this book.

In the meantime, since I still receive a small stipend no matter whether the books are read or not, I encourage you to buy as many copies of this volume as you can find and toss them in the fire. Buy one for a friend to burn. Do not read it, for what happens between these covers is Sinanju business and is none of yours. I will know if you peek, so don't.

If you are a regular Destroyer reader looking for something on your level to read until the next sorry-excuse-for-a-novel comes out, I suggest turning to your local funny pages. Remo and "Ziggy" have much in common. Mostly around the nose.

With moderate tolerance for you, I remain,

—Chiun, Reigning Master of Sinanju

PROLOGUE

"He does not belong. No matter what lies he tells you."

Ancient fury sparked in the depths of his mother's almond-shaped eyes. Beyond her crooked shape, orange flames crackled in the stone fireplace.

The small house was warm through no effort of those who lived there. The same was true for all the homes in the village, for as far back as anyone could remember.

The firewood was always there in the warm house with the solid roof that kept out the driving spring rain and winter wind, all because of *him*. The Impostor.

Those who thanked him didn't know the truth.

He was a fraud masquerading as their protector.

There were no thanks for the Impostor in this house. So what if he kept fires burning and bellies full? In this tiny house, the hatred was worse than the cold. Ancient malice gnawed bellies far worse than any hunger pangs.

"Learn well what he teaches you," his mother said to the boy. "But know that he does not belong. He is a fraud, as was his father before him, all down the line to the first."

The boy had learned early in life that members of

his family alone were not frauds. The only exception was his own father. A soft-spoken man, the husband of his mother was not blood of their blood. Worse, he was brother to the tyrant who fed the village. The boy's mother had married the fool in order to get close to *him*. To her brother-in-law, the Impostor.

A moan came from the corner of the room.

The boy's grandfather. A portly shaman, he sat on a stool, wrinkled eyelids closed tight. The old man spent most days sitting in the corner of the main room. The boy's mother said the old man could speak with the dead. His powers went beyond even that.

Near the shaman, a young woman was preparing the evening meal in a cast-iron pot.

The shaman's other daughter was called Sonmi. Sister to the boy's hectoring mother, she spent her days studying the black arts at the feet of her father. The food the boy's aunt was cooking—like everything else in the village—had been paid for by the Impostor.

Although all this was about to end.

There was no more work.

Gone were the days of pharaohs and kings. The world was ruled by presidents and dictators, locked in the bloodless, twilight combat of the modern age.

Even war was different. At the moment, there was one being fought to the south. At night the villagers would climb to their roofs to watch the explosions of artillery shells. Like all the other wars of the twentieth century, it was all about machines and guns and men on foot advancing and retreating until one side thought it had captured a prize. The artistry of assassination was lost. The world was big and clumsy and dismissive of the old ways.

Because the rules had changed, the Impostor couldn't find work. Who needed a scalpel when he could use a club? Why remove a king's head when a single bomb could obliterate his entire kingdom? The work had gone away, and the desolate shadow of death had descended over the small village.

If the food they ate and the wood they used to cook it came courtesy the Impostor, it would not be so for much longer. When the money he had earned was gone, he would have to draw on reserves bequeathed to the village from those who came before. And one day it, too, would all be gone.

The Impostor's only hope—the only hope for the future of the village—was the young boy sitting on this dirty floor, bathed in the dancing fires of hate carefully stoked and tended by his bitter mother.

"He thinks you will save his family," his mother said as the warm fires burned and the wispy smoke rose in ghostly black threads up the chimney. Drawing up a deep ball of phlegm, she spit on the stone floor. "That is all his family is worth. You are the hope of *our* future, not his. Bring him to ruin. Do it for your family. Such has it been foreseen, such it will be. It is our destiny, and yours."

And the fire of pure evil from his mother's eyes reflected full in the young boy's hazel eyes.

1

His name was Chiun and he was the Master of Sinanju and he was leaving.

Although it was late spring, winter refused to release its grip on the Korean peninsula. Despite the cold morning, the village of Sinanju was alive with celebration. There was rice wine and cakes, cured fish and dried fruit. There was singing and dancers and the laughter of children. All taking place under a sky of perfect white-streaked blue.

Such it was when a Master left. Such had it always been. Tributes and laudations came from those whose needs were sustained by the Master's toil.

The tiny fishing village of Sinanju in North Korea had seen many such celebrations. For five thousand years it had been home to the most feared assassins in human history. The discipline that had risen from the rocks near the shore of the West Korean Bay was the source of all the lesser martial arts. They were but rays, pale reflections of the blinding glory of the sun that was the discipline known as Sinanju.

"Hail, Master of Sinanju, who sustains the village and keeps the code faithfully," called the villagers as Chiun passed by. "Our hearts cry with joy and pain at your departure. Joy that you undertake this journey for the sake of we, the unworthy beneficiaries of your generosity. And pain that your toils take your beauteous aspect from our midst. May the spirits of your ancestors journey safe with you who graciously throttles the universe.''

As Master of the village, Chiun accepted the words with a stoic face. The praises continued to fall on his proudly erect back as he passed through the crowd.

Of course he knew the hymns of honor that trailed him were hollow. There was more beneath the smiling faces. Here the hint of a frown, there the beginnings of a scowl. Facial muscles ached from frozen smiles. They lied to him now because none dared express his true feelings.

It had always been this way. The people of Sinanju always walked uneasily when the Master was in residence. Although tradition dictated that every Master take the pledge not to raise a hand against a member of the village, one never knew. Especially in these days of uncertainty. This Master who walked among them would be the last. All gathered there this day knew it was so.

Chiun. That was all he would ever be. Not Chiun the Great or even Chiun the Lesser, for honorifics like ''great'' or ''lesser'' were bestowed only on those who did not fail. And this Chiun-Who-Would-Have-No-Title had failed like no other Master before him.

''Cursed are we to live in this time, with this Master who has failed us,'' the women said in hushed voices when they thought the failed Master Chiun was out of earshot.

''Silence,'' the fearful men insisted. They cowered at the edge of the crowd, behind the women and children. ''Yes, he has failed. But even in failure he is strong.''

"Not strong enough to find a suitable heir. Not strong enough to protect the village of his ancestors. His strength has waned. The time of the great Masters of Sinanju is over."

Although whispered, their words still carried. Chiun did not let them know he could hear every barbed word.

Such it was for a Master of Sinanju. The ability to detect a lone truthful whisper in a chorus of joyful lies was but a single skill in the arsenal of Sinanju.

He left the crowd to their fraudulent celebration.

He spurned the main road from the village, taking the path that led into the rocky hills above the shore.

Chiun skittered along the treacherous path in seeming defiance of the force of gravity. His surefootedness would have seemed miraculous to many, given his apparent age.

Chiun was old. He did not yet appear ready for the grave, but he was long past the middle of his life. Twin wisps of white hair floated gently at the sides of his head. A thread of matching beard quivered at his proud chin.

Although his outward appearance was that of a man surrendering to the inevitable march of time, in the case of the Master of Sinanju, looks were deceiving.

Looking closer, one could see a man possessed of a powerful inner strength. His hazel eyes were youthful, as was the certain stride that carried him swiftly along the rocky promontory.

The Horns of Welcome rose above the bay. Two great curving arcs of stone that had for countless centuries acted both as welcome and warning to those who dared visit the Pearl of the Orient. Framed between the horns, far out in the black waters of the

West Korean Bay, the oblong blot of a submarine sat like a steel island amid the rolling waves.

The USS *Darter* had surfaced at dawn.

When it first broke through the frigid whitecaps, alarm had registered in the highest corridors of Communist North Korea. Patrol boats that had been in the area were sent to the bay. They circled the silent sub like hungry wolves, gunners and torpedoes at the ready. The sailors expected a battle, possibly reigniting the fire that had been smoldering since the war with the South twenty years before.

But no shots were fired.

It was learned that the American submarine had come to pay tribute to the legendary Master of Sinanju.

Kim Il Sung, Leader for Life of North Korea, knew well of Sinanju and its Masters. Assassins who could hide in shadow and kill in the time it took a man to draw breath. If the sub was here on Sinanju business, it was no business of his. North Korea's premier ordered his boats to stand down.

The patrol boats sped away into the Yellow Sea, leaving the submarine alone in the bay.

Only when the communist boats had gone did the hatch open. A lone man left the submarine and found his way into the village to the Master's house, there to seek an audience with the Reigning Master. Hours later that same man now waited at the shore for the Master of Sinanju.

Chiun would go to him shortly. But there was one stop he had to make first.

The hillside became a plateau. At the top yawned the mouth of a deep cave. Around its entrance grew three trees—a pine, a bamboo and a plum blossom. Moving among the trees was a lone figure.

Although Chiun had seen nearly eighty summers, the old man on the hilltop had obviously lived many more than that.

He was heavyset and bald. Age had whitened his skin. The flesh was pulled taut over knots of fragile bone.

He didn't incline his head Chiun's way. His back to the bay, the aged figure seemed oblivious to his visitor. Yet as Chiun approached, the ancient man spoke.

"There is no beauty to that sailing vessel," the old man said. His voice was thin and quavered with great age. With yellowed fingernails he clipped a sucker from the plum tree.

He nodded back over his shoulder. Only the very tips of the Horns of Welcome were visible this high up. Pincered between the tops of the curved rocks was the submarine.

"A ship should have sails," the elderly man said. "In my day some still had them. Now none do. It is sad that you live in this age without having experienced at least some of the last, young Chiun. It was a magnificent time."

At this the old man finally turned.

When he beheld the ancient man's face, Chiun was forced to mask his deep sadness.

Once bright eyes were clouded with puffs of white.

The blindness was recent and had come on rapidly. It grew worse with each passing day. It would only be a matter of months before he was completely blind.

If his failing vision bothered the older man, it

didn't show. The heavy man offered Chiun a knowing smile.

"Do not waste a moment worrying over me, young Chiun," the aged man said, nodding wisely. "I have seen enough in my many days. Much more than most men. My remembered vision will be enough to sustain me for the time that remains."

Chiun wasn't surprised that the old man had guessed his thoughts. Half-blind or not, there was little that could be hidden from H'si T'ang, the man who had been his teacher.

"Forgive me, Venerable One," Chiun apologized. But his sadness for the man who had given him so much remained. "I have come to take my leave of you."

At this, H'si T'ang nodded once more. "I heard the motors from the government boats and the chanting from the village. When the sun rose full and I saw the shadow of that strange vessel in the bay, I knew." The old man tipped his bald head. "Where do you go?"

"To the West. America's king has summoned Sinanju to his court."

"Ah. And what is the service you are to perform?"

At this Chiun hesitated.

He didn't dare lie. Not that he could have gotten away with it even if he tried. But he couldn't tell the truth. Couldn't admit that a legend, an ancient promise, a *hope* was drawing him to the most barbarian of Western nations.

H'si T'ang sensed his pupil's troubled spirit. Chiun was relieved when the older man interrupted.

"Whatever the service, I am certain it will bring greater glory to the House of Sinanju, son of my son,'' the retired Master said. With a shuffling of feet, he turned his attention back to his plum tree.

Chiun watched his teacher for a long moment.

"You do not have to live here, Little Father," he said all at once. "The Master's House in the village—"

"Was home to me in my time," H'si T'ang broke in. "You are Master now. Therefore the House of Many Woods is yours. Besides," he added, waving a hand of bone at the open mouth of the cave, "this place is familiar to me. Three times in my long life have I entered into the ritualistic seclusion, only to have to reenter the world again. It is easier to remain here than to pack and unpack every few decades."

At his words, Chiun hung his head in shame.

"I am sorry to have failed you, Father," he said.

When H'si T'ang turned, his smiling face had grown stern. "How have you failed me?" the old man demanded. "The first time I entered this cave was when your father took you as pupil. For such is it written that the Master should purify his spirit when his successor takes a pupil of his own. When your father, who was my son, passed into the Void I completed your training. As Master and as your grandfather, I was known as Hwa and Yui. As your teacher, I took the name H'si T'ang. The circumstances surrounding my rebirth as teacher could not be blamed on you."

"No," Chiun admitted. "But that was not the only time."

H'si T'ang waved his words away. "Your child who died was a tragedy that you did not cause and that you could not have prevented—despite what you think. As for your second pupil, he was a child of

Sinanju the village and student of Sinanju the discipline, but he was never one with the essence that is the Sun Source. The best he could do was mimic what we are. At this Nuihc excelled, but his heart was never ours.''

At the mention of his nephew's name, Chiun's back stiffened. The name of his brother's son was unmentionable in the village. Only H'si T'ang would dare speak it.

"As you say," Chiun said quietly. "For now I must go. Take care, Little Father.'' Bowing deeply, he turned.

He had taken only a few shuffling steps when a voice rang out behind him.

"Hold," H'si T'ang commanded.

Chiun froze in his tracks. "Yes, Venerable One?"

The older man motioned with a long, crooked finger.

"Come here."

Chiun did as he was told. When he stopped before his teacher, H'si T'ang reached out with one hand. He took Chiun's chin in a knot of bony fingers.

"This is the last time I will look on your face with these failing eyes," H'si T'ang said. "I want to be sure I remember it."

As he studied his pupil, the translucent flesh of his old, old face pulled into a satisfied smile. When he was finished, his fingers slipped from Chiun's chin. Wordlessly, H'si T'ang turned back to his plum tree.

The ancient man resumed his work. Busy nails clipped another small shoot.

Chiun left his teacher to his pruning. With a troubled shadow across his parchment brow he left the plateau.

Only when his pupil was gone did H'si T'ang stop his pruning. Eyes of milk turned to face the shore. The fuzzy blot of the submarine was barely visible in the bay.

"Have a care, my son," the Venerable One said in a voice so low Chiun's sensitive ears could not hear. "While you are racing off to fulfill one legend, do not allow yourself to be blinded to the second."

Laced with foreboding, his words of caution were carried off on the wind. They were lost in the sounds of celebration that still rose from the squalid main street of Sinanju.

2

The American looked up with bleary eyes.

He had waited so long that he had passed out from the cold. The villagers had revived him. Someone started a fire. Sitting on the edge of a rubber raft, he leaned near the flames, arms drawn in tight to his chest.

When he saw the old Korean approaching, he stood. There was a hook where his left hand should have been.

"You about ready to go?" he grunted. The collar of his trench coat was turned up in a futile attempt to ward off the bitter Korean cold.

Padding up beside the big man, Chiun aimed his chin toward the water's edge where three steamer trunks bobbed in the frothy water like colorful corks. The trunks had been lashed together with wire from the waiting submarine.

"Where is the rest of my luggage?"

"The SEALs brought the other trunks aboard the sub hours ago," the man with the hook said. He was shivering from the cold. He extended his good hand to the raft. "We should get out of here. I don't know what kind of mojo you worked on the North Koreans, but they won't hold off forever."

"Our reputation keeps them away," Chiun intoned.

"You who would petition the House of Sinanju should know that. Are you certain that you collected all of the trunks I left at the steps of the Master's House? You whites are notorious for your sloppy work habits. I do not wish to get halfway to—what is the name of the place we are going again?"

"America. Look—"

"Yes, that place. I do not wish to sail halfway to that place with the ugly name only to have to come back."

"Can't say I blame anyone for not wanting to come back," the man muttered. Twice in his life he had gotten a good look at the Pearl of the Orient. It wasn't a place he'd opt to return to if given half a chance to leave. "There was a total of fourteen trunks. We loaded eleven. The last three are the ones you said could be floated out on their own."

Chiun inspected the three bobbing trunks. Satisfied that they were indeed the right ones, he nodded.

"You may take them in tow," he said imperiously.

Hiking up his skirts, he stepped into the rubber raft. Before sitting, he paused.

Chiun took one last look back at Sinanju. The village was a black rock lodged into unforgiving earth, surrounded by a churning sea of despair. He didn't know how long this journey would take him from his home. If the omens were true, it could be a long time before he saw his homeland again. With sharp eyes of hope and regret he soaked in every stone, every sound, every twist and turn of the jagged shore.

Once the mental photograph was complete, he turned.

Chiun's parchment face formed a stoic mask as he

settled onto his seat. Slender fingers fussed with the fabric of his brocade kimono around his bony knees.

The additional ninety-pound weight of the Korean in the boat proved not a problem to the man with the hook. Somehow the old man seemed able to make himself lighter than air.

With the curve of his hook and his one good hand, the American shoved the boat from the shore.

It was tricky paddling. It would have been easier to get one of the sailors from the *Darter* to help. But his orders had been specific. Minimize exposure of the *Darter*'s crew to anything and everything that had to do with retrieving the old man. Do whatever he had to do to enlist the aid of the Master of Sinanju. But do it alone.

ALONE. That was a word with which the American was well acquainted. *Alone* and Conrad MacCleary were old friends.

In the OSS in World War II, Conn MacCleary had worked mostly alone. Whenever some higher-up wanted to put him on a team, MacCleary's answer was invariably the same: "With all due respect, if I screw up, I die. If someone I'm with screws up, I'm just as dead. If it's all the same, sir, I'd rather be the one doing the screwing."

His lone-wolf attitude would never have been tolerated if not for one simple fact. Conrad MacCleary got results.

Fluent in German, MacCleary had spent much of his time behind enemy lines coordinating Allied spy efforts. In his six years in Germany—both prior to and throughout American involvement in that great conflict—MacCleary enjoyed greater success than all but one other deep-cover U.S. agent.

There was only one shadow in his entire wartime record. Although no one but Conrad MacCleary saw it as a blemish, to him it was the darkest moment of his entire espionage career.

It happened just before the fall of Berlin. The war in Europe was at an end. Bombs were dropping like April rain.

When MacCleary learned that Heinrich Himmler had fled Berlin, Conn gave chase. No history book would ever record the fact but, thanks to MacCleary, the SS head was captured attempting to sneak out of Germany. While Conn was away from Berlin the Russians took the city for the Allies.

Bad timing had drawn him away from his ultimate prize—the mad kraut sausage-sucker, der führer himself.

Someone had to be there. *Someone* had to be first to wrap his hands around the neck of that demented paperhanger. Why not Conn? But thanks to bad timing, the goddamned Russkies got there first.

Only afterward did MacCleary learn that no one had claimed the prize. Finishing his life with an act of ultimate cowardice, Adolf Hitler had committed suicide.

Conrad MacCleary's field of expertise was actually Asian affairs. With the war in Europe over, he was anxious to get over to the Pacific theater. When MacCleary was allowed back into Berlin with the American army, he didn't really want to go when the call came for a translator.

A German captain had been discovered in a bombed-out wing of the SS headquarters. For reasons unclear, the officer had been slated for execution. He had missed his date with the firing squad when the building collapsed around the ears of his would-be executioners.

When discovered by the Russians, the man was babbling. Fearful that he might be aware of some sort of doomsday weapon hidden in the city, they called for a translator.

When Conn showed up in the detention cell, he found a lone German army captain sitting in a wobbly chair.

The man's eyes were glazed. His face sported a week's growth of beard. There were bruises inflicted by SS torturers. The captain rocked back and forth as he sat. Voice low, he repeated something over and over.

Three Russians—a colonel and two conscripts— stood above the German. Their anxious eyes snapped to MacCleary as the tall man entered the cell.

The Russian colonel quickly briefed MacCleary on the situation. As he spoke, the seated German continued to murmur softly to himself, repeating only one word.

"He speaks nonsense," the colonel insisted in heavily accented English. "I speak German well, and that is not a word I have ever heard."

With a glance at the Russians, MacCleary leaned forward. He cocked an ear, listening closely.

The German continued to hiss softly. Eyelids fluttered at half-mast over his twitching eyes.

MacCleary frowned. "Whatever it is, it ain't German," he concluded.

"What does it mean?" asked a Russian colonel.

MacCleary shrugged. He listened hard once more.

Maybe the kraut had some kind of speech impediment. But try as he might, Conn could hear no German in what the man was saying.

"...Sinanju...Sinanju...Sinanju...Sinanju..."

It was like a mantra to the poor battered soldier.

"Beats the hell out of me," Conn admitted eventually, his voice a hoarse grumble. "Just another crazy German in a country of crazy Germans. Let him join Hitler in Hell."

It was the Nazi leader's name that did it. Something triggered in the soldier's face. A spark of raw terror.

The seated soldier snatched MacCleary by the wrist that would one day end in a hook. Fingers dug into bone.

"The Master of Sinanju is coming," the soldier hissed in German. "Tell the führer that death is on the way."

The fear in his wounded face was deeper and stronger than anything MacCleary had seen in his life. The German's bloodshot eyes were pleading. It was as if the fear that his message would not get through was far greater than his fear at what the Germans, Russians or Americans might do to him.

When the German lunged, the two Russian soldiers jumped forward. They pinned the captain back to his seat. The Russian colonel came to MacCleary's aide. It took all their strength to pry the man's hands off Conn's wrist.

"I don't know what's wrong with you, Fritz, but your führer's already on ice," MacCleary snapped in German. He massaged the pain in his wrist with one hand while he flexed the fingers of his left hand.

The captain blinked in confusion. It was as if he were coming out of a dream. "On ice?" he asked.

"Yeah," MacCleary replied bitterly. "On ice. Dead. Courtesy of Little Joe Stalin and a damned politician's conference at Yalta I sure as hell wasn't invited to."

The relief that washed over the face of the captured German captain was great. He released a heavy sigh.

As MacCleary was ushered from the room, the Russians were resuming their questioning. The last thing Conn saw was the two Russian soldiers working over the German. He accepted their blows with a smile. It was as if the captain had already endured all the pain one man could possibly suffer.

It was a strange chapter that, for Conrad Mac-Cleary, should have closed out this part of his personal story of World War II. But for some reason it stuck with him.

The rational part of MacCleary's brain wanted to chalk it up to the craziness of war, but that weird episode with the German captain just wouldn't get into the box. A tour in Asia and the end of hostilities didn't stop him from thinking of that frightened German captain from time to time.

Life went on. For Conrad MacCleary, World War II was just the start of the real spy game.

Although the Cold War presented new challenges, many of the same men who had fought in secret in the Second World War found themselves transferred to a new life and a new cause. There were still battles to be fought, dragons to be slain.

As before, MacCleary largely worked alone. There was only one man he had ever fought beside whom he would have trusted to guard his back during the early CIA days. But that man had taken a break from the game.

Conn had met the best friend he'd ever had while in the OSS. The guy was a cold bastard if ever there was one, yet the two men shared an unspoken bond of friendship. He was a man who could be trusted. But when Conn switched from the OSS to the peacetime CIA, his friend briefly opted for civilian life. Time to complete his education, get married, have a kid. Not Conn. He was part of that holy first generation. The anointed team of warriors to first enter into the decades-long twilight struggle.

It was in 1952, while the Cold War was heating up, that MacCleary next encountered the mystery of his German captain.

Conn didn't meet the soldier himself—if the Russians were true to form, the babbling man was long dead.

It was during the undeclared war on the Korean peninsula. MacCleary was in Seoul in an advisory capacity to General MacArthur. At a special meeting the South Korean military leadership was adamant that the American-led army not come within a country mile of a particular fishing village north of the Thirty-eighth Parallel.

"With all due respect, nothing can get in the way of complete victory," MacArthur had insisted.

"If you choose to invade Sinanju, you do it without our cooperation," a South Korean general replied.

In a corner of the conference room, Conn Mac-Cleary looked sharply at the man.

"Did you say Sinanju?"

The man nodded. There was fear in his hooded eyes. It was matched by the looks of dread on the sweating faces of the remaining South Korean military delegation.

"Is there someone there—what the hell was that title?" Conn snapped his fingers. "Is there someone called the Master of Sinanju there?"

The fear grew greater. Nods all around.

MacArthur was growing impatient with the interrupting CIA man, as well as with the Koreans.

"Is there a point to all this?" the general demanded.

"I'm not sure, sir," Conn replied. "But I'd suggest you do as they say until I can get some research done."

He had quickly ducked from the room and placed a few quiet calls back to Washington. When the call came back, it was not for MacCleary, but for MacArthur.

The general seemed as surprised as Conn at who was on the other end of the line.

"Yes, Mr. President," MacArthur said.

Conn got a clear enough picture from that part of the conversation he was able to hear.

Apparently while commanding America's European forces in World War II, Eisenhower had heard a rumor that the head of this insignificant little speck of a Korean fishing village was somehow—either by direct or indirect means—responsible for Hitler's death. Anxious not to suffer the same fate, the President not only commanded that MacArthur steer clear of Sinanju, he ordered that a gift of gold be delivered to the village, compliments of the United States.

Conrad MacCleary accepted the job as delivery boy for the gold. By now his curiosity was more than piqued. Under cover of darkness, he led a small team through enemy territory to the small North Korean village of Sinanju.

When he arrived with the gold, Conn was disappointed to find the Master was gone. According to the villagers, the head of the village and his young pupil were off somewhere training. Conn had left the gold along with a promise from General MacArthur that no tanks would approach Sinanju.

Although disappointed that he had missed out on meeting this mysterious Master, this time Conn didn't let the matter drop. After all, reputation alone had not just preserved a worthless little fishing village, but had also inspired an American president to send a payoff to a mud-smeared Korean backwater.

The first thing MacCleary did when he got back to the States, was to do some digging into what made this Sinanju and its Master so special.

He was surprised at what he turned up. Sinanju was some sort of training ground for the martial arts. The references were spotty and undetailed, but there were a lot of them.

Conn found an allusion to a Korean from Sinanju in Nero's court. Another was with Hannibal as he crossed the Alps. Some were present at pivotal events in human history. They went where the money was. The legend of Sinanju was that of a shadow force behind events and historical figures stretching back to the earliest recorded history.

It was interesting. Certainly intriguing. But there was no real practical application for what MacCleary learned. What was he supposed to do, run to the newspapers? "Excuse me, sir, but hold page one. I've got a story about a secret cult of assassins living in the Orient. It's so feared and respected that even the President of the United States paid tribute to it rather than risk his neck crossing them."

Conn would be laughed out of every city room from New York to Bugtussle.

Besides, Sinanju in the late twentieth century seemed in decline. According to his research, there were likely only two practitioners of the martial art at a given time. Master and student. From father to son. Passed down for generations. But aside from a blip in World War II, the current Master hadn't made himself known to the courts of the modern world.

Conn was interested, sure. But there was damned little he could do with what he'd learned.

He had filed the information away in a dusty corner of his brain. And there it sat for almost two decades. Until one day that amazing, useless scrap of knowledge resurfaced. And with it, the hope of maybe, just maybe, saving a nation.

THE ROWING GREW choppier as they neared the sub.

The three steamer trunks were tied to the big rubber boat with a rope line. They bobbed obediently in the raft's wake as they closed in on the waiting submarine.

If the trunks started to sink, they'd pull the back end of the raft underwater. Conn wasn't thrilled with the idea of taking a dip in freezing water. Worse was the possibility that he'd have to rescue his passenger from the drink.

MacCleary still couldn't believe the shape of the old man. The stories he'd read back in the fifties had led him to believe that the Master of Sinanju would be, well, younger. This guy looked older than dirt.

The Korean's parchment face seemed troubled to depths beyond Conn's understanding as he stared out across the bay.

"You mind if I ask you something?" MacCleary asked abruptly as he struggled with the oar.

"I do not paddle," the old Korean replied blandly. Saltwater mist speckled his white hair.

"No," Conn said. "When I came to your village before. Back, geez, seventeen, eighteen years ago. When I delivered the gold from General MacArthur. They said you weren't here because you were off training your pupil."

The Master of Sinanju didn't look at MacCleary. His narrowed eyes were locked beyond the big man, on the looming shape of the American submarine.

"What of it?" Chiun asked, his voice thin.

"Well," MacCleary began, "no offense, but... well, shouldn't your pupil be of age by now? I mean, I know some of your history here. In a generation only one Master trains a pupil. Yours should be Master by now, shouldn't he?"

Conn couldn't explain it. But later, when he recalled that moment, he would swear the freezing air of the West Korean Bay dropped by twenty degrees.

Chiun turned his head with agonizing slowness. When his eyes locked on those of MacCleary, the American was convinced that he was gazing into the face of death itself.

Chiun's voice seemed to quell the very waves. "Yes," the old man said. "He should be."

And he said no more.

They were at the sub. Conn had never been so grateful to see American sailors in his life. The young men reached down with helping hands from the ladder of the *Darter*.

The old Korean was right about one thing. His trunks turned out to be seaworthy. They weren't heavier or seeping water as they were hauled up the side of the sub.

Chiun scurried up beside them. The old man's movements were so quick and graceful he looked like some form of seafaring spider. In a trice he was across the deck and up the conning tower. He disappeared through the hatch.

Sitting in the wave-tossed raft, Conrad MacCleary shook his head. ''It's worth every penny to get you on our side,'' he grumbled, dropping the oar at his feet.

The sailors helped the big man from the rubber raft.

3

Phil Rand had no idea why this particular job was so special. But it had to be special to at least *someone* at AT&T. Why else the extra attention?

Try as he might, Phil couldn't see this as anything other than the usual mundane scut work. Just another day at the office. For Phil, the office this day was a gloomy waterside street in New Rochelle, New York.

His crew had arrived at a little after five in the morning. When the telephone company trucks rolled to a stop on Shore Road, a supervisor was already waiting for them.

The predawn gloom seemed tailor-made for the mysterious company rep. The guy looked as though he lived in shadows. He stood there like an eager vampire as Phil and the others climbed out of their trucks.

"You're late," the supervisor said. His tone was chilly in the damp October air.

Phil checked his watch. It was only six minutes after five. "We got caught in traffic," he said, half-joking.

Of course the supervisor was kidding. After all, the guy couldn't be serious. However, the look of displeasure never left his angular face.

"That is unlikely, given the hour," the supervisor

said. "And I am on a tight schedule. I would appreciate it if you got to work as quickly as possible."

Phil sighed deeply. Another day, another hassle.

"Whatever you say," he muttered.

With maps and measuring Phil quickly found the spot he was after. At his direction, his men set to work tearing up a chunk of Shore Road.

It took more digging than Phil expected. They found the cable buried deep. The braided steel line ran in from Long Island Sound, past Glen Island. It stopped dead at Phil's feet. Coiled in the hole like an insulated copper snake was another line that ran through an abandoned sewer line from a point inland. Phil had spent the previous day snaking the second line in from two streets over. The new line ended near the capped one.

"That it?" Phil asked.

The shadowed man stepped to the edge of the hole. Looking in, he nodded sharply.

That was all. Couldn't even be bothered to grunt a yes.

"Yeah, that's the one," Phil instructed his men.

The fact that this was an underwater cable didn't matter to Phil. To Phil and the rest of the men it was just another tedious day on the job. Made all the more annoying by the presence of the humorless, silent supervisor.

Phil didn't know who the man was or why he had showed up for this specific job. He was just some faceless higher-up in the corporate monolith that was American Telephone and Telegraph. One thing was sure. The man's eager, virtually unblinking gaze gave Phil a case of the heebie-jeebies.

Men climbed down into the hole.

"This from Columbia Island?" Phil asked the silent supervisor as his men worked to connect the cable.

"I really cannot say," the supervisor replied. His voice was tart and nasal.

Although day had long broken, the gaunt man still kept to the shadows. Only when the sun had risen fully did Phil realize it was the other way around. The supervisor didn't keep to the shadows; the shadows clung to him.

The man was gray faced and dour. He looked more like an undertaker than a telephone company employee.

It took five full hours to complete the work. The bright red rubber tubing that protected the strands of the copper analogue line were spliced carefully together.

Phil thought that was weird. The individual lines weren't color-coded. But the supervisor assured him that they could start anywhere.

They were done everything and were burying the line by 10:30 a.m. The supervisor waited until the line was covered by six feet of dirt and sand before turning to go.

The New Rochelle Department of Public Works truck had just arrived. In back was a steaming pile of blacktop.

"Excuse me, sir," Phil Rand asked as the DPW truck backed up to the hole.

The supervisor was climbing into his station wagon. Phil noted that it was the same model as his wife's. The '69 they had bought new two years ago.

The supervisor hesitated. For the first time, Phil

noted his name tag. It identified the man as Harold Jones.

"Yes?" Supervisor Jones asked impatiently.

"What's this all about, sir?" Phil asked.

The supervisor didn't miss a beat. "Telephone company business," he said crisply.

As the city dump truck poured tar onto the road, the supervisor drove away. He left Phil Rand and his crew standing, oblivious, at ground zero of one of the most damning secrets in the history of the American republic.

THAT THE PHONE LINE was merely *one* of the most damning secrets in U.S. history was an unquestionable fact to the man who had spent the morning posing as an AT&T supervisor. At this point in his life, he had been privy to enough secrets to know how to categorize them as either big or small.

He had been entrusted with national secrets for almost as long as he could remember. However, now it was different. Before there were always others who were in on the secrets. Higher-ups, as well as peers. Always a circle of knowledge, growing wider or smaller on a need-to-know basis.

That circle had now grown smaller, tighter than anyone could have ever imagined. And the circle closed around the driver's thin neck like a hangman's noose.

As he drove away from the dig site, he unclipped the plastic ID card from the breast pocket of his gray suit.

The Harold Jones identification was phony. Another secret in a life of secrets.

Dr. Harold W. Smith was used to secrets. At least

he thought he was. During the war he had seen his share. In the CIA he had seen even more. But they were all nothing compared to his life now. And that life was only growing more complicated as these latest hours passed.

He took the Boston Post Road up the coast from New Rochelle to Rye. He avoided the heart of the city. Skirting the center of town, he headed up a wooded road.

To his right stretched Long Island Sound. Obscured mostly by trees in the early autumn, he could see the dappled water now and then through breaks in the brightly colored foliage. Boats bobbed on the surface of the whitecapped water. Somewhere far beneath their thin hulls snaked a telephone cable, connected to the same line that was even now being entombed forever by the New Rochelle Department of Public Works.

The phone line had been tricky. It was something he had wanted to do from the outset. But though it would have been convenient, patience was needed. After all, he couldn't very well have it done all at once. Workmen digging a straight furrow to lay a single line from Rye to Washington, D.C., would have drawn far too much attention. The equivalent of drawing an arrow on a map.

No. In the end restraint had won out over any inconvenience he had experienced while waiting.

The line went in piecemeal. In his spare time for the past five years Smith studied the work schedules of many a local telephone company office. When a particular crew's daily work happened to coincide with the route Smith had established, a circuitous order was sent to lay a single section of cable. There was never any doubt that the special type of cable would be available. Smith made certain it was.

To Smith it was like remotely assembling a jigsaw puzzle. The map he had drawn early on for the proposed telephone line was updated as progress was made. It was spotty at first. After three years it was little more than a long dotted line. But over the course of the past two years, that dotted line had slowly, laboriously closed up. Until all that remained was the final connection in New Rochelle.

A man of lesser patience would never have lasted so long at such a project. But, among his other sterling attributes, Dr. Harold W. Smith had patience in abundance. He was also single-minded of purpose. When he began a task, he didn't stop until it was completed.

Which was part of the reason he was chosen for his current position as the man who would save America.

"A cure for a sick world." That was what the man who hired Smith for this impossible task had said.

"America is in trouble, Smith," the young President of the United States told him during one of the handful of early, fateful meetings that set Smith on his new life's mission. "We can no longer handle crime. Government is living within the boundaries of the Constitution while organized crime continues to turn the Constitution on its head. It's a losing battle that the thugs are winning."

That conversation took place eight years ago. Right now, as he drove along the autumn-shaded New York road, it seemed like another lifetime.

At the time Smith had been a CIA analyst nearing early retirement. He had logged more time for king and country than most. As his youth darkened under the looming shadow of middle age, Smith decided to opt out for a more settled life. He was offered and had accepted a professorship at Dartmouth, his alma mater.

His wife was thrilled. Maude Smith couldn't wait for her Harold to assume the role of normal father. At the time, their daughter, Vickie, was in the early stages of some sort of teenage rebellion. Maude didn't much like to talk about it. When she did, she blamed it on the crazy times they lived in. It would be good for all of them for Harold to be at the dinner table like a traditional husband and father.

A new life and a new chance for the Smith family was to begin with the fall semester of 1963. But fate had charted another course for Harold W. Smith.

Smith had been summoned to the Oval Office in the summer of '63. By the time his first clandestine meeting with the President was over, Smith's life had changed forever.

The Dartmouth position was quietly declined. From that summer to fall, Smith worked on the details of a new type of crime-fighting organization. One that would operate outside the confines of the Constitution in order to preserve the very document it would habitually violate.

Smith's organizational abilities and keen mind were without equal. Strategies, funding, staffing were all set up in less than eight weeks. When it came time to name the new agency, Smith chose CURE. It was not an acronym, but a desire. "A CURE for a sick world."

The only thing left was a headquarters.

Washington was out of the question. There were

too many government agencies, too many prying eyes. With the new computer technology, it was possible to operate from a remote location. However, the woods of North Dakota or some hollowed-out bunker beneath the Rockies were not exactly convenient—either for himself or his family. After a two-month-long search, Smith stumbled upon the perfect location for CURE in, of all places, the *New York Times*.

As he drove his station wagon along the winding road, Smith allowed himself a rare smile at the memory of that back-page *Times* throwaway piece.

A high wall rose up from the woods. The road on which he was driving followed the contours of the wall around to a gated entrance. Two stone lines perched atop the granite columns on either side of the main gate. Above, a bronze sign was etched with the words *Folcroft Sanitarium*.

The guard at the booth nodded and waved as Smith passed.

Smith barely acknowledged the man.

He steered his car up the great gravel drive. A somber brick building loomed ahead, cloaked in spreading ivy.

Folcroft Sanitarium had been an exclusive retreat for the rich and eccentric since the 1920s. If a Rockefeller or Getty or Vanderbilt showed signs of what might be charitably termed "mental fatigue," Folcroft was one of the approved places they could be sent. The staff at Folcroft was always caring, efficient and, above all, quiet. After all, if old Uncle Jebediah went squiffy in the head, it was vital to remand him to the care of people who knew enough to keep the good family name from appearing in the papers.

According to the *Times* article Smith had read, Folcroft had lived off its reputation for four decades. Unfortunately as the twentieth century rolled along, the sanitarium's fortunes faded along with those of America's nineteenth-century moneyed aristocracy. By the time the 1960s marched in, it was pretty much expected that the venerable old institution would soon have to close its doors forever.

However, those who predicted Folcroft's demise had not factored in Harold W. Smith.

Smith had come to Folcroft as director in October of 1963. In the past eight short years, he had turned the sanitarium around. In under a decade Smith transformed the mental and convalescent home that was Folcroft Sanitarium into an institution that was even more exclusive than it had been in its celebrated heyday.

On most days Smith felt some satisfaction at the work he had done to revive Folcroft. On this day he had more important things weighing on his mind.

He parked his car in his reserved space at the edge of the employee parking lot. A briefcase that had been designed to look old in order to discourage thieves sat on the front seat beside him. Smith gathered it up and headed for the side door of the building.

Two flights up, he entered the administrative wing. It was a quick walk to his office suite.

A dour young woman with an impenetrable knot of sprayed-stiff blond hair looked up at him as he entered the outer office. A clunky black Smith-Corona typewriter sat on her desktop.

Miss Purvish was Smith's semipermanent secretary. Although only one woman manned his outer office at a given time, he didn't have just one to do the job.

It was all part of the larger problem of security. Although Smith was careful in the extreme, he could not possibly hope to cover every base. It might just be possible for a secretary to see enough, read enough, piece together enough to get some *something* of an idea of what was going on at that big, ivy-covered building on Long Island Sound.

But he was head of Folcroft, as well as head of CURE. And as the former, he could not very well greet the families of potential patients personally. A man in his position without a secretary to guard his outer office would raise suspicion. But a secretary—while necessary if only for appearance sake alone—presented an inherent security risk.

Early on he settled on a scheme that seemed to keep a potential problem from exploding into a crisis. As new director of Folcroft, he initiated a policy of cross training. The various Folcroft secretaries were occasionally required to fill duty shifts in the medical wing of the facility. At the same time, some of the female medical personnel were trained in secretarial work. Smith personally oversaw the scheduling of work shifts and even lunch breaks to prevent the women who worked directly for him from coming into contact with one another.

For eight years the schedule seemed to work. No one secretary was with him long enough to learn anything of value.

This sort of analyzing and overthinking would have driven a lesser man to despair. But for Harold Smith it was just another of the thousand seemingly small things that added to the weight of his crushing daily burden.

Smith gave the young woman at the desk a curt

nod as he entered her office. "Miss Purvish," he said crisply.

"That delivery you expected came while you were out, Dr. Smith," his secretary said. "I had the workmen put it in the basement just like you requested."

"Thank you, Miss Purvish," Smith said. With quick strides he crossed to his office door. His long fingers snaked impatiently to the brass knob.

"What's it for?"

Smith's grip tightened on the doorknob. For an instant he was frozen in place.

His secretary's words didn't exactly shock like a physical blow, yet they registered deeply.

He would have preferred not answering at all. But in moments like these he found that all the women who worked for him tended toward the tenacious. It was typical for their gender. A nonanswer would inspire greater curiosity.

"I intend to use it for storage," Smith said.

"Oh," Miss Purvish said with a confident nod. She was already returning to her typing. "I thought it was for something like that. But it was so big and I didn't see any drawers. It looked like a big steel box."

Her interest mollified, she began pecking away at the stiff keys of her manual typewriter.

The young woman was getting too familiar. As Smith slipped into his office, he made a mental note to rotate Miss Purvish back out to the sanitarium for a few weeks. He shut the door behind him with a muted click.

The inner office was clean and Spartan. A few chairs, a sofa near the door. A couple of plain wooden file cabinets.

Smith hurried to his desk, sliding into his comfortable leather chair.

The big oak desk was already beginning to show signs of age. Nothing lasted like it was supposed to. Not desks, not people and not—it would seem—representative republics.

Smith fretted briefly at the loosening veneer of his desk's surface as he opened his bottom drawer. He pulled out a cherry-red telephone, the only item in the drawer. The phone had no dial.

Smith set the dialless red phone reverently atop the desk, careful to keep the base perfectly parallel to the desk's edge.

Feeling a thrum of excitement in his narrow chest, he bracketed the phone with both hands before sitting calmly back in his seat. With a deep breath, he checked his Timex.

It was 10:55 a.m. Phil Rand and his telephone company workmen had taken longer than anticipated. Even so, Smith had gotten back in time. He had precisely three minutes.

Another deep breath. There was no sense wasting time.

Leaning forward, he searched the underside of the desk with his fingers. Depressing a hidden stud near his right knee, Smith watched as a computer monitor rose like some modern Leviathan from beneath the surface of the desk. A keyboard was revealed at his fingertips.

Smith quickly set to work scanning the digests culled for him by the CURE mainframes.

Computers were becoming more and more a daily fixture in American life. Most banks and many businesses these days were turning to computerized systems. The government was blazing a trail that federal and even local law enforcement was starting to follow. Crude military computer networks were growing interdependent. A global network of computers was sparking hesitantly to life. The CURE director envisioned a day—perhaps even in his lifetime—where computers would become as common an appliance as the television. For the moment the CURE mainframes were a secret part of the vanguard of the coming age.

CURE had many unwitting operatives on its payroll. Thousands of people in all walks of life, peppered throughout the country. A web of informants, none of them knowing the others, not one having any clue they were part of some greater information-gathering system.

The first item of interest was from New York City. A CURE informant in the FBI's New York branch had forwarded a memo to a superior in Washington. Little did he realize that the superior didn't exist and the note had found its way to the computer of Harold Smith.

According to the report, an FBI agent in New York City had turned up dead that morning. Sadly, such a thing was not unprecedented in this lawless age. Smith was about to file the report in the CURE system when something caught his eye.

The dead man was an Agent Alex Worth.

Only when he scanned the man's name did Smith's heart skip a cold beat.

The man was a CURE agent. Of course, he didn't know it. There were only three men on the face of the planet who knew of the covert agency's existence. Worth was not one of them. The FBI man had been placed in the field by a circuitous order from Smith one week ago. And now he was dead.

With renewed interest the CURE director's flint-gray eyes quickly scoured the report. The details of the memo brought a puzzled expression to Smith's lemony face.

There was precious little information.

According to the terse report, the agent had been killed by some inhumanly powerful force. If Smith's source was right, Agent Worth's chest had been crushed. A hasty autopsy revealed pulverized internal organs.

"Odd," Smith said to the empty room.

In his experience men were shot or stabbed or died in one of a hundred familiar ways. This, however, was new.

Ostensibly on order of his FBI superiors, Worth had been sent to investigate some new type of weapon in the arsenal of New York's organized crime. The only clue given up by a dying informant was the name Maxwell. But where this Maxwell might be remained a mystery. And now the man who had been charged with uncovering Maxwell was dead.

Smith would have to send another agent.

CURE's computerized tendrils stretched to the upper reaches of the CIA, FBI, Treasury Department and every other major law-enforcement agency in the nation. Although technically he had thousands of agents at his disposal, there was just one he could personally order into the field. Given the death of Agent Worth, Smith might have considered using him. But his man was already on a mission.

Smith had heard a minor blip out of North Korea three days before. Then nothing. If the Communists had captured or sunk the *Darter,* it would likely have made news by now.

The likeliest conclusion Smith could reach was that Conrad MacCleary was on his way back home with his special package. But it would still be a few more days. He couldn't wait. He would have to send someone else.

Smith was about to issue the proper surreptitious commands via his computer when he was startled by a ringing telephone. For an instant he wasn't certain of the source. Although he'd had the phone in his office for a number of years now, it had never rung.

Before the red phone could ring a second time, Smith scooped up the receiver.

"Smith, 7-4-4," he said, offering the arranged code. As he spoke, he checked his watch—10:58 on the dot.

"I assume we can consider this a successful test, Smith," said the clear voice on the other end of the line. The man sounded impatient. As if the world were somehow out of sync and he was always hurrying to keep up.

"Yes, sir," Smith replied efficiently. "We can now eliminate our face-to-face meetings. In the event of dire circumstances you may contact me using this line."

"Good. I can't say I liked the idea of you sneaking in and out of here like a common thief. The press would eat me alive if they found out about this. Now, as long as you have me here, do you have anything to report?"

Smith hesitated. He considered mentioning the death of FBI Agent Worth, but quickly thought better of it. There were enough complications for CURE coming in the near future. No need to pile more on.

"No, sir. I am taking steps to augment our personnel as we discussed. I will update you when I know more. For now, the safety window for this phone runs for only five minutes. I dare not leave it longer than that, so I suggest we keep this conversation short."

"Very well, Smith. Good luck."

The phone went dead in his hand. There wasn't even the buzz of a dial tone.

Alone in his office, Smith allowed another rare smile of satisfaction. His second of the day.

The years of patience had finally paid off. The White House hotline was now fully operational.

Perhaps this was a turning point for CURE. Maybe after eight long years his agency was finally coming together.

But there was still the matter of the dead FBI agent and this mysterious Maxwell.

Smith's smile melted to a frown as he noted the report on his monitor. Replacing the red phone in his lower drawer, he turned his full attention back to his computer.

4

The USS *Darter* landed in San Diego two days earlier than expected. MacCleary arranged for a regular commercial flight from California to New York. The only problem came at the airport when a clumsy skycap put a small scratch in one of the Master of Sinanju's precious steamer trunks.

Both Chiun and skycap vanished. Just like that.

MacCleary had no idea what happened. One minute they were there—the next, poof.

The only place they could have gone was the nearby men's room. When MacCleary ducked inside, he found the Master of Sinanju exiting a stall. Beyond the Korean, the uniformed porter was upended in a toilet, legs bent at inhuman angles.

When Conn checked, he found no bubbles rising from the drowned man's mouth. MacCleary quickly locked the stall door and jammed it so it wouldn't open. Afterward he handled Chiun's luggage. Carefully.

Luckily, the plane ride to the East Coast was less eventful. He called Smith from the airport after they landed. When their cab drove up Folcroft's gravel drive, the CURE director was waiting on the front steps.

Smith's gray face was already showing displeasure before they even reached the bottom of the staircase.

The Master of Sinanju's fourteen lacquered steamer trunks hadn't fit in a single cab. MacCleary had been forced to hire two more to trail the first. All three Yellow Cabs slowed to a crunching stop at the base of the staircase.

MacCleary was first out of the back of the cab. Even as he was mounting the stairs to catch Smith, Chiun was flouncing from the rear of the lead vehicle. The Korean hurried back to oversee the unloading of his trunks.

At the appearance of the old Oriental, Smith's face fell. When MacCleary stopped beside him on the steps, the initial look of shocked confusion on the CURE director's face was already bleeding to anger.

"Is that him?" Smith demanded.

Down in the driveway, Chiun danced between the three cabdrivers. Darting hands swatted heads in an attempt to whip the cabbies into shape. The grumbling men began hauling the luggage up the stairs and inside the main foyer.

"Yeah. And I know what you're thinking, Smitty," MacCleary said, raising both arms to stave off argument. His hook glinted in the dull autumn sunlight.

"I doubt that," Smith said through clenched teeth. "Is this your idea of a joke?"

MacCleary shook his head firmly. "Wait'll you see what he can do before you throw him overboard, Smitty. And trust me, you do *not* want to mishandle his luggage."

The old man chose that moment to come padding up the stairs in the wake of the last cabbie. To Smith, rather than appearing as a savior, the Korean looked as if he should have been checking into Folcroft as a patient.

"You had better be right about this," Smith warned MacCleary from the corner of his mouth.

Chiun stopped before the CURE director.

"Greetings, President Smith," the Master of Sinanju intoned. He offered a formal bow.

"Presi—?" Smith questioned. The word wasn't past his lips before he heard a scuffle behind him.

When he glanced over his shoulder, he found a Folcroft visitor leading an elderly patient down the main staircase. Although the female patient was oblivious to the tiny kimono-clad figure, her relative took a long, puzzled look at Chiun.

Coming down behind the two women was the trio of cabdrivers. They went to work on the next set of trunks.

Smith bit his tongue until the pair of women had passed and gotten into a parked car and the cabdrivers were hauling the second trio of trunks. Only when no one was paying them any attention did he grab MacCleary by the arm.

Smith pulled the bigger man up into the building.

The first of Chiun's trunks were piled just inside the entrance. Smith steered past them. The first open door he found was to an empty waiting room. Smith took MacCleary inside. To the CURE director's intense displeasure, the old Korean trailed in their wake.

"What is this?" Smith demanded, closing the door. His voice was a low hiss.

"The president thing?" MacCleary asked. "It's a long story, Smitty. Sinanju has a history of working for leaders of nations or guys aspiring to *be* leaders of nations, if you catch my drift. Chiun thinks you want to be president.''

Smith's spine grew so rigid for a moment it looked as if it might crack. ''And I suppose you didn't attempt to disabuse him of something so patently preposterous?''

MacCleary's face split into a smile. ''Hey, I tried, Smitty,'' he admitted. ''But I think he thought I was full of it. He thinks I'm just your lackey. Probably thinks I want to bump you off so *I* can become president.''

Eyes growing wide, Smith shook his head sharply. He looked as if he thought the wallpaper might be threaded with hidden listening devices.

''No one wants—'' He turned from MacCleary, realizing he was arguing with the wrong man. ''No one wants that,'' he assured the Master of Sinanju.

Chiun stood in the corner of the room. He had turned his indifferent back to the two babbling whites.

A wall-mounted black-and-white television set murmured softly at the room. Chiun's button nose was turned upward, his hazel eyes directed at the action on the screen.

Stepping over, Smith reached up and shut off the TV. The afternoon soap opera that had been playing collapsed to an incandescent blotch before fading from sight.

''Excuse me, Master Chiun—'' Smith paused. ''Forgive me, but is that the appropriate title?''

Eyes flitting from the darkened TV set, Chiun's parchment face was flat.

''You do not speak Korean?'' he asked.

''No, I don't,'' Smith admitted.

Chiun allowed a small nod. ''Then in English that

will suffice. Either that or Gracious Master of Sinanju.''

"I, er, prefer Master Chiun if it's all the same to you.''

"As you wish, President Smith," the old Korean said.

"That, on the other hand, is a title that is not appropriate," Smith said rapidly. "I am not certain what Mr. MacCleary has told you—"

"Hey, he didn't get it from me," Conn interjected.

"—but you may call me *Dr.* Smith," the CURE director finished.

Chiun's weathered face brightened. "Ah, you are a physician."

"Not in the sense with which you might be familiar. I have a doctorate in clinical psychology, among others."

"President Smith is a head doctor," MacCleary explained with a knowing wink.

"Stop it, Conn," Smith snapped.

"You cure ailments of the brain?" Chiun suggested.

"Not as such. Not physical ailments, anyway. And I have never practiced psychology. Do you see?"

Chiun nodded. "But of course," he said, his tone perfectly even. "You are a physician who is not a physician who does not practice the healing arts. How very wise."

This man is a lunatic, the Master of Sinanju thought to himself. He smiled and nodded at Smith.

"I don't think he understands," Smith said to MacCleary.

"But of course I do, Your Highness," Chiun told Smith.

"Chiun understands enough," Conn promised Smith.

"I am not a highness, either," Smith insisted, ignoring MacCleary. "Master Chiun, this is a delicate situation. I cannot give you the details of our mission here. I can only say that it will attract unwanted attention if you address me as Highness. And since I was not duly elected by the voters of this nation, nor do I have any desire to become president, it is wholly inappropriate for you to address me by that title, as well."

"Elected?" Chiun asked, arching a suspicious brow.

"Yes," Smith said. "America votes for its president—our king, if you will. It is the people here who choose the man who leads the country."

"So it *is* true," Chiun said, stroking his thread of beard wisely. "One hears rumors, of course. They tried a thing like that in Rome once. It didn't take."

"Yes," Smith said cautiously. "In any event, I would appreciate it if you call me Doctor."

But the Master of Sinanju shook his head firmly. "Would that I could obey, but I can see that title is neither appropriate nor adequate, for any quacksalver with a jar of leeches considers himself a doctor. And your regal bearing, handsome visage and piercing eyes tell me you are much more than a common bloodletter." Before Smith could argue more, the old man held up a staying hand. "However, since I am but a humble servant, I will honor your request, though it drives a dagger deep in my crude heart to do so."

Smith allowed a slip of relief to pass his bloodless gray lips. "Thank you, Master Chiun."

"No, no," Chiun said. "The thanks are mine. Thanks that you would honor one so lowly and unworthy as I to bask in the radiant glow of your reflected majesty."

Smith decided to quit while he was ahead. Offering an uncomfortable "you're welcome" to the Master of Sinanju, he turned his full attention to MacCleary.

"Set up some exercises," Smith ordered. "I would like to see what it is we're buying."

Conn's face cracked into a wicked smile. "I think you'll be pleasantly surprised," he promised.

He headed out the door. Smith began to follow but felt a bony hand clamp his elbow. When he looked down, the upturned face of the old Korean was filled with cunning.

"I understand completely, Your Royal Presidential Highness," Chiun whispered slyly. "You do not want to make your intentions known before the commander of your palace guard. That is wise, for a king has welcomed betrayal into his court who fully trusts his closest knight." He patted Smith's forearm. "We'll talk later."

With a broad wink Chiun ducked past Smith and headed out into the hallway to check on his trunks.

Alone, Smith gripped the door frame until his knuckles turned white. His sick eyes strayed to the fuzzy wallpaper.

With renewed worries of hidden microphones, the CURE director left the small waiting room.

THE NEXT DAY was Saturday.

There was normally only a skeleton work crew at Folcroft on weekends. Smith made certain that there was less staff than usual. It was early in the afternoon, after lunch but before visiting hours, when the three men met once more in Folcroft's basement gymnasium.

The gym was on the far side of the big building, beyond the already closed cafeteria. At MacCleary's insistence, Smith had informed the duty staff that any strange noises they might hear this day would be caused by plumbers working on the sanitarium's ancient boiler-fed heating system.

"Good afternoon, Emperor Smith," Chiun said as he padded into the big room in the company of Conrad MacCleary.

This was the title the old Korean had decided on the previous night.

Smith reluctantly accepted it for the time being. On consideration, he realized that it wouldn't cause too many raised eyebrows given the mental state of many of Folcroft's patients. And there would be plenty of time to convince the Master of Sinanju to drop the honorific, assuming things worked out the way MacCleary seemed to think they would.

Ever punctual, Smith was standing alone in the gym reading the day's newspaper. He fully expected MacCleary to be late. After all, he usually was. Assuming it was the Master of Sinanju who had held Conn MacCleary to the preordained time, Smith folded his paper and tucked it neatly up under his arm as the men stopped before him.

MacCleary had been drinking. Smith could smell the stale booze on the big man. Not enough to be drunk. Just an eye-opener to steady the nerves for what lay ahead.

"You're going to be amazed, Smitty," Conn assured him.

Smith reserved judgment. He calmly placed his newspaper on a small shelf near a wall-mounted black phone. Crossing his arms, he waited near the door for MacCleary to set up for the demonstration.

He was surprised when MacCleary eschewed the floor mats that were rolled in the corner of the gym.

Smith assumed that this Sinanju martial art was like all the others. Given the reputation of the House of Sinanju, he thought Chiun might be faster than other martial artists, but he assumed a demonstration would still involve a lot of tumbling, shouting and breaking of boards.

The CURE director knew he was in for something different when the old Oriental padded to the far side of the gym.

A few yards away from Smith, MacCleary waited at the faded foul line of the basketball court.

When Chiun was in position across the hall, MacCleary reached under his rumpled jacket.

Smith was looking from one man to the next, confused at what sort of demonstration this might be. Only when he glanced back at MacCleary did he see the gun.

MacCleary had pulled out a .38 Police Special.

Smith felt his stomach freeze. He was running at a full sprint over to MacCleary even as the big man was taking a careful bead on the wizened Korean who stood, calmly awaiting doom, on the other side of the gym.

Even before he reached MacCleary, Smith knew he'd be too late. When it came, the single shot was like thunder in the gymnasium. The fat slug screamed across the gym.

Smith saw Chiun. The tiny man seemed to crumple

and fly from view, flung back by the force of the gunshot.

"Have you gone mad?" the CURE director snarled, coming up beside MacCleary.

Conn's face was blandly amused. He held the gun beyond reach of Smith's grabbing hands. His hook was resting casually in his jacket pocket.

"Relax, Smitty," MacCleary said. "Take another look." He aimed his chin across the room.

Smith glanced over to where the ancient Korean lay. His mind was already reeling as he tried to think of how they would be able to dispose of the body.

But there was no body.

The tiny Korean was standing where Smith had last seen him, a placid expression on his wrinkled face.

"Thank God," Smith sighed, relieved. "You missed."

MacCleary shook his head. He seemed insulted at the mere suggestion. "Like hell. You ever know me to miss?"

Smith hesitated to answer.

"That's 'cause I don't miss," MacCleary concluded. And to punctuate the point, he raised his gun and fired again.

This time Smith kept his full attention on Chiun.

He thought he saw something. The same flash of movement he had caught from the corner of his eye the first time. But it moved faster than his brain and eyes could reconcile. And faster, it would seem, than a bullet in flight.

When the bullet struck the wall, sending up a faint puff of concrete dust, Chiun was standing five feet away from the spot where he had been. His face held no expression as he smoothed invisible wrinkles in his kimono skirts.

"How is this possible?" Smith asked, amazed.

MacCleary shrugged. "It's Sinanju," he said.

Across the vast gymnasium, a reed-thin voice chimed in.

"General MacCleary is correct, Emperor," Chiun called.

"General?" Smith said, raising an annoyed eyebrow. He turned a gimlet eye on MacCleary.

Conn's broad face was pure innocence. "Hey, don't blame me if the guy recognizes officer material when he sees it."

He squeezed off another casual round.

At first Smith once more thought he saw movement. Only when this latest bullet missed did he realize what he was seeing was a mirage. The ghostly afterimage of a body twisting impossibly from the path of a speeding bullet.

"Incredible," Smith said.

"A gun is merely a device that goes boom, Emperor Smith," Chiun called. "And Sinanju has long learned not to fear loud noises."

"But the bullet," Smith said. "How is it possible for you to avoid being struck?"

"You call it a bullet. Master Thuk called it a spear. Before that was rocks. There is no difference."

Smith thought there was a huge difference between a hurtling bullet and a thrown rock.

MacCleary didn't seem to care about the specifics of what Chiun was doing. He was in awe of the mysterious little Oriental who had been a living puzzle tickling the periphery of his daydreams for the past twenty-five years.

Raising his handgun, MacCleary fired again and again. To Conn it was like some joyous game.

Sometimes Chiun was close—sometimes he was far away. Even Smith took a few turns. They had to have shot at the old Korean a hundred times from a hundred different angles. And each time the wizened figure would pop up unharmed a few feet from where he'd last stood.

When the ammunition was spent, MacCleary finally rolled out some of the practice mats. Chiun padded up to join him.

Conn MacCleary was a powerful man. Not only had he never backed away from a good brawl, Smith knew from experience that he was generally the one to instigate them.

MacCleary stripped down to his T-shirt before turning to face Chiun in the center of the largest mat.

It was ridiculous, *comical*. Here was Conrad MacCleary—all six foot two and two-hundred-plus pounds of him—towering over a five-foot, ninety-pound Korean. There was a hint of animal anticipation on MacCleary's rugged face. For his part the Master of Sinanju was an imperturbable pool.

When MacCleary lunged, Chiun seemed to be studying the treetops visible through the gym's high second-story windows.

MacCleary knew any hopes he might have had of catching the old Oriental off guard were dashed the instant he saw the dull blue exercise mat racing up to meet him. He struck the hard padding with a lung-depressing thump. Stale air burst from his mouth.

He hadn't even seen Chiun move. Nor, apparently, had Harold Smith. Unlike with the bullets, this time the CURE director hadn't seen even a hint of movement.

"Amazing," Smith said, eyes wide behind the spotless lenses of his rimless glasses.

"Such is it for those employers who wisely stock their armories with the silent sword that is Sinanju," Chiun said. "A bargain at twice the price."

On the floor MacCleary had gotten his breath back. "Cram the sales pitch," he snarled.

He tried to take down Chiun with a sweeping foot.

For the next half hour, MacCleary was bounced and tossed like a sweating beanbag all around the skidding blue mats.

"You little yellow bastard," MacCleary growled, panting to catch his breath. Though bruised from the exercises, there remained a mirthful glint in his bloodshot eyes. His blotchy face glistened with sweat.

Chiun tipped his birdlike head to Smith. "Begging the Emperor's pardon," he said, "but do you have many generals?"

By this point Smith was lost in thought. As the afternoon had progressed, he slowly came to the realization that this crazy scheme might work after all.

"What?" the CURE director asked, snapping from his reverie. "Oh, er, no," he said. "He is my only one."

"A pity. Traditionally one ends a demonstration such as this by offering the head of his worthy opponent to the prospective employer."

"I'd like to see you try." Conn grinned. He raised his hook near his shoulder, his other hand directed forward.

"That is not necessary, Master Chiun," Smith quickly interjected. "MacCleary, back off."

With great reluctance Conn did as he was told.

"I told you we had a winner here," MacCleary panted.

Smith couldn't disagree. "Very good," he said. "Master of Sinanju, we would like to formally retain your services."

Chiun offered a bow that Smith assumed signified some kind of acceptance. "Sinanju desires only to serve America's true ruler." He tucked his hands inside the voluminous sleeves of his kimono, latching on to opposing wrists. "Now, this dead man you would have your unworthy servant instruct," Chiun asked. "Is he here in your palace?"

The old Korean seemed a little too nonchalant. For the first time Smith saw a hint of eagerness in the Master of Sinanju's hazel eyes.

Smith shot a wordless glance to MacCleary.

"I told him a little bit about his trainee back in Korea," Conn explained. He wiped the sweat from his face with his T-shirt.

"I suppose it doesn't matter," Smith said reluctantly. "You would have found out when you met him."

"When will that be?" Chiun asked. Again the eagerness.

A notch formed on Smith's brow. "Soon," he promised. "There are just a few loose ends to tie up first."

"Very well," Chiun said. "I will be in my quarters awaiting his arrival. Emperor." With a nod of his head that barely disturbed his tufts of white hair, he spun from the two men. On shuffling feet he left the gym.

"He is a man of mystery," Smith commented.

With an introspective hum he went to retrieve his newspaper.

"Yeah," MacCleary said. As he trailed behind Smith, he put on his shirt and tucked it in. Every muscle ached. "If by 'mystery' you mean an A-number-one, rice-eating ass-kicker."

Smith didn't respond. He took his paper from the shelf. As he did, his eye was drawn to a below-the-fold headline.

There was a short article about an execution that was scheduled to take place at Trenton State Prison in New Jersey the following week. While it had made some news, it wasn't as big a story as it might have been even ten years earlier. The world had been turned so completely upside down these days that people were beginning to lose their capacity for either shock or outrage.

MacCleary caught Smith stealing a look at the article. Buttoning his last few shirt buttons, he read the headline over the CURE director's shoulder.

"Poor bastard," MacCleary muttered after a quiet moment.

"It is necessary," Smith insisted without emotion. But though he tried to mask it, there was a hint of remorse in his gray eyes. Paper in hand, Smith left the gym.

"It still stinks," MacCleary said to himself once he was alone. His voice was so soft it didn't even echo off the distant gymnasium walls.

With a sweep of his hand, he clicked off the lights. As he left the room, one thought played through his troubled mind: *No one even knows why he's going to die.*

5

Everyone knew why Remo Williams was going to die. The chief of the Newark Police Department told his close friends Williams was a sacrifice to the civil-rights groups.

"Who ever heard of a cop going to the chair...and for killing a dope pusher? Maybe a suspension, maybe even dismissal, but the chair? If that punk had been white, Williams wouldn't get the chair."

To the press the chief said: "It is a tragic incident. Williams always had a good record as a policeman."

The reporters weren't fooled. They knew why Williams had to die. "He was crazy. Christ, you couldn't let that lunatic out in the streets again. How did he ever get on the force in the first place? Beats a man to a pulp, leaves him to die in an alley, drops his badge for evidence, then expects to get away with it by hollering 'frame-up.' Damn fool."

The defense attorney knew why his client had lost. "That damned badge. We couldn't get around that evidence. Why wouldn't he admit he beat up that bum? Even so, the judge never should have given him the chair."

The judge was quite certain why he had sentenced Williams to die. It was very simple. He was told to.

Not that he knew why he was told to. In certain circles you don't ask questions about verdicts.

Only one man had no conception of why the sentence was so severe and so swift. And his wondering would stop at 11:35 that night.

Remo Williams sat on the cot in his cell chain-smoking cigarettes. His dark brown hair was shaved close at the temples where the guards would place the electrodes.

The gray trousers issued to all inmates at New Jersey's Trenton State Prison already had been slit nearly to the knees. The white socks were fresh and clean with the exception of the gray spots from ashes he dropped.

He had stopped using the ashtray days before. He simply threw the finished cigarette on the gray painted floor each time and watched its life burn out. It wouldn't even leave a mark, just burn out slowly, hardly noticeable.

The guards would eventually open the cell door and have an inmate clean up the butts. They would wait outside the cell, Remo between them, while the inmate swept. And when Remo was returned, there would be no trace that he had ever smoked in there or that a cigarette had died on the floor.

He could leave nothing in the death cell that would remain. The cot was steel and had no paint in which to even scratch his initials. The mattress would be replaced if he ripped it. He couldn't even break the bulb above his head. It was protected by a steel-enmeshed glass plate.

He could break the ashtray. That he could do, if he wanted. He could scratch something in the white enamel sink with no stopper and one faucet.

But what would he inscribe? Advice? A note? To whom? For what? What would he tell them?

That you do your job, you're promoted, and one dark night they find a dead dope pusher in an alley on your beat, and he's got your badge in his hand, and they don't give you a medal but fall for the frame-up, and you get the chair.

It's you who winds up in the death house. The place you wanted to send so many hoods, punks, killers, pushers—the scum that preyed on society. And then the people, the right and good people you sweated for and risked your neck for, rise in their majesty and turn on you. All of a sudden, they're sending men to the chair—the judges who won't give death to the predators, but give it to the protectors.

You can't write that in a sink. So you light another cigarette and throw the old butt on the floor and watch it burn. The smoke curls and disappears before rising three feet. Then the butt goes out. But by that time, you have another one ready to light and another one ready to throw.

Remo Williams took the mentholated cigarette from his mouth, held it close before his face to see the red ember feeding on that hint of mint, then tossed it on the floor.

He took a fresh cigarette from one of the two packs at his side on the brown, scratchy wool blanket. He looked up at the two guards whose backs were to him.

They had never walked the morning hours on a beat looking in windows and waiting to be made detective. They'd never been framed with a pusher who, as a corpse, didn't have the stuff on him. They went home at night and left the prison behind them. They were the clerks of law enforcement.

The law.

Remo looked at the freshly lit cigarette in his hand and suddenly hated the mentholated taste, which was like eating Vicks. He tore off the filter and tossed it on the floor. He inhaled on the ragged end deeply and lay back on the cot, blowing the smoke toward the seamless plaster ceiling.

Remo had strong, sharp features and deep-set brown eyes that crinkled at the edges, but not from laughter.

Suddenly, Remo's facial muscles tightened and he sat up. His eyes suddenly detected every line on the floor. He saw the sink, and for the first time he really saw the solid gray metal of the bars. He crushed out the butt with his toe.

"How much time do I have?" Remo asked. The words were slow coming out. How long had it been since he had spoken?

"About a half hour," one of the guards said. He was a tall man and his uniform was too tight around the shoulders. "The priest will be here in a while."

Remo closed his eyes. They were dry.

"I haven't been to church since I was an altar boy," he said. "Hell, every punk I arrest tells me he was an altar boy, even the Protestants and Jews. Maybe they know something I don't. Maybe it helps." He sighed as he lay back down on the cot. "Yeah, I'll see the priest."

Remo drummed his fingers silently on his stomach. What was death like anyway? Like sleep? He liked to sleep. Most people liked to sleep. Why fear death?

In a few minutes he heard the soft padding of feet in the corridor, louder, louder, louder. They stopped outside his cell door. Voices mumbled, clothes rustled, keys tingled and then with a clack the cell door opened.

Remo blinked in the yellow light. A brown-robed monk clutching a black cross with a silver Christ stood inside the cell door. A dark cowl shaded the monk's eyes. He held the crucifix in his right hand, the left apparently tucked beneath the folds of his robe.

"The priest," the guard said to Remo. To the monk he said, "You've got five minutes, Father."

The cell door shut and the key clicked in the lock.

Remo sat up on the cot, his back to the wall. He motioned to the empty space beside him on the cot.

Holding the crucifix like a test tube he was afraid to spill, the monk sat down. His face was hard and lined. His blue eyes seemed to be judging Remo for a punch instead of salvation. Droplets of perspiration on his upper lip caught the light from the bulb.

"Do you want to be saved, my son?" he asked. It was rather loud for such a personal question.

"Sure," Remo said. "Who doesn't?"

"Good. Do you know how to examine your conscience, make an act of contrition?"

"Vaguely, Father. I..."

"I know, my son. God will help you."

"Yeah," Remo said without enthusiasm. If he got this over fast, maybe there'd be time for another cigarette.

"What are your sins?"

"I really don't know."

"We can start with violation of the Lord's commandment not to kill. How many men have you killed?"

"Including Vietnam?"

"No, Vietnam doesn't count."

"That wasn't killing, huh?"

"In war, killing is not a mortal sin."

"How about peace, when the state says you did, but you didn't? How about that?"

"Are you talking about this conviction?"

"Yes." Remo's voice was small. He stared at his knees.

"Well, in that case…"

"All right, Father," Remo interrupted suddenly. "I confess it. I killed the man." The lie came easily.

His trousers, fresh gray twill, hadn't even had a chance to get worn at the knees. Remo noticed that the monk's cowl was perfectly clean. Spotlessly new. He looked up at that hard face beneath the cowl. Was that a smile?

"Coveted anyone's property?" the monk pressed.

"No."

"Stolen?"

"No."

"Impure actions?"

"Sure. In thought and deed."

"Blasphemy, anger, pride, jealousy, gluttony?"

"No," Remo said, rather loudly.

The monk leaned forward. Remo could see the tobacco stains on his teeth. The light, subtle smell of expensive aftershave lotion wafted into his nostrils. The monk's voice was a whispering rasp. "You're a goddamned liar."

Remo jumped back. His hands moved almost as if to ward off a blow. The priest remained leaning forward, motionless. And he was grinning. The priest was grinning. The guards couldn't see it because of the cowl, but Remo could. The state was playing its final joke on him: a tobacco-stained, grinning, swearing monk.

"You're no priest," Remo said.

"Shh," cautioned the brown-robed man. "Keep your voice down. You want to save your soul or your ass?"

Remo stared at the crucifix, the silver Christ on the black cross and the black button at the feet.

A black button?

"Listen. We don't have much time," the man in the robe said. "You want to live?"

The word seemed to float from Remo's soul. "Sure."

"Get on your knees."

Remo went to the floor in one smooth motion. The crucifix came toward his head. He looked up at the silvery feet pierced by a silver nail.

"Pretend to kiss the feet. Yes. Closer. There's a black pill. Ease it off with your teeth. Go ahead, but don't bite into it."

Remo opened his mouth and closed his teeth around the black button. He saw the robes swirl as the man got up to block the guard's view. The pill came off. It was hard, probably plastic.

"Don't break the shell," the man hissed. "Stick it in the corner of your mouth. When they strap the helmet around your head so you can't move, bite into the pill and swallow the whole thing. Not before. Do you hear?"

Remo held the pill on his tongue. The man in the robes of a monk was no longer smiling. Remo glared at him.

Why were all the big decisions in his life forced

on him when he didn't have time to think? He tongued the pill.

Poison? No point in that.

Spit it out? Then what?

Nothing to lose. Remo tried to taste the pill without letting it touch his teeth. No taste. The monk hovered over him. Remo nestled the pill under his tongue and said a very fast and very sincere prayer.

"Okay," he said.

"Time's up," the guard's voice commanded.

"God bless you, my son," the monk said loudly, making the sign of the cross with the crucifix. Then, in a whisper, "See you later." He padded from the cell, his head bowed, the crucifix before him and his left hand flinting steel.

Steel?

Remo caught just a glimpse of a curving hook before the monk vanished in the hallway outside his open cell door.

Someone was telling Remo it was time to go. The prison guard. Remo swallowed very carefully. Tongue clamped down over the pill, he walked out to meet his fate.

HAROLD HAINES DIDN'T like it. Four executions in seven years, and all of a sudden the state had to send in electricians to monkey with the power box.

"A routine check," he was told. "You haven't used it for three years. They just want to make sure it'll work."

Whoever they were, Haines never saw them. They'd come to do their tinkering the previous night. That was hours ago. Now, on the morning he was scheduled to execute that maniac killer cop, Williams,

Harold Haines was having to give his own equipment a less than thorough once-over.

The executioner's pale face tilted toward the head-high regulator panel as he turned a rheostat. Out of the corner of his eye he glanced momentarily at the glass partition separating the control room from the chair room.

Haines shook his head and turned the juice back down. The generators resumed their low, malevolent hum.

"Is something the matter?" asked a crisp voice.

Haines jumped in shock, spinning.

A tall, middle-aged man in a three-piece gray suit and carrying a metallic attaché case was standing very nearby beside the control panel. The executioner had thought he was alone. This man with the lemony voice had slipped into the small room like a silent ghost.

"Who are you?" Haines snapped.

"The warden's office told you I was coming," replied the stranger. He had the bland look of a career bureaucrat.

Haines remembered Warden Johnson mentioning something about some state observer wanting to be on hand to witness the execution from the control room.

"Oh," Haines sighed, nodding. "Oh, yeah. They did." With a grunt he turned back to the control board. "He'll be here in a minute. It's not much of a view from here, but if you go to the glass partition you can see fine."

"Thank you," said the man with the attaché case.

The man in the gray suit didn't move toward the window. He waited until Haines involved himself with his toys of death. Once he was certain he was not being observed, he cast an eye over the steel rivets at the base of the generator cover. Counting carefully to himself, he stopped at the fourth rivet. The rivet was brighter than the others.

The man glanced around the room. Certain once more that Haines wasn't paying attention, he pressed the attaché case against the fifth rivet, which moved an eighth of an inch.

There was a faint click. The man moved quickly away from the panel toward the glass partition. Through the thick glass, the electric chair was reflected in the spotless lenses of his rimless glasses.

Less than a minute later the door to the chair room opened. Remo Williams stepped in behind the warden. Two guards came in behind.

Remo didn't struggle. Stepping into the center of the room, he sat in the chair by himself.

The guards placed his arms on the chair arms and fastened them in place with metallic straps. Kneeling, they clamped Remo's legs with more straps.

In the control room the lemon-faced man watched as the condemned man pursed his lips. Williams seemed to be rolling his tongue inside his closed mouth. The movement stopped and Williams just sat there, calmly awaiting death.

Harold Haines hustled from the control room for a few moments. He emerged in the chair room. After drawing a cap over the prisoner's head, the executioner did one last check around the chair. Satisfied that everything was in working order, he hustled back into the control room.

The next few moments were always anticlimactic.

The warden asked the condemned man if he had any last words.

Williams didn't say anything. His eyes were closed and his arms were limp. It looked as if he was out cold.

Passed out, Haines thought. Mr. Tough Guy Newark, New Jersey, beat cop had passed out in the chair. Well, Harold Haines would wake him up, all right.

Warden Johnson stepped back from the chair and nodded toward the control room. Sweating, Haines slowly turned up the twin rheostats. The generators hummed.

Williams's body jolted upright in the seat.

Haines eased off the rheostats slowly.

The warden nodded again. Haines threw another jolt into Williams as the generators hummed.

The body twitched again, then sagged into the seat.

Inside the control room, Haines cut off the juice and let the generators die.

This was the fifth man to die in Harold Haines's chair. Experience didn't lessen his great relief. When it was over, Haines let loose a long gasp that almost sounded like a whoop of joy. Only then did he suddenly remember that this time—unlike the previous four times—he wasn't alone.

The gray-faced bureaucrat who had come to view the execution would never understand his relief. Haines glanced around the room, already trying to find words of explanation.

He found that he needn't have worried. Harold Haines was alone. His visitor was gone.

FOR A HAZY FEW MOMENTS Remo awoke in a confused cloud.

He didn't know how long he had been out. Days. Weeks?

He had bitten down on the pill. The sweet, warm ooze had made him drowsy. He was out when the electric jolts came. Not enough to kill. Just enough to simulate death.

Sleep still clung to the cobwebs of his brain. He thought he heard someone speak his name. When he opened his eyes a bone-tired slit, he thought he glimpsed a face. It was wrinkled and old and reminded him of something he had seen in a dream long ago.

Remo couldn't see very well. There was something heavy wrapped around his own face. Bandages. Only his eyes and lips were exposed.

The old vision of a dream long gone was talking in an angry singsong.

"A white? You would have me train a white? Why stop there? Why not have the Master train for you a chimpanzee? Put it in a diaper and sit it on a unicycle and have it peddle around the American countryside flinging sticks and dung at the enemies of your crown. Believe me, it would strike more fear into their hearts than this whatever-he-is."

"I told you, *this* is your pupil," insisted a second voice, this one as sour as a pail of squeezed lemons.

Lying in the fog of semisleep, Remo groaned.

"I think he's coming around," the lemony voice said.

A moment later Remo felt a pinch at his arm. A sedative. The warmth of sleep melted through him once more.

The voices floated down to where he was sinking into the bottom of a deep, dark well.

"I will do what I must, for I have made an agreement," said the first voice reluctantly. "But I will not enjoy it."

"No one is asking you to."

"Good," insisted the singsong voice as Remo faded into sweet oblivion. "Because I guarantee you I won't."

6

When he finally regained full consciousness, the first thing Remo Williams saw clearly was the grinning face of the monk looking down at him. Over the face glared a white light—a mockery of a halo. Remo blinked.

"Looks like our baby's gonna make it."

Remo groaned. His limbs felt cold and leaden as though asleep for a thousand years. His wrists and ankles burned with pain where the electric straps had seared flesh. His face was sore, as if someone had been punching him repeatedly while he slept. His mouth was dry, his tongue like a sponge. Nausea swept up from his stomach and enveloped his brain. He thought he was vomiting, but nothing came out.

The air smelled of ether. He was lying on some sort of hard bed. He turned his head to see where he was, then stifled a scream. His head felt as if it was nailed to the mattress and he had just ripped out part of his skull.

Kaboom, kaboom, kaboom. His temples screamed. He shut his eyes and groaned again. He was breathing. Thank God, he was breathing. He was alive.

When a nurse offered sedatives, the monk refused them.

It took hours for the pain to subside. Remo was in and out of sleep the whole time, grateful to be alive. When the pain finally fled and Remo fully awakened, the monk with the hook was chasing a nurse and two doctors from the room.

Locking the door, the man rolled a tray to Remo's bed. With his hook he lifted the gleaming silver dome. Beneath were four lobsters, oozing butter from slit red bellies.

"My name's Conn MacCleary." He spooned two lobsters onto a plate and handed it to Remo.

"Bully for you," Remo said, cracking open a lobster claw. He scooped out the rich white meat with a small fork and swallowed without even chewing. His stomach rumbled. He was amazed at how hungry he was.

"You've been out for two weeks." MacCleary's voice became a low grumble. "I was worried we might have lost another one," he said to himself.

Remo had found the draft beer that MacCleary had wheeled in with the food. He drank greedily.

"I suppose you're wondering why you're here."

"Mmm," Remo said, reaching for the second lobster. Crushing the claw in his hands, he sucked out the meat.

"I said I suppose you're wondering why you're here," MacCleary repeated.

"Yeah," Remo said absently as he dipped a white chunk of lobster meat into a mug of melted butter. "Wondering."

Remo saw that something had been stamped on the side of the mug. The faded legend "Property Of Folcroft Sanitarium" was written in blue ink. It was the sort of stamp a business might use on furniture or expensive equipment. By the looks of it, the words on the mug had worn out several times and had to be reapplied. There were shadowy remnants of the phrase beneath the current one. Remo wondered briefly what exactly Folcroft Sanitarium was and what kind of nit would waste his time stamping and restamping a cheap, stained, easily replaceable coffee mug.

MacCleary had drawn a chair up next to Remo's bed. He frowned as the kid studied his mug of butter. He hoped for a moment that he hadn't wasted CURE's resources shanghaiing a flake. Probably the ordeal. After all, few men who had been executed had ever lived to tell the tale.

When Remo put down the mug and resumed eating, Conn started talking. He talked about Vietnam, where a young Marine named Remo Williams had entered a farmhouse alone and killed five Vietcong. He talked about death and life. He talked about patriotism and country. He talked about CURE.

"I can't tell you who runs it from the top," MacCleary said, "but I'm your boss." He stared into Remo's cold, brown eyes. In that moment he knew he was looking into the eyes of a born killer. "I promise you terror for breakfast, pressure for lunch, tension for supper and aggravation for sleep. Your vacations are the two minutes you're not looking over your shoulder for some hood to put one in the back of your head. Your bonuses are five minutes when you're not figuring out how to kill someone or keep from getting killed.

"But I promise you this." MacCleary lowered his voice. "Some day America may never need CURE, because of what we do. Maybe some day kids we

never had can walk down any dark street any time
and maybe a junkie ward won't be their only end.
Some day maybe honest judges can sit behind clean
benches and legislators won't take campaign funds
from gamblers. And all the union men will be fairly
represented. We're fighting the fight the American
people are too lazy to fight—maybe a fight they don't
even want won.''

Standing, MacCleary turned from Remo and paced
at the foot of the bed. ''If you live six months, it'll
be amazing. If you live a year, it'll be a miracle.
That's what we have to offer you.'' He stopped dead,
resting hook and hand on the base of Remo's bed.
''What do you say?''

MacCleary's eyes were reddened, his face taut.

Sitting in bed, Remo was picking lobster meat from
between his teeth with a fork. ''You frame me?''
Remo asked.

''Yeah,'' MacCleary said without emotion.

''Good job,'' Remo said. He reached for another
lobster.

''I'M NOT GETTING any younger,'' Remo said, irri-
tated. He leaned against a set of parallel bars in the
Folcroft gym.

For some reason MacCleary had made him dress
in a white costume with a white silk sash. The older
man had said it was necessary in order to show proper
respect.

''Hold your horses, kid,'' MacCleary called. He
was waiting near the open door at the far end of the
gym.

''This better be worth it,'' Remo grumbled.

It was more than a week since he'd awakened from

his drug-induced sleep. Remo's face was still sore. He had caught his reflection in the glass door of an emergency fire-hose box on the way to the gymnasium. The bruising was healing.

It was still a shock to see his own reflection—to look in a mirror and see someone else staring back. His cheekbones seemed higher, his eyes even deeper than before. When he'd finally seen his reflection in the silver serving tray that first day, Remo's own eyes had unnerved him.

MacCleary had told him the plastic surgery was necessary. No point going through such an elaborate frame-up only to leave the victim with his own face. Just another thing CURE had stolen from him.

Remo was absently taking inventory of his own face with his fingertips as MacCleary waited near the gym door. A .38 Police Special dangled from MacCleary's hook.

Remo wondered if he was going to get some more gun training. He had been given a little instruction this past week, mostly on how to casually fire a gun at a point-blank target. He thought he had gotten pretty good at it. When he tried it out on MacCleary with a blank pistol two days ago, however, a blinding flash caught his eyes and he was suddenly sprawled on the floor. He didn't know what had happened, not even when MacCleary, laughing, lifted him to his feet.

"You're learning, kid," MacCleary had said. But through the bluster, even MacCleary seemed a little surprised by the speed of his own reaction.

"What the hell did you do?" Remo asked. He was flexing his hand. His fingertips tingled. "How'd you move so fast?"

"I didn't. Not really. You wanna see fast, just wait."

Remo seemed doubtful. "What'd you hit me with?"

"Fingernails," MacCleary said, offering a boozy smile as he handed back Remo's pistol. "Remind me some day to tell you about the most boring submarine ride in history."

But that was days ago and this was today and Remo was wondering why he was standing in borrowed pajamas while MacCleary was looking out the gymnasium door with that crooked, knowing smile plastered across his face.

"Here he comes," MacCleary called all at once.

When Remo looked up, he almost laughed. But the figure shuffling into the gym was too pathetic for laughs.

The aged man was five feet tall with skin the hue of old walnut. Two wisps of white hair floated above shell-like ears. His scalp was otherwise plucked bald. A single thread of beard clung to his chin. The skin was wrinkled like old parchment. The ancient Oriental wore a simple red brocade kimono and plain wood sandals.

He said not a word. With the weariness of some unseen burden he crossed over to Remo.

MacCleary fell in behind the old man. He seemed almost deferential to the wizened Oriental. The gun still dangled from MacCleary's gleaming hook.

The two of them stopped before Remo.

"Chiun, this is Remo Williams, your new student."

The old Korean's lack of enthusiasm was obvious. He stood silent, hands tucked deep in the sleeves of his kimono as he stared at the callow white thing before him.

Remo stared right back. "What's *he* going to teach me?"

"The Master of Sinanju is going to teach you to kill," MacCleary said. "To be an indestructible, unstoppable, nearly invisible killing machine."

The Oriental snorted.

Remo glanced from MacCleary to the old man and back again. "Master of what? C'mon, Conn, who is he really, your dry cleaner?

"No washie shirtie, Pops," he said to Chiun.

Chiun didn't address Remo. Releasing a displeased hiss, he turned to Conrad MacCleary.

"Did you dress it up like that?" the Korean asked.

"Yeah. I thought you said you wanted him to dress respectfully," MacCleary said.

"Hey, I'm a him, not an it," Remo said. He was frowning at Chiun. For some reason he thought he had heard the old Oriental's voice before. It was like something from a dream.

"*This* is your idea of respectful?" Chiun said to MacCleary. "To dress him in these kung-fool pajamas? And what is this?" He flicked Remo's white belt.

MacCleary shrugged. "He's a student, right?"

Rolling his eyes, Chiun offered a muttered prayer of atonement to his ancestors.

"Are you *sure* I'm supposed to be his student?" Remo asked. "Maybe Upstairs got their wires crossed."

"Don't knock him," MacCleary said. "If Chiun wanted, you'd be dead right now before you could even blink."

At that, Remo laughed derisively. "Whatever you're drinking, cut the dose, Conn."

"Don't believe me, huh?" MacCleary said. "In that case, I've got an idea. You want to shoot him?" He rolled the .38 lazily on his hook.

"Why should I?" Remo asked. "Just sit him on the front steps and call the hearse. The shape he's in, he'll be dead before they back out of the garage."

MacCleary said nothing. He just continued to swing the pistol back and forth, a glimmer of mirth in his blue eyes.

The room seemed to grow very still. Even the cobwebs at the high, raftered ceiling ceased swaying in the stale eddies of cold autumn air.

"You're serious," Remo said, voice level.

MacCleary took the revolver from his hook and slapped it into Remo's palm. "Give yourself a chance," he instructed gruffly. "Let him start at the other end of the gym. Try it point-blank, and you'd be dead before you pulled the trigger."

Remo felt the weight of the gun in his hand.

"If this is a trick, I don't get it."

"No trick," MacCleary said. "It's exactly what it seems, give or take. Feel free to shoot him. If you can."

The gun felt cold in Remo's hand. He glanced at the Master of Sinanju. "How do you feel about this?"

"Guns cheapen the art," the Master of Sinanju intoned, face impassive. "But from what I can see, you are completely artless and in need of every advantage you can get. Just be certain you point the little hole the right way."

"You *want* me to do this?" Remo asked.

Chiun exhaled a tiny puff of anger. "What I want,

you will never know, white. Now, let us get this demonstration over with. The sooner we are done here, the sooner I can leave this land of crazed emperors and besotted generals.''

Remo examined the gun. Dark shell casings. Probably extra primer. It was a real gun with real bullets.

These guys were serious.

He looked to MacCleary.

"If I shoot him, do I get a week out of here?" he asked.

"A night," MacCleary answered.

"So you *do* think I can hit him."

"Nah, I'm just stingy, Remo. I don't want you to get too excited." MacCleary's smile never fled. His hook rested on his hip.

"A night?" Remo said. "You're not lying?"

"A night," MacCleary assured him.

Remo considered for a long moment. "Sure," he said. "I'll shoot him."

He figured it was a joke. Some kind of bizarre test. Even as the old Oriental padded to the far corner of the gym, Remo was watching MacCleary out of the corner of his eye. He fully expected that the big man would put a stop to this before it went too far. But MacCleary just stood there, the same idiot's grin plastered across his face.

The Master of Sinanju stopped and turned. White cotton-stuffed mats were hanging against the wall behind him.

When Chiun was in position, Conn took a step back.

"Ready?" he asked.

Remo sighted down by barrel instead of the V.

Never trust the sights on another man's gun. The distance was forty yards.

"Ready," he answered.

"Go!" yelled MacCleary.

And the old man was suddenly gone.

Like that. Vanished like a puff of steam.

And in the deepest pit of his stomach, on a level beyond simple knowledge, Remo Williams realized he'd been had.

When the old man reappeared two yards to the left and five yards closer, Remo knew all bets were off. He aimed for the scrawny chest and squeezed the trigger twice.

Chiun was no longer in the same spot. Cotton chunks flew from the mats as the shots thunked into the wall beyond the spot where the Master of Sinanju had been.

Remo's belly turned to liquid.

It was impossible. This frail old man was somehow able to move faster than a bullet. But no one moved that fast.

Yet there was Chiun once more, skittering, twirling, closer still and moving fast.

Even through the shock, Remo was pulling the trigger. Another shot rang out in the gym.

Another miss.

Remo gave him a lead. *Crack!*

Still he kept coming. Fifty feet away. Wait for thirty. Now. Two shots reverberated through the gymnasium and the old Oriental was suddenly walking slowly.

No bullets left.

With an anger as visceral as the shock he had felt a moment before, Remo threw the pistol at Chiun's head. The old man seemed to pluck the gun from the air as if it were a butterfly. Remo didn't even see the hands move. Chiun stopped before Remo. There was a flurry of movement, and when the old man handed the pistol back to Remo, the barrel had somehow been twisted into a knot of black metal.

Remo's jaw dropped.

As Remo stared at the twisted gun barrel in his hands, Conrad MacCleary stepped forward. His smile was gone, replaced by an expression that was all business.

"What do you think, Chiun?" MacCleary asked.

"Pitiful," Chiun answered, stroking his thread of beard thoughtfully. "He actually wavered at the start. A shameful display of misplaced compassion. Still, I like him better than you, MacCleary. He came to his senses. That is better than nothing, I suppose." His expression made it clear that it wasn't much better than nothing at all.

"What the hell is this?" Remo asked, finally finding his voice. He offered the lump of a gun to MacCleary. He found himself ignored yet again.

"Furthermore, he reeks of beef and alcohol," Chiun persisted. "And he is fat. In his current dismal condition, this pudgy, wheezing thing could only bring disgrace to Emperor Smith's crown. If he is to be my student, the first thing I must do is put him on a diet."

"He doesn't look fat to me," MacCleary said. "But you're the boss."

Remo had had it with being ignored. He forced his way between MacCleary and the old Korean.

"Hey, Chan, I asked you a question," Remo

snapped. He grabbed the little Oriental by the arm. Or at least he thought he did.

For Remo Williams, the world suddenly got very bright. His legs turned to rubber and he was falling to the floor, a terrible hollow feeling in his burning chest.

"Yeeowch!" Remo cried as air exploded from his lungs.

"And he is rude," Chiun clucked impatiently. "We are trying to have a conversation," he admonished Remo. He turned back to MacCleary. "Now, what were you saying?"

"Hnnnnhhhhhhhhhhhh," gasped Remo.

"Chiun, he's turning blue," MacCleary said worriedly.

The Master of Sinanju glanced at his would-be pupil. Remo's cheeks were puffed out, threatening to pop his plastic-surgery scars. His eyes bugged from their deep sockets. He clutched his belly, sucking for air that wouldn't come.

Chiun tipped his head as he studied Remo's complexion. "Yes, I agree with you, General MacCleary," he observed, nodding. "Blue is an improvement. If we wait long enough, maybe he will turn the right color."

Remo was on his knees gasping for breath. He seemed about to pass out.

"Chiun," MacCleary insisted.

The old Korean exhaled impatiently. "Oh, very well," he said. Slender fingers sought Remo's spine. "Hold your breath," he ordered. "Now bend."

Remo was in no position to argue. He stopped trying vainly to suck in air. He bent farther in on himself.

Deft fingers manipulated a knot of muscles on his back.

The air abruptly flooded back into his lungs. It was as if the old Oriental knew the location of some hidden switch between life and death.

Remo exhaled. The pain was gone. He looked up in amazement at the wrinkled parchment face.

"How'd you do that?" Remo asked.

"What do they teach you people in school?" Chiun said, with growing exasperation. His fingers fled Remo's back. "All muscles, because they depend on blood, depend on oxygen. Since it is obvious your lungs have been inert for more than one score years, you will first learn to breathe. *After* you unlearn how to breathe."

Remo climbed to his feet, still trying to comprehend all that had just transpired.

"You'll be training with Chiun for a while," MacCleary said. "You've got limited access to the sanitarium. Stay out of the regular patients' wing and the executive offices. Chiun has said he'll need the grounds and maybe the sound for some training. And remember, if and when you encounter any Folcroft employees, not a word about us, Remo. Only a few of us here even know about CURE. Me, you and my boss. Chiun's aware of some stuff, but not all the details."

Remo shook his head, as if coming out of a trance. "What if I tell them what's really going on here? Send them to get the cavalry? Or better yet, the newspapers?"

"Chiun will prevent you from doing so. Don't doubt he can. And even if you managed to tell someone—doctor, nurse, groundskeeper, guard—we'd have to kill them. You'd be responsible for an innocent life. We don't exist, Remo. Not me, not you, not Chiun, not Folcroft. That's why it's especially important that you never make a friendship here.''

Remo looked at Chiun. The Master of Sinanju stood at Remo's side, arms folded across his narrow chest. The brown slits remained impassive over stern hazel eyes.

"Trust me," Remo assured MacCleary. "No problem of that happening."

"Likewise," said Chiun with equal certainty.

"No one asked you, Chairman Mao."

And the next thing Remo knew, his lungs were on fire once again and the floor was flying back toward him. Somehow this time the white karate sash that he would never again be permitted to wear was wrapped tight around his neck.

7

On the evening of their second day of training, Remo
Williams began to practice breathing.

After his first meeting with his new pupil in the
Folcroft gymnasium, Chiun not only assumed it
wouldn't be easy, he was certain it would be impossible. This thing they'd given him to train was, after
all, white. Not only that but he was a white who had
seen more than twenty summers. Still, he had to start
somewhere and so he started with breathing. Who
knew? Maybe this white would be able to absorb
something. He quickly found his first instinct was correct.

"I already know how to breathe," said the rude
white thing whose name, ugly as it might be, was
Remo. "Watch."

Remo inhaled and exhaled a few times.

"See? I get a gold star in breathing. Now, how
'bout we move along to breaking boards? I saw a guy
do that once at the academy. It was pretty neat. You
think I'll be able to do that one day?"

"No."

"Oh." Remo was disappointed.

"Since you are white and therefore graceless in
form and act, I think you will be lucky if you do not

accidentally dislocate your shoulders while tying your shoelaces.''

"You're a real Rebecca of Sunnybrook Farm, you know that?'' Remo said sourly. "I think those guys upstairs are paying you to boost my confidence a little, not knock the stuffing out of it. And by the way, why are you always harping about us whites? If white is so bad, why do the good guys always wear white hats? Huh? Riddle me that.''

He let the question hang between them.

Although tempted, Chiun resisted the impulse to eliminate this imbecile would-be pupil. He drew on wells of patience that, for five thousand years of Sinanju Masters stretching back before the dawn of time, had remained hitherto untapped.

"Am *I* wearing a white hat?'' Chiun asked thinly.

"No,'' Remo admitted, hastily adding, "But don't think that proves your point. In fact, I think it proves mine. You haven't exactly been nice to me since we met. What are you doing now?''

Eyes closed, Chiun had been slowly counting to ten. "Do you always talk so much?'' the Master of Sinanju asked.

"Show me how to break a board with my hand and I'll stop,'' Remo said. "Does it hurt when you do it? The guy at the academy screamed bloody murder when he did it. I'm not sure he screamed 'cause it hurt, though.''

Chiun opened his eyes. "Hold your breath in the pit of your stomach for five seconds, then release.''

"Why five seconds?'' Remo asked.

Chiun hissed angrily. "Why two lungs? Why one turnip-sized nose? Why breathe at all?''

"Okay. That's sarcasm. Five seconds it is.'' Remo

sucked in a deep breath. He immediately let it back out. "Wait, you got a watch?"

"Timepieces are a confidence trick invented by the Swiss," Chiun explained. "Count in your head."

"Got it," Remo said. "It's a count by hippopotamus."

"What?" Chiun asked, voice flat.

"You know. One hippopotamus, two hippopotamus, like that. It leaves a break between the seconds so you don't rush them. Some people prefer Mississippi. Are you a Mississippi man?" Remo's questioning face was sincere.

Chiun went to Smith's office.

"I quit," said the Master of Sinanju.

"We have a deal," the CURE director replied firmly. "Until Remo's first service."

Reluctantly, Chiun returned to his quarters. When the old Korean reentered the room, he found Remo flopped on the floor watching television.

"I thought you said you were leaving," Remo said. He didn't look up as the Master of Sinanju padded in.

"It appears I am a hostage to my ethics," Chiun complained to himself.

"Yeah, that's rough," Remo said, hardly listening. He was busy watching an *F-Troop* rerun.

"Your breathing is still terrible," Chiun pointed out to the beached white thing wheezing on his floor.

Lying on his back, head cradled in his interlocked fingers, Remo attempted a semishrug. "I'm just happy I'm breathing at all. They plugged me in like a short-circuiting waffle iron, you know. I almost died."

"And if you had, I am certain the chimps of the

world would still be mourning the loss of their king,''
Chiun said. He suddenly noticed something. ''Is that
my best sleeping mat you are squatting on?'' the old
man demanded.

''Oh,'' Remo said, sheepish. ''Is this yours?''

A single touch left Remo rolling in agony on the
floor of Chiun's quarters. As the young man writhed
in pain, the Master of Sinanju returned to Smith's
office.

''I can do nothing with that thing,'' Chiun pleaded.
''He has no respect for me. He has no respect for my
property. I would have an easier time training this
one.'' He waved a bony hand at Conrad MacCleary,
who was sprawled on the sofa near Smith's closed
office door.

''That is out of the question,'' Smith said firmly.
Behind him, a big picture window of special one-way
glass overlooked Long Island Sound. ''MacCleary is
too old. We need a man who will last for at least
several years. A young man just might be able to
survive. Besides, Conn's prosthetic makes him too
easy to spot.''

Chiun threw up his hands. ''Then give me a young
man. In Sinanju the training begins not long after
birth. Give me an infant and perhaps I can do something.''

''We cannot wait that long, Master Chiun,'' Smith
said somberly. ''Like it or not, Remo is your pupil.''

The old man muttered something in Korean that
had no relation to the flattery he normally lavished on
Smith. Still griping to himself, he stormed from the
room.

Reaching across the arm of the couch, MacCleary
nudged the door until it clicked shut.

"Those two are off to a rocky start," Conn suggested.

"They do not have to like each other," Smith said. He was studying his computer monitor.

"And what was that crap about me being too old?" MacCleary said. "I'm only four years older than you."

Smith didn't raise his eyes from his desk. "Yes," he said. "And I'm too old for fieldwork, as well." After reading a few lines of plain text from his screen he offered a low "Hmm."

"What's wrong?" MacCleary asked.

Smith glanced up, a worried expression on his face. The grave look confirmed MacCleary's worst fears.

"Damn," Conn said. "I *thought* that was your something's bad 'hmm.' What is it?"

"I told you of the FBI agent who was killed while investigating the Maxwell matter," Smith said. "I dispatched two others to follow up. They've disappeared."

MacCleary sat forward on the sofa. "You sure?"

Smith nodded. "According to the FBI, they have failed to report in. My unofficial source within that agency who is keeping me informed on the matter has said that they are now listed within the Bureau as missing."

Conn shook his head. "This isn't right, Smitty," he said. "I thought this Maxwell thing was supposed to be small potatoes. Just some new Mob enforcer."

"That is what my early intelligence indicated. Using CURE's resources, I assumed we should have been able to locate him and turn him over to the proper authorities."

"Yeah, well, so much for the proper authorities,"

MacCleary said. "One's dead and two others are probably with him." He stood. "I suppose you're sending me in."

MacCleary was surprised by the CURE director's answer.

"No," Smith said. "Although that which is permitted us in the operational line of duty has recently been expanded, we shouldn't rush off half cocked. We need to preserve this authorization for only the most dire circumstances."

Standing on the worn carpet, MacCleary threw up his one good hand in frustration.

"It's *killing,* Smitty," Conn growled. "You won't die if you say the word. We've been okayed to kill in the line of duty. *Finally.* We've been pissing our pants like a bunch of scared choirboys for the past eight years, afraid to get our hands bloodied in this. Now we've got our chance, and I say use it. Three dead feds is good enough excuse for me."

But Smith was adamant. "No," he repeated. "This Maxwell—whoever he is—is just another face on organized crime. There have been many before him, and there will be many more after him. I will not risk your life or the exposure of this agency to go after one man. Not at this time. Not when we are on the verge of something that could finally turn this war to our advantage."

There was a fire in Smith's eyes. MacCleary had seen that look before. It was there when the two had met in World War II. It was there, too, when Smith returned to the CIA after his postwar studies to become superior of Conrad MacCleary, who had barely graduated high school. And it was there eight long years ago when the two men had secretly met on a motor launch in the Atlantic ten miles east of Annapolis to discuss a new covert organization.

The gleam in Harold Smith's eye was pure, unadulterated patriotism. The kind that was born in a hot, insect-filled hall in Philadelphia on July 4, 1776. The kind that had been consecrated in blood on fields in Lexington and Gettysburg, on beaches in Normandy and Iwo Jima, and at a thousand other places in between. The kind of raw, certain patriotism that was once part of a great nation's soul and that, sadly, was rapidly falling out of fashion in schoolrooms and government halls all across the fruited plains.

"You're going to sic Williams on him? The kid's greener than horseshit. He won't be ready for months."

"Then we will wait months," Smith said. "Yes, we have been given new authorization. But I am not so anxious to use it that I can't exercise patience. Let's give Williams time to complete his training. Has Master Chiun indicated how long he thinks it will take to bring him up to speed?"

"No," MacCleary said sullenly. "And don't forget, Chiun isn't the only one. Remo's got other trainers out there, too. Weapons, disguise, the whole James Bond works."

Smith nodded. CURE's new operative would be given the best possible instruction in all facets of fieldwork.

It was a schedule that had given MacCleary great difficulty. The situation with Chiun was unique. Unlike the Master of Sinanju, the other trainers couldn't be brought here to Folcroft. Not without breaching security. Nor could they be active-duty agents themselves, for fear they might alert higher-ups within their respective organizations. The men who would be teaching Williams would be doing so at remote locations. All were former intelligence agents, and none would know for whom they were working.

"It's unfortunate that we couldn't use a single trainer," Smith said. He was staring thoughtfully at a point beyond MacCleary. A framed black-and-white drawing of Folcroft sketched in ink hung on the wall next to the door.

"Yeah," MacCleary agreed. "But as good as Chiun is, even he can't cover all the bases."

Smith tore his eyes off the drawing. "Very well," he said. "Accelerate what you can. I don't want to put him in the field too soon, but there's no reason we can't move things along as quickly as possible."

"Okay, Smitty. I'll start taking him to the sessions personally starting next week."

His heart wasn't in the words. MacCleary was clearly annoyed that he wasn't being allowed to go into the field.

He turned to go. MacCleary was grabbing the doorknob when Smith called him.

"Conn."

When MacCleary turned back around, he found a contemplative frown on the CURE director's face.

"If you need to trim any of Remo's lessons, do so elsewhere," Smith said quietly. The lines of his forehead formed a V over his thoughtful gray eyes. "Don't allow the other sessions you've arranged for him to cut into his time with Master Chiun."

MacCleary allowed a sharp nod. Flipping the doorknob with the curve of his hook, he skulked into the outer room.

Once he was alone, Smith looked over the report

of the two dead agents one last time. When he was through he spun his chair around. Through the one-way glass of his office window he looked out across Long Island Sound.

This Maxwell business was the same as all the rest. The risk of death was always there to the men Smith deployed. But in eight years it hadn't gotten easier.

How many other Maxwells were out there? How many more agents could he commit to the field to combat them? How many more would die at his command?

MacCleary seemed to think this Williams had something special. He had seen the young man in action in Vietnam two years previous. MacCleary was impressed. That opinion had had a lot of clout with Smith. After all, Smith knew that Conrad MacCleary did not impress easily.

With Williams aboard, Smith hoped to banish some of the doubts that had plagued him since the start. But they were still here. As always. Haunting his waking soul.

"Will anything we do ever be enough?" Smith inquired softly of the sound.

There were no glad portents in the endless, silent waves that lapped to foam on the jagged shore.

Leaving Long Island Sound to tend its eternal business, the director of CURE swiveled wearily back to his patiently waiting computer.

8

When he saw the bodies of the two FBI agents, Luigi
"Vino" Vercotti nearly blew lunch. A pretty amazing
thing, given the cast-iron nature of Vino's stomach.

Vino hadn't gotten his nickname for love of the
grape. At least not in the sniffing, sampling and spitting sense of the artsy-fartsy wine-club set. Vino liked
to watch while other people drank wine. He especially
liked watching while his brother Dino was sitting on
the unlucky wine-taster's chest. It was generally at
this time that Vino was pinching his victim's nose
shut with his pudgy fingers.

Vino liked to drown people in wine. He had decided on this method early on for two reasons. First,
it was unique and would doubtless earn him an interesting nickname in New York's Viaselli crime Family, to which he belonged. Second, it was a good
cover for murder. Most of his victims were assumed
to be drunks who had imbibed too much and paid the
ultimate price. No one could argue with the success
of his unique method of eliminating enemies of Don
Carmine Viaselli. While many of his peers had been
on the endless merry-go-round of court, trial, prison
and appeal, murder by drowning had kept Vino out
of jail his entire adult life.

Not that it was always easy. Sometimes a victim

kicked so violently his shoes would fly off. One guy in Hackensack had even busted the window of Vino's Cadillac. Sometimes they bit their tongues bloody or chewed so hard on the neck of the glugging bottle that they bit clean through the glass.

But in the end, death was almost always clean and quiet. That was one of the things Vino Vercotti prided himself on. The neatness with which he went about his chosen work.

Vino Vercotti couldn't help but think of the thirty or so men he had sent to peaceful, drunken oblivion as he viewed the mess spread out across the cold warehouse floor.

There was blood everywhere. None of his victims had gone out like this. This wasn't clean. And judging from the mess that had been made, the men hadn't died quietly.

"What the hell happened with these guys?" groused Dino Vercotti. The younger Vercotti stood next to his brother, face pinched as he eyed the gruesome scene.

"You think I know?" snarled Vino. He was breathing through a handkerchief. "You think I *care?* I'm thinking how we gonna clean this up, that's what I'm thinking. I got no time to worry about the what here."

The warehouse was stuck out in the middle of New Jersey's swamps. The place was big and drafty. Wind whistled around the rattling windowpanes. Good thing. The cold and the wind kept down the body smells.

Damn, the blood and gore was *everywhere*.

Vino couldn't believe he'd been picked for cleanup duty. He should have ranked higher than this. Dirty work like this should have gone to guys like Marco Antonio or Emilio Lepido. Bottom-rung dwellers.

"That a leg?" Vino asked. "That looks like a leg."

Dino peered close. "Not unless legs got noses."

When Vino squinted, he saw nostrils in what he'd thought was a thigh. A pair of squinted-shut eyes were above them.

"Sheesh, this ain't right," Vino complained angrily. "I do neat with my stiffs. Cops clean up my bodies practically send me a goddamned Christmas card to thank me, the stiffs are so neat. I wanna know why I gotta clean up someone else's bodies who ain't even considerate enough to leave a body as neat as I leave a body?"

He would have been annoyed at Dino if his brother had responded to his rhetorical question. As it was, when the reply came from someone other than Dino, Vino Vercotti nearly jumped out of his skin.

"Some lessons are not about neatness," a thin voice said from Vino's elbow.

When the brothers twisted around, they found a man in a black business suit standing between them.

The guy was just *there*. As if he'd been born standing in that spot on the warehouse floor. Except he had absolutely not been standing there all along. There had been no one else in sight when the two Vercotti brothers entered the warehouse a minute before. Vino was sure of it. It was as though the stranger had appeared by magic.

When Vino got a good look at the man's face, his own expression grew harsh.

The man's broad face was as flat as a frying pan. His hooded Oriental eyes were mirthless.

"Are *you* the guy we're supposed to meet?" Vino asked.

"I am Mr. Winch," the man said, his voice cold.

Vino noted that his pronunciation was too precise, too good for someone born and raised in the good old U.S. of A.

"You Vietnamese?" Vino demanded. "'Cause I don't do deals with no Vietcong."

Mr. Winch's flat face hinted at disgust. "Do not be an idiot," he spit. "You two are here to perform a service. Do so quickly, for I have no time to suffer fools."

Vino didn't like the idea of taking orders from some gook who might or might not be Vietcong. But he had been given orders from on high and—he had been told—it was his neck if this Mr. Winch wasn't kept happy. Despite their misgivings, Vino and Dino went to work.

They had been given a special car for this assignment. An old Ford Thunderbird with rusting fins and broken taillights. Dino drove the car in through a garage door, which Vino quickly closed back up. They parked the car in a blood-free spot on the warehouse floor.

Although they knew they'd be on body-cleaning duty, neither Vercotti brother had anticipated such a big mess. Vino pulled out a big leaf tarp which he spread on the floor at the edge of the blood pool. They took a couple of big plastic garbage bags from the trunk of the Thunderbird.

Working down the dry heaves, Vino and his brother set about gathering up the arms and legs. Vino kept his sleeves rolled up to keep his cuffs out of the blood.

As the brothers worked, Mr. Winch slipped into the shadows at the side of the warehouse.

It soon became clear to Vino that there was someone else back there. At one point when he was coaxing a rolling head into a plastic bag with a chunk of broken plywood, Vino caught a glimpse of Winch and his companion.

It was only in silhouette. Mr. Winch wasn't a large man. Whoever he was talking to was smaller than him. Maybe only five feet tall.

Probably another gook. Vino had seen the news enough to know they made those Vietnamese small. The better to strap dynamite to them and sneak them into U.S. Army camps.

Vino kept a watchful eye for dynamite as he cleaned.

The torsos went in bags all on their own. Vino was surprised there were only two. It seemed that there was too much of a mess in the warehouse for only two corpses.

Vino noticed something else odd as he was working. It was the way the body parts had been severed. Despite the large amount of blood and the random scattering of limbs, on closer inspection he found that every single appendage looked to have been cleanly amputated.

Something here wasn't right. A hacksaw would have chipped bone and made jagged tears in flesh. This was more like a smooth-edged blade had been used. A butcher knife or surgeon's scalpel. Yet there was no evidence of tools anywhere around. And even if there were, this Mr. Winch of the Vietcong didn't look strong enough to force a smooth blade through solid bone.

"I got a bad feeling here," Vino whispered to his brother as they dropped a pair of bags on their tarp. He snapped to attention when it was Mr. Winch who responded.

"Feelings for a killer are dangerous things," came the thin, cold voice.

Vino's head shot up.

Winch was back. No longer in the shadows, the Oriental now stood at the fender of the Thunderbird. There was no sign of the other mystery person he'd been talking to.

Mr. Winch smiled. It was merely a function of the facial muscles. There was no emotion behind the expression.

"You are a killer of some sort, correct?"

Some of his Mob associates considered him slow, but Vino Vercotti was sharp enough not to admit anything. Whether or not this guy had an in with Mr. Viaselli, there was no way he was going to confess outright to ever having killed.

"I get around," he grunted.

"You don't have to say it. You reek of it. Of death."

Vino and Dino didn't admit anything. They loaded the penultimate bag of mangled body parts into the car trunk.

"*Everything* reeks of it here," Vino said, disgusted.

"Not everything," Winch said. "Not yet anyway."

His last words were spoken so softly they were swallowed up in the sounds of cursing and crinkling plastic. The two Vercotti brothers stooped for the last bundle.

"It is an interesting thing about killers," Winch

mused as they hauled the sack to the car. "Some—a very few, granted—but *some* are truly born to kill. They may never know it, may walk through their daily lives oblivious to the darkness lurking below the surface, but sometimes a moment comes. A split second that puts them to the test. These moments are rarer than born killers themselves, but when they come—" this time Winch's smile was sincere "—the men who do not think themselves killers are shocked at the ease with which they kill. The calm with which they obliterate a life. They are shocked by the very *lack* of shock they feel."

Now Winch was just babbling nonsense. The more he talked, the better Vino felt. The seed of fear that had been germinating in the pit of Vercotti's stomach was slowly dying with each word. By now he wasn't even listening.

"That's just great," Vino muttered as he dumped the last bag of body parts into the trunk of the big car.

"But because they are so hard to find, true born killers hardly ever fulfill their destinies," Winch lamented. "Fortunately, there is an alternative. It requires taking someone who is not naturally suited for dealing death and, by stages, bleeding the humanity from him."

"Sounds about right," Vino agreed, disinterested. He hadn't even heard most of what Winch said. "This blood's pretty soaked in," he said, nodding to the floor. "We should be able to burn it off okay. Soak it in gas and light it up. The building should be fine. Ceilings are high enough and the posts are far enough so it won't catch. You know where there's a fire extinguisher around here, just in case?"

When he turned, Vino was surprised to find that he'd missed something in the cleanup. On the floor near the bumper of the car was a severed arm.

That shouldn't be. Vino had personally collected three arms. And he'd seen Dino grab up another. There were only two guys dead in the place. So where could this fifth arm have come from?

In the instant before words came, in that slivered moment when he was pondering the fifth arm that was lying on the floor where it had not been a second before, Luigi ''Vino'' Vercotti became aware of a lightness in his shoulder.

When he glanced over, he found that his sleeve now ended just beyond the end of his turned chin.

Horror set in. Vino's eyes flew to the floor where his severed right arm twitched, fingers curling reflexively.

Only then did the pain come.

He saw his horrified brother stumbling back. Reaching under his jacket for the gun beneath his armpit.

Vino's mind reeled. He saw Winch. Standing placidly near the car. Too far away to be the cause.

A flash of movement. Close up.

Then he remembered. There was someone else here. The person Winch had been talking to in shadow.

As Vino grabbed for the spot where blood pumped from his naked shoulder socket, feeling bone beneath his shaking palm, he saw someone dart up before him.

He caught a glimpse of soft yellow hair. Barely registered a pair of electric-blue eyes.

A too pale hand shot out, fingers drawn tight.

The pain came like an exploding star. Vino's left arm joined the other on the floor. He screamed.

By now Dino had managed to draw his gun. Hand shaking, he sent a single fat slug at the little dervish that had appeared like a vengeful demon near his howling brother.

He was too close to miss. Yet somehow he did. Worse, the bullet that should have hit the small apparition thudded hard into Vino Vercotti's chest.

Vino went down. His knees hit concrete. The instant they did, a bare foot lashed out.

With a sound reminiscent of a popping champagne cork, Vino's head tumbled off his neck. The decapitated body fell, blood pumping a red river from its severed neck.

Wheeling from the dead man, the small killer turned full attention on Dino Vercotti. In a panic now, Dino unloaded his magazine at the person who had killed his brother.

Somehow the killer managed to dodge and weave around most of the bullets. When one of them finally hit his target, Dino nearly jumped for joy.

The bullet struck the killer in the upper arm. The instant the screaming lead kissed flesh, the murderer of Vino Vercotti stopped dead. A look of fearful incomprehension blossomed full on the very pale face.

He was open now. Vulnerable. This time, Dino wouldn't miss. He aimed at the small chest.

"This is for Vino, you little prick," Dino growled.

Before his hairy finger could caress the trigger, he heard an angry exhalation from the other side of the car.

Winch. Dino would take him out next. Right after he'd dealt with his brother's killer.

But in the instant he was pulling the trigger, he felt a presence nearby. A gentle displacement of air.

His flickering eyes briefly caught a glimpse of Winch.

Impossible. Winch was on the other side of the car. People didn't move that fast. Dino's brain was still insisting this was so even as the hand of the man that could not be there was ending the Mafia man's life.

Winch struck Dino Vercotti in the forehead with an open palm. Skull fragments launched back into Dino's brain. As a look of dull shock spread across his five-o'clock shadow, the hoodlum toppled back on the cold concrete floor.

Winch turned away from the body. Disgust filled his flat Oriental face.

"Miserable," he proclaimed.

The killer of Vino Vercotti was recovering from his shock. A pale hand clutched his arm where the bullet had grazed his left bicep. The fear that had flooded his blue eyes after being shot was now directed at Winch.

"I'm sorry," the killer said.

The apology seemed to anger Winch all the more. Marching over, he slapped the small killer hard across the face. The stinging blow echoed like a rifle crack against the high warehouse ceiling.

"You favor your hands," Winch snapped. "You will use only your feet for the next exercises."

"Yes, Master."

Turning, Winch gathered up Dino Vercotti's body. Although the dead man outweighed him by a good eighty pounds, Winch carried him easily. He hung the corpse from a crooked nail that jutted from one of the supporting roof columns.

"You are a pathetic disgrace against living targets," Winch sneered. "Practice on this dead one."

With that, he turned and walked away, leaving the bleeding murderer alone with the two corpses.

The killer, a boy of no more than fourteen, squeezed the spot where Dino Vercotti's bullet had torn his frail flesh. Warm blood oozed between his slender fingers.

As hot tears burned his pale blue eyes, the child walked slowly over to the hanging dead man.

9

When Chiun returned to his Folcroft quarters, Remo was still rolling in agony on the floor.

The Master of Sinanju released the young man from his pain with a soft touch on the neck. Instead of expressing the proper thanks for the lesson in politeness that had been thoughtfully bestowed on him by the Master, the loathsome white beast expressed typical unpleasantness.

"You son of a bitch," Remo panted. Sweat dripped from his forehead, rolling down his face.

Despite the residual pain that still sparked every nerve ending, Remo didn't say what he really wanted to say. The previous day he had made the mistake of calling Chiun a gook and wound up doubled up on the floor in pain for an hour.

"You do that to me one more time and the next time I shoot you it's gonna be for keeps," Remo threatened.

"Now that I have some idea the depths of your stupidity, I pray that next time you truly do forget which direction to aim the little hole," Chiun sighed. "But since your granite forehead would likely stop the bullet from penetrating whatever it is that fills the space where your brain should be, I fear we will still be stuck with each other for the foreseeable future."

Chiun made Remo sit cross-legged on the floor. It was hard for Remo to pull his legs into the lotus position.

"What's with you getting all turned on over floors? Why can't we sit on chairs like people?" Remo griped.

"Civilized men sit on the floor," Chiun said.

"Og the freaking caveman sits on the floor. Even Borneo headhunters have stools."

Chiun gave him a baleful look. "You have an option—" He stopped. "What is your name again?"

"Remo," Remo said with a sigh.

Chiun crinkled his nose as if smelling something unpleasant. "Are you certain that's right?"

"I think I know my own name."

"I suppose." Chiun didn't sound certain. "You have an option, Remo. You may listen to instruction while in pain or you may listen while not. But either way you will listen."

Remo had had his fill of pain for the day. "All right," he muttered. "I won't bitch about sitting on the floor till my ass goes numb like some dirt-eating aborigine. Happy?"

"No," Chiun replied. "But I fear I am as close as I will get with you as a pupil."

Some of his trunks were piled in the corner. Chiun went over to the black-lacquered one with the silver inlay. Digging inside, he removed a plain black metronome, which he brought over and sat on the floor near Remo's folded knees.

Remo looked at the metronome. With hooded eyes he looked around the room. Finally, he looked at Chiun.

"Someone swipe your piano?" Remo asked thinly.

"This is going to help you to breathe," Chiun said. He sank like a dropped rose petal to the floor across from Remo.

Remo sighed. "Again with the breathing? Look, Pops, you say I'm not breathing, but I'm pretty sure I am. Can't we just split the difference and say air's getting in me by some act of divine intervention and be done with it?"

"I did not say you didn't breathe," said Chiun. "It is obvious something is reaching your lungs in those brief respites your tongue enjoys between words. After all, if there was not some breath, you would not be able to propel your gorging, oafish body from one greasy hamburger stand to the next. What I said was that you do not breathe right."

With the tip of one long fingernail he set the metronome to clicking.

"The work of the metronome is twofold," Chiun explained. "I have noticed that you are like most whites in the way in which you are easily distracted. The repetitive movement and clicking sound should occupy your infantile mind."

Remo, who had already been tracking the hypnotic bounce of the metronome, looked up with a frown.

"What's the second reason?" he asked, annoyed.

"To show you how you should breathe. Two beats inhale, two beats hold breath, two beats exhale. Pull the air down into the pit of your stomach. Begin."

Remo thought this entire exercise was stupid and pointless. But he had already been victim one too many times of the old Korean's flashing hands. Rather than risk more punishment, he decided to humor the codger.

He followed the course of breathing. Chiun's bony

index finger kept time with the metronome's movement. As Remo found himself reluctantly tracking the old man's hand, he felt something odd trip in his chest.

It was strange. For a moment he thought his heart was fluttering. He had heard that some people's did that every once in a while. But he soon realized it was more than that.

It was as if something had always been there. Lurking inside him but never used. Chiun's special breathing seemed to flip some dormant inner switch.

Following the prescribed two beats, he drew the air in deep. Holding it for two more, he allowed it to slip out.

His lungs responded deeply to the breathing. His heart seemed to take up the rhythm. And for the first time in his life, Remo *felt* the blood coursing through him.

It was some kind of hypnotism. Had to be. After all, breathing was just breathing. But there definitely seemed to be something more to it than that. It was like a feeling, a dream. Something once known, long forgotten.

For the first time in his life Remo felt...alive.

"Wow," he said, "that's weird."

Closing his eyes lightly, he breathed in deep, as he was told, down into the pit of his stomach. There was something about this simple act of measured breathing that was impossible for him to describe. It was a sense of awakening. As if the farthest, smallest parts of his body had been sleepwalking for his entire adulthood. For an instant Remo felt a sense of oneness with life itself.

So enthralled was he with the strange sensation,

Remo didn't notice the odd expression that had blossomed on the face of the Master of Sinanju.

Chiun was watching his pupil intently, his hazel eyes narrowed to razor slits as he studied the young man performing his earliest breathing exercises.

In Sinanju, breath was all. So important was it that all Masters began their training with it. But it was a known fact that the lessons had to begin early in life. A baby was always preferable to a grown child, since after a certain age it became difficult to unlearn incorrect habits. As a person aged, it became impossible to overcome the damage wrought by a lifetime of improper breathing. This was why so few Masters in Sinanju history dared waste precious time attempting to train pupils any older than ten years of age.

But, as he watched the white man before him, Chiun almost began to question his own senses.

This Remo—this white thing with the stench of charred beef emanating from his every pore—appeared to have mastered in an instant the special breathing that generally took a new trainee many months to learn. What's more, as the proper breath took hold, Remo had instantly aligned his spine.

It was impossible. Yet here it was.

For a moment the Master of Sinanju's heart soared as he felt a strange stirring of amazement. And of hope.

Of course, the white thing ruined it.

Remo opened his eyes. "Hey, that was pretty spiffy," he commented. "Say, you got a smoke?"

Chiun didn't answer. His disgusted expression said all. With a sharp gesture he instructed Remo to resume his breathing exercises.

Remo no longer complained. Despite his skepticism, he was reluctantly drawn into the exercise. His eyelids fluttered shut and he resumed the breathing. This time, without the benefit of the metronome. He fell into the proper breathing naturally, as if it had been with him all his life.

Chiun was certain this was a fluke. An aberration, a lapse into perfection that would soon correct itself. When it did not and the white persisted in his perfect breathing, Chiun fell into a watchful silence.

For the rest of the day Chiun sat mute as his new pupil breathed. And in his unspoken heart, the last Master of Sinanju reflected on what all this might mean. For him, as well as for the future of the House of Sinanju.

MacCLEARY CAME to Chiun's quarters later that evening.

When he opened the door he was relieved to find Remo still alive. It had been so quiet in the hall he was afraid Chiun had killed America's newest superweapon.

The Master of Sinanju said nothing to either MacCleary or Remo. As the two men left, the old Korean was padding silently from the common room to his bedroom.

"What did you do wrong to piss him off?" MacCleary asked once he and Remo were walking down the basement hallway.

"Actually, this time I think I did something right," Remo replied.

There was a calm to the former Newark beat cop that MacCleary hadn't seen since Remo had awakened from his coma. MacCleary decided not to press it.

Conn had set up weapons drills for Remo in an abandoned meatpacking plant in Jersey City. Remo's instructor was an ex-CIA operative who claimed to have assassinated Fidel Castro back in 1962. He swore repeatedly that the Castro the world had been watching for the past decade wasn't the real Castro but was actually a Castro impersonator with a CIA bugging device hidden in his false beard.

"The guy's nuttier than Aunt Fanny's fruitcake," MacCleary whispered to Remo. "But anything you need to know about killing with guns, he can teach you. Oh, and if you know what's good for you, don't ask him his name."

"Great," Remo muttered as he dragged a lazy toe across the dirty floor. He was still practicing Chiun's breathing techniques. "More dippy spy bullshit."

"Not really," MacCleary said. "He's got this thing about his name. He kills anyone who asks it. Have fun."

Remo was stuck with the nameless gun expert for the next six days. He learned everything about every kind of gun. From taking them apart and putting them together, to ranges and accuracy and how to jam certain weapons.

The whole time he was put through the drills, he continued to practice his breathing. It actually got easier as time went on. By the sixth day when MacCleary came to bring him back to Folcroft, Remo no longer had to concentrate to maintain the proper pattern. It was such a natural thing it seemed that he'd been breathing that way all his life.

When he pushed open the door to the quarters he was sharing with the Master of Sinanju, he found

Chiun sitting alone in the center of the common room. The old Korean was watching television.

"Wipe your feet," Chiun said without looking up.

"I missed you, too," said Remo.

Before he'd even crossed the threshold, the Master of Sinanju's face was puckering unhappily.

"You have been smoking," the old man accused.

Remo flashed a guilty smile. "Just a couple," he admitted. "And that was two days ago. You have one hell of a nose."

"That is because I do not clog my senses and pollute my lungs with poisonous tobacco smoke."

As he spoke, the Master of Sinanju detected something else wafting to him on the gentle eddies of basement air. He let out a shocked gasp of air.

"You have been firing guns!" Chiun hissed. He rose from the floor and whirled on his pupil like a wrathful typhoon.

Remo rolled his eyes. "Tell me about it," he griped. "Only a couple thousand times. You should have seen the psycho MacCleary hired to— Hey, where are you going?"

But Chiun didn't answer. With a determined frown on his parchment face, the wizened Korean breezed past the confused young man. Leaving Remo in their basement quarters, Chiun marched up to Folcroft's second-floor executive wing.

Miss Purvish had been temporarily rotated out into the hospital wing of the sanitarium. A new woman filled her chair. The nameplate on her desk read Miss Stephanie Hazlitt. Smith's latest secretary was working diligently at her typewriter when Chiun marched in.

"Oh, hello," Miss Hazlitt said when the old man

stormed through the hallway door. "Can I help you with something?"

Chiun ignored her. As the young woman protested, the old Korean slapped open Smith's door.

"What exactly is it you want me to do with him?" Chiun demanded as he breezed into the inner office.

By now the shock of Chiun barging unannounced into his office had worn off. The CURE director calmly depressed the stud that lowered his computer terminal inside his desk. When Miss Hazlitt stuck her head around his office door, Smith waved her away. Glancing at Chiun, she pulled the door shut, leaving the two men alone in Smith's office.

Only when the door was closed did Smith speak. "We have a contract," he announced by rote.

"No, we do not," Chiun said. "What we have is an agreement. A Sinanju contract is a different matter, which we will discuss at another time. I am not here for that now."

Smith's face was suspicious as he looked up over the tops of his glasses. "What, then?"

"This Remo. Is he my pupil or isn't he?"

The CURE director frowned, sensing a trap. "He is, obviously," Smith said cautiously.

"Then why have you given over precious time when he should be training to the shooting of guns?"

"Ah, I see." Smith leaned back in his chair. "Master Chiun, while I value your services highly, Remo needs to be fully trained in other areas. Areas beyond your expertise."

"Nothing that exists beyond the knowledge of Sinanju is worth knowing," Chiun sniffed, waving his hand.

"I respectfully disagree," Smith replied. "Sinanju

is an ancient philosophy that is unfamiliar with the demands of the modern world. There are many aspects of fieldwork with which you are doubtless unaware.''

"Pah, fieldwork," Chiun snapped contemptuously. "You have used this nonsense phrase before. Do you wish to train an assassin or a harvester of wheat?"

"Please try to understand, Master Chiun, there are things that Remo will encounter in his service to us that will be beyond your ken. This isn't meant as an insult—it is merely a statement of fact. The demands of the modern age require a modern approach."

Chiun made a disgusted face. "Yes, by all means. Use your modern approach. Fill his hands with shooting guns and line his pockets with nuclear booms. And when the radio-controlled boom parts break and the forged steel snaps, he will be left defenseless, for you will have harmed him irreparably in the most important part of his training."

"I assure you that Remo's training in all areas will be extensive."

"There is only one area that needs extensive training," Chiun replied. He tapped a long fingernail against the thin skin of his forehead. "That is here. When you tell him that guns will protect him, you allow him false comfort. By filling his brain with pretty songs that it wants to hear, you are only putting him at risk, for his brain is weak and will trust the siren songs your gunsmiths sing to it."

Behind his desk the CURE director absorbed the old man's words in thoughtful silence. Pursing his bloodless lips, he leaned back in his leather chair.

"Do you have a personal stake in this, Master Chiun?" Smith asked abruptly.

Chiun bristled. "You have hired me for a task," he sniffed. "I merely wish to fulfill it in a manner that does not harm the reputation of the House of Sinanju."

"That is likely, given Sinanju's historical reputation," Smith conceded. "However, MacCleary said you were not interested in taking this job when he first offered it."

Chiun became a five-foot post of haughty indignation.

"Can you blame me?" the old Korean asked hotly. "Here I was, an old man meditating peaceably in the solitude of my retirement years, when through my door stumbled your MacCleary, reeking of fermented grain and blabbering something about a Constitution that needed saving. When he stubbornly refused to leave, I was forced to accompany him, for if he had stayed any longer he might have corrupted the children of Sinanju to his wicked ways of vice." He pitched his voice low. "Really, Emperor Smith, you would be wise to choose another general as your aide-de-camp when you assume your place as President of this nation. Inebriates, while sometimes amusing, provide too great a distraction at court."

Smith shook his head. He was not about to let the wily Korean distract him from the issue at hand.

"Let us set aside for the moment your mistaken assumption that I have designs on the presidency," Smith said, steering back to the original topic. "The fact is you became interested in taking this job only when you learned how we planned to recruit Remo. That he would have to die to be brought into the organization."

"A false death," Chiun interjected levelly.

That had been a problem very early on. When Chiun had learned that his pupil would not be truly dead, he threatened to return to Sinanju. It was only when Smith accused him of trying to break a solemn Sinanju contract that he relented.

"But you didn't know at the time that it would be a false death," Smith insisted. "It is MacCleary's contention that somehow in our method of recruitment, we stumbled into a Sinanju legend of some sort. By reputation I know that your House has beliefs as old as the art of Sinanju itself. If this is the case, I believe I have a right to know. After all, I am not paying you for divided loyalties."

Chiun didn't immediately respond. His gaze was directed at a spot in the carpet where traffic had begun to wear the material thin. The thread of beard at his chin at first trembled, then stilled as an otherworldly calm descended on the old man's tiny frame. For a long moment he considered his employer's words. His hands were clutched in knots of white bone at his sides. At long last, he lifted his head.

Chiun's hazel eyes locked on those of Harold Smith.

"It is not a legend, but a prophecy," the Master of Sinanju admitted. "Passed down from the Great Wang, he of the New Age, of the Sun Source. The first true Master of Sinanju of the pure bloodline." He began reciting from memory. "'One day a Master of Sinanju will find among the barbarian lands of the West one who was once dead. This Master will teach the secrets of Sinanju to this pale one of the dead eyes. He will make of him a night tiger, but the most awesome of night tigers. And he will be created Death, the Destroyer, the Shatterer of Worlds.'"

By the time he was done, his words were so soft and ominous that Smith had to strain to hear.

Smith was a practical man who as a rule left matters of the ethereal to priests and poets. But though he trucked exclusively in the physical realm, the old Korean's words and the seriousness with which he delivered them sent a shiver up the CURE director's rigid, normally sensible spine.

"You cannot believe Remo to be this man," Smith said.

"That is a Sinanju matter and is not for me to share, even with my emperor," Chiun replied tightly. "However, you need not be troubled by my loyalty, for I have given my word to serve and so I shall. Furthermore, if he is the one, then I am destined to be wherever he is. If that place is in your service, so be it."

Smith knew that Sinanju had not survived for so long by breaking contracts. And he was wise enough not to question the word of the Master of Sinanju.

"Thank you, Master Chiun," Smith said. He stood. Somehow it suddenly seemed inappropriate that he should be sitting. "I cannot say that I understand what you have told me, but I appreciate your candor. As for Remo's training, I have already given word to MacCleary to increase the time for your sessions. For now Remo will continue training with other instructors, but I will keep an open mind. If you can demonstrate to me that your training alone is sufficient, I will consider remanding him entirely to your supervision."

"As you wish, O Emperor," Chiun said.

The Master of Sinanju offered a semiformal bow,

which the CURE director returned. Afterward Chiun padded from the office on silent sandals.

Alone, Smith retook his seat. With one hand, he adjusted his rimless glasses. The other hand he drummed on his smooth desk surface.

"Hmm," Smith mused.

Reaching beneath his desk, a touch raised his computer monitor and keyboard. He brought up CURE's personnel files, accessing the file of the new man Williams.

In code, Smith entered the word "Destroyer" at the top of Remo's personnel file.

The Master of Sinanju had just solved a niggling little problem that had bothered Smith since the start. CURE's new field agent needed a code name. Obviously Smith couldn't use Williams's real name.

The blob of a green cursor blinked over the last letter in *Destroyer*. The name somehow felt right.

With a look of mild satisfaction, Smith returned to his regular day's work.

10

Thanksgiving passed without any of the traditional trappings. At the start of his training Chiun put Remo on a restrictive diet of fish, rice and water. On Thanksgiving day Remo tried to sneak a few slices of turkey roll and some whipped potatoes from the Folcroft cafeteria. As punishment, the Master of Sinanju made him go without food for two days.

At Christmas someone taped a cardboard Santa to the front of Folcroft's main reception desk. Remo was grateful for the reminder, for by then he had lost all track of time.

New Year's Day of 1972 came and went with no fanfare. It was early in February when Conrad MacCleary came to visit Remo and Chiun in their basement quarters.

Remo was lying flat on his back on the concrete floor. The Master of Sinanju stood above him, arms crossed imperiously over his bony chest.

"Taking a break?" MacCleary commented.

"Get stuffed," Remo grunted.

He sounded as if he were exerting himself. In fact, there were signs of strain on his face. His neck muscles bulged.

When MacCleary looked closer he saw to his amazement that his initial assumption was wrong.

Remo wasn't lying on the floor at all. The young man's arms were extended down by his sides, hands resting near his hips. At least at first glance it *looked* as though they were resting.

Only the flats of Remo's palms were touching the floor. The rest of his body was raised a half inch in the air. Even the heels of his bare feet weren't touching. His hands were supporting the entire weight of his body.

"That's amazing, Chiun," MacCleary said. His eyes narrowed as he studied Remo's straining wrists. They seemed much thicker than when he'd first arrived at Folcroft.

The old Korean did not look MacCleary's way. He continued to watch his pupil, a vaguely dissatisfied expression on his parchment face.

"To the white world, perhaps," Chiun replied tersely. "The lowliest in my village of Sinanju are able to perform the same simple exercise for twice the duration and with no strain. But one makes do with what one has to work with."

MacCleary wasn't too sure about the veracity of that statement. After all, he'd been to Sinanju. He was willing to bet that the only people there to work up a sweat since before the Bronze Age were the Masters of Sinanju themselves.

"Everything's ready for your trip," MacCleary announced.

Remo relaxed his grip on the floor. He slumped to his back, a hopeful expression forming on his exhausted face.

"You going somewhere?" he asked the Master of Sinanju eagerly. "You want me to help pack?"

At that MacCleary laughed long and hard. He was still laughing when he left their quarters.

"That was a bad laugh, wasn't it?" Remo said warily.

MacCleary had arranged for two plane tickets. Chiun and Remo's flight was direct from New York to Texas. A car was waiting for them at the airport just where MacCleary said it would be. Remo found the keys in the visor.

MacCleary had given Remo a map before they'd left Folcroft. He followed the highway and side streets dutifully, eventually coming to a stop beside a high chain-link fence. By the time he shut off the headlights, night had fallen.

In recent weeks Remo had taken to wearing black chinos and a matching T-shirt. His simplified wardrobe seemed to suit him, plus allowed for better freedom of movement during the endless tedium of Chiun's exercises.

In the car Chiun gave Remo an old glass canning jar of some horrible-smelling black substance. When he took one whiff of the junk, Remo's face fouled.

"If this is your idea of a picnic, I'd rather have a bowl of your famous Fish Head and Rice Surprise."

"It is to help mask your glow-in-the-dark whiteness."

Remo looked at the jar again. He looked back at Chiun.

"Umm..." he said very, very slowly.

Chiun exhaled angrily. "You don't eat it, nitwit. Rub it on your skin."

"Oh," Remo nodded, relieved. "Much better idea."

Remo set about blackening his face and bare arms.

"What's the gig?" he asked the Master of Sinanju as he finished darkening his light skin. "We finally doing a hit?"

Chiun sat with him in the front seat. Even in the weak dome light, his yellow silk kimono shimmered brilliantly.

"*I* am performing a service to my emperor," Chiun replied. "Don't forget your neck."

"That's a hit, right?" Remo asked as he dutifully darkened the back of his neck. "I mean, that's what we do."

Chiun's chin rose high from the collar of his kimono, making him look for all the world like an insulted turtle.

"We?" he demanded. "*We?* There is a me and there is a you. Where, Remo, have you gotten the impression that there is a 'we' in anything either the 'me' or the 'you' does?"

"Don't get your knickers in a twist," Remo grumbled. "I just meant 'we' in the sense that we're both assassins."

At this the Master of Sinanju stifled a laugh. "You, an assassin? You?" Tears of mirth filled his eyes. "The only thing you have assassinated, other than that herd of unfortunate beef cattle that surrendered life to fill your worthless cow-gobbling gullet, is my patience."

Wiping his eyes, Chiun popped the car door. In a silent crinkle of yellow silk, he slipped out onto the dirt road.

"Wait," Remo called, "aren't you going to camouflage?" He held out the canning jar of smelly black goop.

Chiun's good humor evaporated. With a withering

look, the old man turned and began marching up the road.

"Maybe they can electroshock those mood swings out of you back at that loony bin," Remo muttered.

He capped the jar and ran to catch Chiun.

They had driven past a main gate a few miles back. If this was a typical Texas ranch, Remo decided Texas ranches were better guarded than most military installations. There were sentries all around the front. There was no way they'd be able to get in the front door.

He assumed they were supposed to be on the other side of the fence. They had walked a few dozen yards when Chiun stopped abruptly. Hands slipping from his voluminous kimono sleeves, the old man surveyed the high fence.

"Okay, how do we get from point A to point B?" Remo asked as he looked through the chain link.

He'd barely asked the question before he felt a tug at his arm. Before he knew what was happening, he was hurtling through the air. Up and over, he cleared the high fence. The ground on the far side raced up to meet him.

Remo was sure he'd break his neck. But the instant he should have hit cold Texas prairie, a pair of sure hands snapped his falling body from the air. In a flash he found himself standing once more on solid ground.

Beside him stood the Master of Sinanju. Chiun put a shushing finger to his wrinkled lips.

Remo couldn't believe it. He shot a look through the fence to where he and Chiun had been standing a moment before. There was no one there. The old geezer couldn't be twins. Somehow he'd thrown Remo over the fence and got to the other side himself in time to catch him.

"How the hell'd you do that?"

"Silence, oaf," Chiun hissed. "Stay close. And try not to trip over those clumsy slabs of mutton you call feet."

Remo wanted to say more, but the moment he opened his mouth a flashlight suddenly clicked on a few dozen yards away. An amber beam raked the area near where Remo and the Master of Sinanju stood. Boot heels scuffed earth.

Remo held his breath.

He assumed the best course of action would be to stay put. Chiun apparently thought otherwise.

A strong hand latched Remo's forearm. Dragging him like a wayward child, the Master of Sinanju steered a beeline across the field, away from the searching flashlight beam.

Soon the dark shadow of a mansion rose up from the ground before them.

The path they took wasn't the one Remo would have picked. Everything in his experience told him that they should opt for caution, sneaking around the perimeter, dashing from shed to fence post—anything that would provide cover on their stealthy approach to the mansion.

Remo thought there were too many foot patrols and dogs for this to be a typical Texas ranch. But who knew? Maybe all Texas ranches were like this one. After all, Remo wasn't exactly a world traveler. His stint in the Marines had taken him to Parris Island, South Carolina, for boot camp. Afterward was his tour in Vietnam. Oh, and once there was a day trip when the nuns took his class to the Statue of Liberty, where Remo had gotten in dutch with Sister Mary Antonine for spitting out of Lady Liberty's crown. Other than that, Remo had never really strayed far from Newark. Nothing in his life experience thus far indicated that this wasn't a typical Texas ranch. Still, it didn't feel right.

He was thinking that maybe he should mention his concerns to the Master of Sinanju when the old man suddenly stopped dead. Remo nearly plowed into him.

"Keep your stupid observations to yourself," the old man whispered.

He continued on.

Remo resisted the urge to crack wise. By now they were too deep in enemy territory for him to piss off Chiun.

He was amazed at how easy this was to Chiun. The Master of Sinanju should have been a walking bull's-eye in yellow silk. But the old man seemed to have an instinct for being exactly where no one was looking in the precise moment they weren't looking there.

There was a moment of anxiety when Remo realized that—if he chose to—the Master of Sinanju could vanish from his sight, too, leaving Remo alone to deal with all the guards and the dogs and the fences.

At the house, they crossed a slate patio and slipped through a set of thick glass doors.

With Chiun in the lead they headed through a formal dining room and into a main foyer. They paused, clinging to shadow as another patrol passed by. Unlike the men outside, this guard wore a black suit and tie. Once the man was gone, Chiun and Remo moved to the main staircase.

They headed up, side by side.

The Master of Sinanju seemed to have a clear sense where to go. Down an upstairs hallway, he found a closed bedroom door and slipped inside. Remo followed.

Two figures slept beneath a mound of covers. The sound of heavy snoring rose from the tangle of blankets.

A wall socket night-light cast V-shaped shadows up the wall near the bedside. In the light Remo caught a glimpse of the slumbering woman.

She looked vaguely familiar. He couldn't imagine where he could know her from. Trying to place the woman's face, he followed Chiun around to the other side of the bed.

The light was better here. It shone directly up onto the sleeping face of the woman's bedmate.

He was a man in his sixties, although he looked at least ten years older. Big ears, bulbous nose and drooping jowls.

The instant he saw that famous face, Remo realized where he'd seen the woman before. She had been on television many times hosting White House functions.

He blinked in shock. It all made sense. The extra guards, the Texas ranch. In a flash of fear-fueled clarity, Remo realized he was standing in the bedroom of the former President of the United States.

They were at the bedside. Remo tugged at Chiun's kimono sleeve. "That's the President," he hissed.

"He rules no longer," Chiun replied in a voice so low it barely registered to Remo's straining ears.

"But what's he doing here?" Remo stressed.

Chiun gave him a baleful look.

"Right," Remo said. "What are *we* doing here?"

"The former king possesses knowledge that endangers my emperor," the Master of Sinanju replied.

Remo had heard plenty about Chiun's emperor in the past few months. Although he had never met the man himself, the mysterious figure was MacCleary's immediate boss at CURE. Whoever he was didn't matter. He had finally given an order Remo Williams would not allow to stand.

"No, Chiun," Remo said softly. His words were like cold thunder in the dark room. "You're not killing a United States President. No way. Not while I'm in the room."

In the bed the woman stirred. She gulped uncertain air before tugging the blankets snugly up under her sharp beak.

Chiun shot Remo a toxic look. "Put away your fife and drum," he whispered acidly. "I am here to remove this one's knowledge, not his life."

Remo's whispering had registered on the slumbering ears of America's former chief executive. With a snort his eyes began to flutter open. Quickly, before the man could fully awaken, Chiun reached out. Slender fingers pinched a cluster of nerves on the sleeping man's shoulder.

The President's eyes sank peacefully shut.

Chiun brought his lips close to one big ear, whispering in a voice so soft Remo couldn't hear. When the Master of Sinanju straightened a moment later, the former President's face was a sagging mask of calm contentment.

"What did you say to him?" Remo whispered.

"I told him that I am a prisoner of lunatics who wish me to teach a sloth to be a swan," Chiun said

to remember a face. Mostly he remembered the eyes. They were flat, hooded. A killer's eyes.

The man in his dream was Oriental, which was strange because he didn't know that many Orientals. Odd that he'd be dreaming about one. But, he realized, in spite of what the psychiatrists might think, dreams rarely made sense. They were just a lot of hooey. Like this one.

In spite of the eerie feeling he knew it couldn't have been real. No one could have been in his bedroom.

The old politician pushed himself to a sitting position. The chill of early morning made him shiver. No surprise. At this point in his life he was rarely warm.

In the weak gray light he felt around the nightstand for his wristwatch. It wasn't there. Odd. He could have sworn he'd left it there the night before. The watch had been a gift from his wife on their fortieth wedding anniversary. He'd catch hell if he'd lost it. No. His wife would find the watch when she got up. She was good at those things.

His cold feet found his slippers. He was pulling on his robe as he tiptoed from the room into the hallway.

He met no mysterious strangers on his way downstairs. Just the same staircase with the same banister and the same third step that squeaked when you stepped on it just right.

In spite of many grueling years in politics, he was still an early riser. Even at his age this was generally his favorite time of the day. But today the dream had ruined it. For some reason he couldn't shake that uneasy feeling.

On shuffling feet he went to the front door. When

he pulled it open, he was so startled by the sight that greeted him he almost had a heart attack right then and there.

There was a kid standing on the steps. Just standing there. Alone and calm at five in the morning.

It wasn't the paperboy. At least not the one he knew.

The politician was about to ask the kid if he was filling in for the regular paperboy when he noticed the morning paper already rolled up on the bottom step. And this kid—whoever he was—didn't have a bag for papers.

"Who are you? What are you doing here?" the politician demanded as he squinted beyond the fair-haired boy.

There wasn't a bicycle on the sidewalk. No place for him to have slung his paper bag.

The kid said nothing.

"If you thought you were going to steal my paper, you've got another think coming, young man," the politician warned. "You young people will drive this country to ruin."

He glared at the boy. The boy stared back. There was no glimmer of emotion in his electric-blue eyes.

"Are you on the drugs?" the politician queried. "All right, then. Give me your father's telephone number. I'm sure he'll want to know you're hepped up on goofballs and standing out on people's steps in the middle of the night."

The voice that answered came not from the boy on his steps, but from the front walk.

"His father is dead," a thin voice answered.

On the walk was a man. When he saw who it was, the politician took a shocked step back.

It was him. The Oriental from his dream. Only this time he was real and he was standing calmly on the politician's sidewalk, just as he had stood calmly beside his bed to make sure he had the right man.

The politician had been right all along. Someone *had* been inside. In his own home, in his own bedroom.

And even as the politician blinked away his shock, the Oriental continued speaking.

"You will understand, it is more efficient this way," the stranger in the tidy black suit explained. "He is young and clumsy and would doubtless have awakened your wife. This way in his sloppiness he will not have to kill her, as well."

The last words rang hollow in the politician's brain. *Kill.* His waking dream had become a nightmare. He instantly snapped alert.

He would jump inside and slam the door. There was a phone in the front hallway. He would bolt the door and call the police. As he was dialing, he'd holler upstairs for his wife to lock the bedroom door.

He grabbed the door handle.

He could do this. Just some kid and a crazy Chinaman. He'd be safe inside.

His hand wrapped around the brass.

A final, desperate glance back.

The Oriental was still on the sidewalk.

The kid was on the steps. Standing funny now. Bent at the hip. Standing on one leg. Like a plastic pink flamingo lawn ornament. The leg was gone. Gone?

No, not gone. Here it was. Moving slowly.

No, wait. Moving fast. Faster than anything the politician had ever seen.

The boy's toe caught the old man in the Adam's apple. The power thrust carried the foot clear through the neck until it reached the brittle spine.

The head of Senator Dale Bianco did precisely what it was supposed to do given the circumstances. It popped neatly off his neck and bounced off the aluminum siding of his suburban Maryland town house. It made one big dent and then dropped into the rhododendron bushes.

There was a sliver of guilt in the boy as he watched the headless body fall back into the foyer. By sheer force of will, he crushed it.

He had worked the foot perfectly. Just as he'd been practicing. Precisely as he had been trained. The boy looked back to his teacher for a hint of approval, a flicker of satisfaction. *Anything.*

The Oriental wasn't even looking. He had already turned away. As if the perfect death that had been delivered—as if the *boy* himself—were less than nothing.

The boy stood next to the senator's body for a moment. Finally, he began slowly padding down the walk after his teacher. There was nowhere else for him to go.

12

Harold Smith found Conrad MacCleary passed out in Folcroft's hospital wing.

MacCleary was sitting in a patient's room, clutching a nearly empty bottle in his hand. He held the bottle down near the floor, hidden by the leg of the chair in which he was slumped. His hook rested on his belly.

Smith wasn't surprised MacCleary was in here. Although he didn't like the thought of his rough-and-tumble ex-CIA comrade in arms spending any time mingling with the sanitarium's civilian staff, this was a unique situation.

In the bed next to where MacCleary sat dozing lay a Folcroft patient. The boy had been brought to the facility two years earlier after an automobile accident had put him in a permanent comatose state. All the doctors who'd examined him insisted the boy's condition was irreversible.

Although Smith prided himself on his ability to remain emotionally detached—from patients and even from his own family members—his old friend didn't possess the same ability. MacCleary oftentimes embraced the maudlin, reveled in the lugubrious. And there was no telling where or how strongly his sentimentality would rear its ugly head.

Even though the teenager in the bed was beyond all hope of medical science, it hadn't stopped MacCleary from coming to this room every day, day after day. It hadn't kept him from sitting in the warm sunlight that poured in from the high, clean window or from smoothing the crisp white sheets and of, eventually, passing out dead drunk in the same green vinyl chair over and over. No one else ever came to see the kid. MacCleary would be damned if he let him rot away in his tidy little room with his clean sheets, alone and forgotten.

Smith understood that this was a special case. Still, he would have preferred it if MacCleary directed his emotional energies to more productive activities.

With a bleak expression he took the big man by the shoulder, shaking him awake. Conn snorted loudly, opening his bloodshot eyes. When he saw who had awakened him, MacCleary shut his eyes with tired impatience.

"The nurses stealing paper clips again, Smitty?" he said. His hoarse voice was phlegmy.

"We need to talk," Smith said tightly. "In my office."

MacCleary's eyes rolled open once more. It was the tone Smith used that got his attention.

"Is it big?" Conn asked.

"Potentially," Smith admitted. The grim look on his face told a more certain story.

Grunting, MacCleary heaved himself up out of his chair. He dropped the bottle into the big pocket of his overcoat. Struggling to maintain his balance, he lumbered after Smith.

As they were leaving the room, MacCleary suddenly touched Smith on the sleeve.

"Smitty."

When Smith turned, MacCleary was glancing back at the boy in the bed. When he looked back at the CURE director, his eyes were moist.

Smith nodded. "I understand."

That was all. For two old friends like these, no more words were necessary.

They took a flight down from the third floor of the hospital wing. A set of fire doors led to the administrative wing. MacCleary was coming around by the time they entered Smith's office suite.

Although Miss Hazlitt had recently been rotated back to the hospital wing, Miss Purvish had not yet returned. This time behind the outer desk was a plumpish woman who looked to be somewhere in her late thirties. Although, MacCleary realized once he'd gotten a good look at her, she was the sort who looked older even when they were young.

"Who's she?" MacCleary asked blearily.

"This is Mrs. Mikulka," Smith explained tightly. "She was transferred from the medical wing to fill in for Miss Purvish for the time being."

"Hello," the woman said nervously.

"I like the other one better," MacCleary slurred.

The woman's face reddened with worry and embarrassment.

"Please pay Mr. MacCleary no mind, Mrs. Mikulka," Smith apologized as he hustled the big man into his office.

Smith shut the door behind them.

"I will not bother to lecture you yet again on your drinking," the CURE director said tersely. "But I would appreciate it if you would attempt to keep yourself reined in when you are around the Folcroft staff.''

''Yeah, okay,'' MacCleary grunted, waving his hook. He flopped onto the sofa. ''Anything you say, boss.''

Smith could tell MacCleary was peeved. That was the only time he used the term ''boss.'' There was little respect behind it. Back in the OSS they had been equals. The ''boss'' showed up only when Smith became MacCleary's superior upon his return to the espionage game after completing school.

''The Maxwell situation may have just reached critical mass,'' Smith said gravely, taking his seat. ''As you know, I had recently started up the investigation again when several CURE informants hinted that something big might be coming out of the Viaselli crime syndicate in New York. However, the three federal agents I had assigned to the case have all disappeared in recent days.''

''Yeah, they're dropping like flies,'' MacCleary said. ''What's that bring the total to now? Six? Seven?''

''Seven *agents*,'' Smith said. ''But at the moment they have become the least of my concerns.''

The CURE director's tone was funereal. MacCleary knew that tone. And knew enough to be instantly wary of it.

''Why? What's happened?'' MacCleary asked evenly.

Smith's gaze was unwavering. ''Senator Dale Bianco was murdered this morning outside his Maryland home.''

MacCleary slowly absorbed the CURE director's words.

Conn normally didn't bother with politics. Still, he was aware of Bianco, largely due to the senator's vocal crusade against organized crime.

"You think this is related to New York?" Conn asked.

Smith nodded. "Possibly. The method of death was…unorthodox. While he wasn't killed in the same manner as the first agent I sent to look into the Maxwell affair, the extreme, atypical nature of his death suggests that they could be connected."

"I take it he wasn't shot, stabbed or suffocated."

"Decapitation," Smith said.

MacCleary issued a soft whistle. "That's a new twist," he said, slumping back in the couch. He stared at the floor.

"I had pulled back from investigating the Maxwell matter pending completion of Remo's training. However, this could have an impact on my original game plan. Senator Bianco was part of a committee looking into organized crime. He and some of the other senators from that committee were scheduled to meet in New York in a few weeks."

"They're sure as hell gonna cancel now," Conn said.

"No, they are not," Smith said. "I suspect that, if anything, this will strengthen their resolve."

"Idiots," MacCleary muttered. "Leave it to politicians to not know when to duck and cover."

The old CIA man spoke with deep bitterness. The decade that had just ended was witness to the shooting deaths of three prominent Americans, including the President who had sanctioned the creation of CURE.

Conn knew that no age was as completely innocent

as people liked to believe. He had seen too much in life to believe in fairy tales. But for many years, thanks to the secret work of men like Conrad MacCleary, the lie had been true for most Americans. Now that was all changing. In his life he had seen the evil that used to lurk in shadow step out into sunlight. America's innocence had been murdered by a sniper's bullet.

Smith's nasal voice cut through Conn's dispirited haze.

"At the moment no one is taking credit for Bianco's death," the CURE director said. "So far the papers have been kept in the dark. They believe the cause of death was a sudden heart attack. That's a stroke of luck for us. As long as they believe that, we'll be able to step up our investigation without fear of interference."

MacCleary sighed loudly. "So what? If the Mob has started wiping out politicians, America'll be better off. I say we pin medals on every guinea who helps thin that herd."

Smith's face darkened. "You don't mean that, Conn," he admonished. "And even you must see that only the honest politicians are at risk. The Mafia would not murder a politician who was working for them."

"Okay, we go with plan B," MacCleary said. "You know, the one we've used for the past eight years where we don't do anything but talk about the problem? Better yet, we let the Mob wipe out the last honest politicians in the country and then slap the cuffs on whoever's left standing."

Smith's flat eyes never wavered. "No cuffs," he insisted somberly. "Not this time."

The CURE director's tone was clipped, efficient.

Across the room MacCleary felt the boozy haze bleed from his brain.

Smith's meaning was clear. It had been months since CURE had been given permission to use the ultimate sanction against America's enemies. They had been twiddling their thumbs ever since, not daring to employ their new mandate. MacCleary had been afraid Smith had lost his nerve.

"So, we're finally gonna go for it," Conn said quietly. "It's about damned time."

Beneath his gruff tone was an underlying awe. They were about to embark on something momentous. And frightening.

"If Remo is close to ready, I will commit him to the field," Smith said. "How is his training progressing?"

"Before they left, Chiun said he was coming along way ahead of schedule," MacCleary said.

Smith's face relaxed. Finally, some good news.

"If it's a matter of days, perhaps we can put this off a little longer," the CURE director said. "Does Master Chiun believe he can have him up to speed within a week or two?"

MacCleary shook his head. There was a hint of sad mirth in his tired eyes. "Not quite. Chiun thinks he could maybe have him ready in fifteen years. Ten if he goes the lazy Western route and cuts a few corners along the way."

Smith blinked. "Is that a joke?" he asked.

"He sounded pretty serious to me."

The CURE director considered deeply. "Obviously, he is not serious. He's simply exaggerating to make a point. He must think Remo isn't ready for fieldwork.''

"I'm not sure about that, Smitty," Conn said. "I know Chiun's pretty out there with all that kissing up and bowing and Emperor Smith bull-hockey, but he doesn't strike me as the exaggerating type for stuff like this. I'll make sure I pin him down on it when they get back.''

"*I* will talk to Master Chiun," Smith insisted. "When do you expect them to return?"

"I'm not sure," MacCleary admitted. "After he finished the job you gave him, Chiun took Remo out into the desert for some kind of Sinanju survival training. It's been weeks already. Could be quite a while more. Chiun's been working him pretty hard.''

"What time of day does Remo report in?"

MacCleary shook his head. "I told him not to bother calling. Chiun will keep him from taking off. And nothing was pressing when they left. Plus the guy's not too sharp for remembering codes or call times or tracing protocols, Smitty. We won't hear from them until they get back.''

"That is unfortunate," Smith said with a frown.

"I guess it was bad timing letting them go now. Especially since this could wind up being a wasted trip. I'm still not sure Chiun wasn't just whistling up all our asses about that selective-amnesia thing.''

"You are the expert on Sinanju," Smith pointed out.

"Yeah, but that one seems far-fetched even to me.''

Smith considered his words. "I have seen enough of Master Chiun's abilities to not disbelieve him out of hand," he admitted. "As it is, the knowledge of

CURE is limited to the two of us and the sitting President. Remo will eventually have to be briefed in greater detail. Four is enough. If Sinanju truly does have a technique that can block certain memories, we will be protecting not only this agency but the former Presidents themselves."

"I doubt any President would rat us out, Smitty," MacCleary said. "Although if one does spill the beans, my bet's on the beady-eyed bugger we're stuck with right now."

"My fear is not that they would voluntarily give us away," Smith explained. "Who knows what secrets they might unwittingly divulge as they age? Something as innocent as the onset of senility or a simple slip of the tongue could prove disastrous for us. If Master Chiun is not simply boasting and it is possible to make an outgoing President forget about CURE, we will be protecting them, as well as us."

"It'd sure make my work easier," MacCleary muttered. His gaze was far-off.

Smith understood his old comrade's unspoken thought.

Three times in the past eight years CURE's security had been breached. Up until recently, deadly force had only been allowed in dealing with security matters. Each of the three times MacCleary had handled the details, and the men who had learned of CURE had simply disappeared.

Although MacCleary had killed more men in the line of duty than he cared to think about, it hadn't gotten any easier with age. Through the years, the faces of his victims had stayed with him. An accusing, Hell-sent choir that haunted his darkest midnight hours.

"Unfortunately, our original security protocols still stand, Conn," Smith said quietly. "Chiun told me the amnesia technique is not infallible. He told me there was one instance where it came undone. I cannot run that risk with someone who has learned of our activities."

"I gotcha, Smitty," MacCleary said. His tired eyes studied the dusty corners of the austere office.

At his desk Smith cleared his throat. "The Maxwell matter needs to be looked into," he said. "And since we don't know how long our new enforcement arm will be away—"

MacCleary didn't let him finish. "I got this one, Smitty," he said, standing.

Smith nodded. "Here is the data I have collected on Maxwell." He pushed a manila envelope across his desk. "We still don't know who he is, but the link to him is a man named Felton. Everything we have is in there."

Stepping over, MacCleary took the envelope. He was slipping it into his coat pocket when something suddenly occurred to him.

"Oops. I forgot."

MacCleary fished beyond the envelope Smith had given him, digging deeper into his coat pocket. He pulled out a plain white envelope and tossed it across Smith's desk.

"Present from an old pal of mine," Conn said. "Just what the doctor ordered. You do *not* want this guy filling your high-blood-pressure prescriptions."

With slender fingers Smith peeked into the envelope. With an approving nod, he closed the flap.

Smith rounded his desk and walked MacCleary to the door. His latest secretary didn't look up as the two men exited the office. She continued typing diligently away, engrossed in her menial work. Smith allowed a brief glance of approval at the woman before turning his full attention to MacCleary.

"Good luck. And be careful."

MacCleary gave a tight smile. "Always am," he said.

For men who had shared so much of life, nothing more needed to be said. MacCleary left the office suite.

Once he was gone, Smith gave a final glance at his latest temporary secretary.

The woman was working steadily away, clattering on her clumsy manual typewriter. She didn't give the impression of someone trying to look busy in front of her employer. She seemed genuinely engrossed in her work. A conscientious employee. A minor miracle in this day and age.

Smith turned wordlessly from the outer room. He closed the door to his own Spartan office behind him, shutting out the staccato clatter of the typewriter.

Back at his desk, he settled in his chair.

The plain white business envelope MacCleary had passed to him sat over the spot where his computer monitor was hidden. With one hand he drew the envelope to him.

Lifting the flap, Smith shook the envelope. A single, small object fell out into his open palm.

This was the final part of CURE's ultimate safeguard. Smith had ordered MacCleary to get one for each of them.

Smith had expected it might become necessary when he assumed the directorship of CURE. But the probability had become a definite the moment CURE had been granted permission to take on an enforcement arm.

Smith held the small white pill between thumb and forefinger. If not for the shape, it might have been mistaken for an ordinary aspirin. The pill had been fashioned in the shape of a tiny white coffin.

It was the only way out of CURE Harold Smith or any of them would ever know.

Wondering how long it would be before one of CURE's inner circle would have to fall on the sword, Smith gently tucked the cyanide pill into the pocket of his gray vest.

13

Don Carmine Viaselli wasn't afraid.

Given the same circumstances, other, *lesser* men might be afraid. But they were men of small minds and low character. They were not men like Carmine Viaselli.

Had someone else been in his shoes, Don Carmine actually wouldn't have blamed them if they felt afraid. After all, as the *capo di tutti capi* of the New York Mafia, he had plenty he could have been scared about.

There were the other Families. Nearby he had to worry about the Renaldis of Jersey, the Constazas of Philly and the newly empowered Patriconnes of Rhode Island. As the East Coast Families grew stronger, each of them threatened the territory of New York's Don Carmine.

Closer still were the factions in his own crime Family. In particular the Scubiscis in Manhattan were making noises. Pietro Scubisci still professed loyalty to Don Carmine, but he was showing all the signs of someone starting to flex his muscle. He was angling to take over from Viaselli.

Although the local police weren't a big problem, they still needed constant watching. Yes, anyone who mattered was already on the payroll. But every once

in a while some young hotshot got it in his head that
he was going to take on Don Carmine's operation.
This was always a concern, since the lid had to be
kept clamped tight at all times. If a cop got too full
of himself, he quickly found himself walking a beat
in Spanish Harlem. Or, in the case of the more stubborn members of the New York Police Department,
he'd find himself walking the special beat—off a pier
into the Hudson River.

The regular cops were a concern, but they weren't
anything to be scared of. With them it was like trying
to herd rats. A lot of scratching and clawing. A pain
in the ass that had to be kept in line.

For other men these worries piled up into fears.
Next came ulcers, heart trouble and an early grave.
That was the usual route for ordinary men. And, the
truth be told, until one year ago this was the route
Don Carmine was taking.

"Carmine, you don't look so good," the traitorous
Pietro Scubisci had said one afternoon, back when
headaches were things to worry about for Don Carmine Viaselli.

They were meeting at Don Carmine's 59th Street
fortress on the fourteenth floor of the Royal Plaza
Hotel.

Carmine had just returned from the bathroom. In
his hand, two Alka-Seltzers fizzed in a Waterford
glass.

His deep eyes, which usually betrayed false
warmth, were sickly. The healthy color of youth no
longer brushed his ashen cheeks. Over the past decade
he had steadily shed weight—at first a good thing,
but now it was too much. In late middle age he
seemed a husk of the man he had once been.

"I'm fine," Don Carmine grunted.

This Pietro Scubisci was forever looking for an opening, for a weakness in his Don. Carmine would have eliminated him, but Scubisci was well connected and respected. It would be hard to remove him without creating yet another headache. So he endured the conniving viper in his midst.

"No, really," Scubisci insisted. "You look kinda bad. You sure you feeling okay?"

He was only pretending to be concerned. Always with Pietro Scubisci there was the conniving undertone.

As he spoke, Scubisci fished around in a paper bag that he'd brought up to the apartment. The bag was stained dark. When Scubisci moved it, a slick line of grease stained the coffee table's glass surface.

"No, I'm not okay," Don Carmine admitted. "What I'm sick of is you and that paper bag of yours. Why you always gotta bring that bag with you all the time?"

"My wife makes the best fried peppers you ever tasted," Pietro Scubisci insisted. "Whatever you got's making you sick, they'll fix you right up." He produced a shriveled greasy green wedge from his omnipresent bag, offering it to his Don. "I promise you, Don Carmine, you ain't had a fried pepper till you had one of my Francesca's fried peppers."

Carmine's stomach rebelled at the smell. "Get that thing away from me," he snarled.

Scubisci shrugged. "You don't know what you're missing," he said, popping the fried pepper into his mouth. Crunching the paper bag shut, he put it down near his shoes.

Don Carmine didn't even care that the noxious-smelling bag would certainly stain his rug. With one hand braced on his knee he slugged down his Alka-Seltzer, wiping his mouth with the cuff of his dress shirt. The liquid left a thick, salty taste on his tongue.

"They're after us, Pietro," Don Carmine said, placing the crystal glass to the coffee table with a click.

"Who?" Pietro Scubisci asked.

"The government," Carmine said softly.

Scubisci snorted. "What's new?" he said. "I been around this longer than you. I seen enough of these G-men, all thinking they're hot-shit Eliot Nesses. All I know is they come and go and we're still here."

Pietro Scubisci had a habit of speaking like the old authority on all things Mob related. He was only ten years older than Carmine, but looked much older. Scubisci had looked like an old man since his twenties.

"Something's different now," Don Carmine insisted. "I've noticed it in the last five years, maybe a little more. The government's getting too good. They're coming after us on all fronts. Things they shouldn't know, they're finding out. I'd say they were getting lucky, but I don't believe in luck, Pietro. I think there's something big out there. Something that's going on where we don't see it."

"Eh, it's the same it's always been," Scubisci said. "You're just jumping at shadows. Comes from being around as long as we have."

"No, Pietro. It's there. I can *feel* it."

The Don spoke with utter conviction. He seemed so certain of this phantom something-or-other that even Pietro Scubisci paused.

"You sure, Don Carmine?" he asked quietly.

"I would bet my life on it, Pietro," Carmine replied. "I don't know what it is yet, but we are under attack."

After an instant's hesitation, Pietro Scubisci shook his head. For a moment he had almost been drawn in.

Pietro rolled his stooped shoulders. "So what?" he said. "I mean, I don't think there's nothing there, mind you. But so what if there is? What can we do about it?"

Carmine's face steeled. "A big threat requires a big response. Knock them down so hard they're afraid to get back up. Whack them so hard they ignore you, 'cause it's easier to pretend you don't exist than to do battle with you."

It was obvious that Carmine Viaselli had given this invisible threat some thought.

"You gonna take on the whole government, Carmine?" Scubisci had asked with a rasping chuckle.

Carmine Viaselli did not laugh. "If I could find a way, Pietro. If only I could find a way."

When that meeting with Pietro Scubisci had ended one year ago, Don Carmine Viaselli still didn't have a plan. How could you have a plan when you were fighting an enemy as big as the United States government? An enemy with so many faces, with unlimited financing, with so much raw power that you might as well try shooting at shadows? An enemy that now—if Carmine's gut was correct—had crossed over the line into lawlessness to achieve its ends.

It was a fight that couldn't be won, and Don Carmine knew it. After dwelling on the problem for weeks, he had finally decided to call it quits. Let someone else take over the show. Someone like that backstabber Pietro Scubisci.

Why not? Carmine had the money to retire. Take the wife and youngest kids and move someplace nice, like Vegas.

He was actually thinking about packing his bags that morning ten months ago when he met his unlikely savior.

Carmine had walked into the living room of his Central Park apartment only to find a stranger standing there.

It was impossible. His enforcer, Norman Felton, had set up the security precautions personally. Felton was the best. There was no way anyone should have been able to penetrate this far. Yet someone had.

Carmine Viaselli stopped dead. His heart pounded in his chest. All his worries, all the sleepless night, all had come down to this moment.

"You from the government?" he demanded. His eyes darted to the room's four corners in search of more federal agents.

The stranger was alone.

The Oriental in the black suit offered something that, on another man's face, might have passed for a smile.

"I represent myself, not a government. I have heard of your problem. I wish to offer myself as the solution."

"Who are you?"

"My name is immaterial as far as our business is concerned. But if you must call me something, you may call me Mr. Winch."

"I'll tell you what I'll call," Don Carmine threatened. "I'll call the cops, that's what I'll call."

"You are welcome to do so," Mr. Winch said. "However, would that be wise? I know that you bribe many of them, but you do not own them all. Who is to say that the ones you get won't be the ones who you fear are after you? After all, do they not work for your government?"

Don Carmine studied the Oriental with slivered, suspicious eyes. There was something about him. Carmine Viaselli had seen enough of it in his day to know what it was. This man possessed an aura of death.

"How you know about my troubles?"

"I hear things," Mr. Winch replied. "It is an easy enough thing when one knows what to listen for."

"You some kind of hit man?" Carmine asked.

This time Mr. Winch's smile was genuine. "I am the original kind," he promised.

Don Carmine's back stiffened. He thrust out his proud Roman chin. "You here to whack me?"

"I am here to offer you my services. You have a problem that needs attention. Ordinarily, I do not like to stay in any one place for very long, but at the moment my situation requires a certain amount of stability. I suggest a business arrangement from which we will both benefit."

Don Carmine knew in his marrow that he was talking to a cold-blooded killer. Maybe the coldest he'd ever met. But given the circumstances, he wasn't about to trust this Winch.

"I have a man who does this sort of work for me," Carmine Viaselli said.

"An amateur," Winch replied.

"Just the same, he's my man," Viaselli said. "I

don't know you, and I won't be intimidated into hiring you.''

Winch shrugged, a delicate, birdlike movement that failed to wrinkle the fabric of his perfectly tailored suit.

"Then don't," the Oriental said. "It does not matter to me. One of you is like the next. If not you, I will go to one of your enemies." He turned and walked away.

That was that. No arguing, no more discussing.

Don Carmine trailed Winch into the hallway. His men there seemed surprised to see the Oriental. Obviously, they hadn't seen him come in.

"I don't like that you got in here," Carmine said as Winch got onto the private elevator.

"Yes. I can see how that would be disconcerting."

His broad, flat face was without emotion as the elevator doors closed with a ping.

The instant the doors shut, Don Carmine turned to his men. "I want that son of a bitch wiped," he ordered.

The call was made from upstairs. Three of Don Carmine's best men were waiting in the lobby for Mr. Winch when he left the elevator two minutes later.

What happened next, no one was quite sure.

According to witnesses, the three Viaselli Family soldiers had approached Winch with guns drawn. That much the few eyewitnesses could swear to. There was a gunshot. Everyone knew that. It was after that things got fuzzy.

There was a blur of something in black that no one seemed able to follow. An instant later, when the blur resolved into the shape of the strange Oriental, there were three fewer Viaselli soldiers among the living.

Winch had deposited one man headfirst into a sand-filled standing ashtray. The thug had drowned on a mouthful of ashes and stubbed-out cigarette butts.

The second lay in a mangled heap behind a potted plant.

The third was missing altogether. He was found an hour later in the basement. Somehow Mr. Winch had thrown him down the elevator shaft—seemingly impossible, since the doors were already closing when the men attacked. He fell only one story, yet had injuries consistent with a twelve-story fall.

When news of what had happened reached the fourteenth floor, Don Carmine quickly sent more men after Mr. Winch. These soldiers had no guns. Waving white handkerchiefs, they caught up with Winch on the sidewalk a block from the Plaza. Offering profound apologies from Don Carmine, they escorted Mr. Winch back upstairs.

When Mr. Winch stepped off the elevator to the fourteenth floor, Don Carmine was waiting for him, an eager expression on his wan face.

"Do you give lessons?" Don Carmine blurted.

"Not to you," Mr. Winch replied.

"Not for me, for my men," Don Carmine said.

"No," Winch said. "Not for you, not for any of them, not for any price."

"Very well," Don Carmine said, clearly disappointed. "But you will work for me?"

"If your financial terms are acceptable to me."

"Whatever you want, you got," said Don Carmine, who felt relief for the first time in months. "You'll be my personal bodyguard. You keep my body safe, you'll be a rich man."

And so the deal was struck.

Carmine soon learned the reason Mr. Winch needed to stay in one place. It was that spooky little kid.

The New York Don was a little worried the first time he'd seen the fair-haired teenager. He figured he'd hired himself a gook bodyguard with a thing for young boys. He quickly learned that the perversions Winch was committing against that kid had nothing to do with sex.

The boy was terrified of Winch and idolized him at the same time. He had that same confident walk and that same killer's stillness as Winch. It was eerie enough coming from a grown man, but doubly so coming from a fourteen-year-old kid. The boy never talked to Carmine or his men. Only to Winch and only in that fruity gook language.

Whatever the kid's purpose, he wasn't a distraction to Mr. Winch. Winch proved himself useful in dealing with the waves of government men who were breathing down Don Carmine's neck. Whenever one of them got close, Mr. Winch removed him. Zip, bang, boom, just like that.

The bodies were remanded to Don Carmine's regular enforcer for disposal. Norman Felton had some untraceable method of disposing bodies. Felton never told his Don how the bodies were made to vanish, and Don Carmine never asked.

Every once in a while Mr. Winch got a little too exuberant and took out a couple of Don Carmine's own men. For training purposes, he said. Carmine wasn't terribly happy when this happened, but he kept his mouth shut.

For Carmine Viaselli, the idiosyncrasies of Winch and whatever he was doing with that kid of his didn't matter. He now had a weapon in his arsenal like no other Mafia leader.

Winch was so effective against the piddling government agents who came against Carmine, the Don eventually decided to use his weapon for a greater purpose.

Carmine decided that he would do precisely what he had said to Pietro Scubisci all those months ago. He would take his weapon and use it against the U.S. government. He would bring the war to them and force them to leave him in peace.

He would make them bleed. And the baptism of hot blood would bring permanent peace to Don Carmine Viaselli.

BLOOD WAS on Carmine Viaselli's mind this night. He was lounging on the sofa in his luxury apartment, sipping bourbon as he watched the evening newscast. On the screen, Walter Cronkite was wearing the serious face he put on when reporting the most dire news. He looked like a constipated buzzard. In somber tones he reported on the heart attack that had killed Senator Bianco.

"Shit," Don Carmine grunted. *"Heart attack."*

His mocking words were answered from the shadows.

"Your media does have a habit of reporting inaccuracies as absolute truths," said the thin voice.

Carmine jumped so high he spilled his drink. He glanced to his right. Mr. Winch stood next to the sofa.

"Dammit, I wish you'd stop doing that," Carmine snarled, wiping bourbon from his pajama bottoms. "And what's with this heart-attack bullshit? You were supposed to kill him in a way that sent a message. What message is a heart attack, except maybe cut down on the linguine?"

"Do not worry," Winch assured him. "In spite of what they are saying, your message has been sent."

"Yeah?" Carmine mumbled. "It better have been. I mean, three more agents last week. They just don't back off."

"Nor, I suspect, will they now," Winch said.

"What do you mean?" Carmine asked. "If they know we aren't afraid to take out a senator, they'll back off."

Winch raised a condescending brow. "Hardly," he said. "If you truly do have enemies, they are sure to retaliate. This was a message, but a weak one. You must do more."

"Then I'll kill a hundred senators," Don Carmine said. "I'll kill the goddamned President if I have to."

He heard a gasp beyond the closed living-room door, followed by a muttered prayer in Spanish.

It was his maid. She was polishing the woodwork in the next room. Carmine was too indulgent of her, but she'd been working for him for almost twenty years. He'd have to speak to her again about listening in on his private conversations.

"That is possible," Winch conceded. His voice in these meetings was always so soft it didn't carry beyond Viaselli's ears. "However, the last time I did that, I recruited an agent to perform the actual deed. With certain techniques of concentration he performed admirably. For a white."

Don Carmine didn't know whether or not Winch was joking. The look on the Oriental's flat face indicated he was not.

"As I have told you," Mr. Winch said blandly, "I do not seek notoriety."

"Then we'll stick with the Senate. Kill enough of them to deliver a message. Any left when that special committee on crime comes to New York, you take them out then."

"As you wish," Mr. Winch said. He melted back into the shadows and was gone.

Don Carmine looked back to the flickering TV. "Let 'em send the biggest guns they got. By the time I'm through with that committee, they'll need a sponge to mop up the puddle."

Smiling wickedly, he took a deep swig of bourbon.

14

On the morning of their tenth day in the desert, Remo Williams looked up at his teacher, Chiun, the Reigning Master of the House of Sinanju.

"I'm thirsty," said the Master's pupil.

As he spoke, he climbed the rope. As he had the previous hour. And the hour before that. The cool early-morning breeze tossed his short dark hair.

"What did you do with the water you drank back at the motel?" replied the Master.

In his reply, the student was typically coarse.

"What do you think? I pissed it out."

Chiun shrugged. "I won't be blamed for your lack of control." Sitting cross-legged, he studied the desert sun as it burned up like a lake of red fire over the flat horizon.

Remo had made it to the top of the rope. At eye level with Chiun now, he stopped.

"What lack of control? Water runs through me. I don't know about you—I know you're perfect and all—but even you must have to tap a kidney every once in a while."

Chiun's brow lowered. "Yes, I am perfect. And I might add that it is high time you noticed. As for the rest, tell me, Remo, are all the subjects of this barbarian land as crude and insolent as you?"

"Pretty much," Remo grumbled. "Welcome to America."

Frowning deeply, he slid back down the rope.

The Master considered the sheer awfulness of what his pupil's words might entail. Shuddering, the Master returned his gaze to the pretty sunrise.

His abusive pupil refused to give him a moment's peace.

"I'd like some water," Remo pressed from the bottom of the rope. His hands gripped the fat knot before he began scampering back up again.

"And I would like a proper emperor. Even one of the lesser Caesars would suffice. I would like to be somewhere other than this nation of bloated hedonists. I would like a good pupil to teach Sinanju and not some white thing who would learn a few karate tricks."

Remo paused. "Wait, I thought I was learning Sinanju."

Chiun's gaze had been far off. Blinking away the cobwebs of sad memory, he looked down at his pupil. The desert sky tinted red his cotton-white tufts of hair.

"There is the Master and there is the pupil. I am Master. But you, Remo, are not the pupil." His voice was filled with soft regret.

"What the hell am I, then, chopped liver?" Remo asked testily. He still clung to the rope, unmoving.

There was no strain on his face. The effort such a feat of strength would cause another man was no longer present. It had been weaned weeks ago from this amazing white thing.

"It is not your fault," Chiun said. "Tradition dictates that the Master take a pupil from the village of Sinanju. Such has it been, such will it always be."

"Why?"

There was no sarcasm in Remo's tone. Just interest. By the look on Chiun's face, it was clear he couldn't believe Remo thought it necessary to even ask such a question.

"Because Koreans are, by temperament and breeding, naturally better suited to the difficult task of learning," Chiun replied matter-of-factly. "Some Japanese might be able to absorb some. A random Chinaman could, perhaps, pick up a move or two, if he wasn't too busy picking the pockets of other thieving Chinamen. The other, lesser Asian peoples are hopeless to a man. The Vietnamese eat dogs, Philippinos smell funny. And do not even get me started on the Thais. The races are all downhill after that. Indians and Arabs are a waste of the land they breed over and the air they breathe. Blacks are merely burned whites except angrier, and whites are bleached blacks with more television sets. Why would we go to inferior outside races for a pupil when we have perfection in our own backyard?" His voice dropped low. "Although, truth be told, most Koreans I could take or leave."

The pupil absorbed the Master's words with thoughtful silence. This was good. At last the Master had given the pupil something weighty enough to absorb his flitting white mind. When the pupil finally spoke, his eyes held a gleam of devout sincerity.

"You're a racist," proclaimed the pupil.

"What is that?" Chiun asked.

"It's someone who thinks he's better than everybody else just because he happened to be born a certain way."

"Ah, this have I heard," Chiun said. A pleased smile spread across his face. "Thank you."

"That isn't a good thing, Chiun," Remo said flatly. "It isn't right to feel superior to other people."

Obviously, the pupil truly believed this. The Master could see the words he spoke were heartfelt.

What is this lunatic land to which the wicked fates have brought me? the Master thought. To the sincere pupil with the wrong ideas of race, he said, "Tell me, Remo, if the sun tells the stars that their light does not shine as brightly as its own, is the sun being racist?"

"Yes," Remo said. "Because the sun is just a star like all the other stars. They're just farther away. It's no different. In fact, some of the other stars are bigger and brighter if you match them up side by side with the sun."

Chiun was aghast. "Who told you such nonsense?"

"Science. And it's not nonsense. It's the truth."

Chiun shook his aged head. "Thank the gods you are not the one destined to be my pupil. There is far too much foolishness that would have to be unlearned first. Even so, you have been adequate in some ways so I will give you some free advice that will help you as you bumble through life: The truth is everything you were not taught in school."

He went back to studying the sunrise. The red sky had burned away to yellow. The disk of the sun flamed white as it peeked over the horizon.

"They did okay with what they had," Remo said. "And whatever you think of us whites as a race, and no matter what you were hired to do by the guys upstairs, I think I'm learning more than you or they bargained for.''

At this the Master fell silent.

It was true. This Remo, this white with the rude tongue and the vile beef-fueled appetites, *was* learning Sinanju.

It had not been Chiun's intention. He had come to this land in search of a legend. To find, as it was written, the dead night tiger that he would make whole in Sinanju. What he found was a gorging white thing. This Remo could not be fulfillment of the legend, could not become Shiva, the Destroyer. And yet there was something there.

Chiun had planned to teach a few tricks. But he found to his amazement that this Remo was capable of much more than mere tricks. Almost without realizing it, Chiun had begun to pour the ocean into a teacup because, miraculously, the teacup was accepting it. It was most disturbing. Chiun would have to pray to his ancestors for guidance.

''And I'd still like some water,'' brayed the pupil.

''When you are done your exercises,'' Chiun said.

''When's that gonna be? You've had me dangling out here like a fish on a line for the past three hours.''

With his chin he pointed up the length of rope.

The thick braided line ended at an ancient chunk of corroded metal. To Remo it looked like something that had been left in the desert since the gold rush days. Chiun had found it on the desert floor near where they had parked their Jeep. Right now, if Remo twisted just right as he hung from the rope, he could just make out their Jeep. It was parked on a lonely, rutted desert path a thousand feet below where he dangled out in open air.

They had come to Arizona after leaving Texas.

At first there was something that felt right about the Arizona desert. Remo had no idea why. It was a feeling of something old and instinctive that made his bones ache for family. A strange thought for an orphan from Newark, New Jersey. Especially given the company he was with.

For the days since their arrival here, Chiun had been putting Remo through his paces. There was a lot of climbing and jumping and scampering from rock to rock.

Remo had been forced repeatedly to pull his hand from the darting fangs of a flashing rattlesnake. This, he was told, to increase his hand-eye coordination. "Incentive," was the word Chiun used as justification for this exercise.

Hours of running in bare feet on sand had caused Remo's soles to blister, then callus. He was repeatedly scolded for doing it wrong. The right way, he learned, was when he did not leave "those mammoth churned-up hoofprints" in his wake. The one time Remo managed to run through the soft desert dust without leaving a single discernible mark, he thought he heard the Master of Sinanju utter a solitary word of praise. He knew he was mistaken, however, for when he looked the old man was wearing his usual nasty scowl.

Still, all in all it was better than Folcroft. At least he was outside. But this latest exercise was ridiculous.

They had climbed up to the top of the butte in the wee hours of the night, without aid of rope or piton or any climbing gear whatsoever. Once they were at the top, Chiun drove the metal post deep into the rock.

Even though he'd been watching at the time, Remo

still had no idea how the old man had done it. It looked as if he'd just jammed it in, like sticking a straw into a thick milkshake. Remo was sure the post would give. But somehow the metal was secure.

The post hung out over desert. Remo was given a length of rope and told to go and secure it to the far end. Once he had done so, Chiun sat to await the sunrise while Remo was forced to climb up and down the rope endlessly.

Just a few short months ago Remo would not have thought it possible to do something like this even once. But he was in his third hour now and had not yet broken a sweat.

"So what are you saying, if I was Korean you'd let me have a drink of water?" Remo groused as he climbed and slid, climbed and slid. His hands were beyond rope burns.

"If you were Korean, you would know enough to be grateful to me for all I have done for you," Chiun replied.

The old man had stopped watching the sun to turn his attention back to Remo.

Chiun was careful to keep his face bland as his pupil continued to perform his exercises flawlessly. It was an amazing thing. Most Korean boys would have given up after the first half hour. In the light of a new day, Chiun noted that the pupil's wrists were coming along nicely.

"Yeah? Well, I'm not a freaking camel, for Christ's sake."

Seated at the edge of the butte, Chiun frowned. "Do not invoke that name in my presence," he sniffed.

At the top of the rope now, Remo stopped. "What name?"

"That Nazarene carpenter," Chiun replied. "I assume you are a Christian of some sort. You people usually are."

"I'm Catholic," Remo replied. A gust of desert sand pelted his face. He gritted his teeth against it. Still stationary on the rope, he rocked back and forth in the wind.

"Worse," said Chiun.

"What do you mean worse? What's wrong with Catholics?"

"What *isn't* wrong with Catholics? You may start with that busybody carpenter. Did you know that he ruined the reigns of not one but two King Herods? Of course you didn't. Because it wasn't written down in your precious white Bible. By his birth alone he forced poor Herod the Elder into the tragic and rash act of executing the firstborn son of every family in Egypt. Does your Bible tell of the sleepless nights that plagued Herod for days after initiating that unfortunate social policy? No. It was a week before his appetite returned, but was that recorded? Of course not. Here was a poor, sensitive man going through terrible emotional upheaval, but does anyone care? No, they don't. It is always Jesus this and Jesus that."

"My heart bleeds for good King Herod," Remo said dryly.

"As it should."

"I was being sarcastic."

"Of course you were."

"I like Jesus," Remo said.

"You would," Chiun replied.

There was a long moment during which the only sound was the wind that sang between them.

"Okay," Remo said finally. "Here's the deal. I'm done with hanging around out here. My arms are like rubber and I'm halfway to total dehydration, so I'm coming in and if you want to stop me you can push me off this cliff. At this point it'd come as a welcome relief."

Reaching up, he grabbed the bar. Hand over hand he climbed to the flat top of the butte. He dropped to the soles of his feet next to the seated Master of Sinanju.

"It is about time," Chiun said. He rose to his feet like a swirling desert dust devil.

"What's about what?" Remo asked warily. He rubbed gingerly at his shoulders. They were far beyond ordinary pain. His arms felt as if they'd just been plugged into his sockets from someone else's body.

"I was wondering how long it would take for you to realize the pointlessness of this exercise. Most Korean boys have sense enough to see it for what it is at the outset." He marched to the edge of the butte. "We have wasted enough time playing games. Recess is over. It is time to start the day's training."

His pronouncement made, the old man slipped over the mesa's edge and was gone.

Remo stood alone for a moment. The desert morning was clear and beautiful.

"Look on the bright side," he muttered to himself. "Maybe on the way down I'll fall and break my neck."

Cradling both sore arms, he trudged reluctantly to the edge of the mountain.

15

MacCleary brought the manila envelope Smith had given him back to his quarters at Folcroft.

During the four months of planning that culminated in Remo's staged execution, Smith had overseen the remodel of Folcroft's old, abandoned psychiatric isolation wing. In the 1920s, the closed-off basement corridor had been home to Folcroft's most dangerous patients. It was now CURE's security wing. This was where Remo was brought after his execution, where the plastic surgery was performed and where CURE's enforcement arm had recovered.

Conn had taken over another room in the otherwise empty hall. Once Remo had sufficiently healed and was remanded to Chiun's care, MacCleary had the run of the special wing.

Alone in his small room, floor cluttered with empty liquor bottles, MacCleary studied the data Smith had collected. There wasn't much. They already knew that the new Mob enforcer was somebody named Maxwell. Somehow this Maxwell was tied in with Norman Felton, a suspected hit man with ties to New York's Viaselli crime Family.

Other than a few photographs of Felton and Viaselli, that was pretty much it.

Conn was disappointed there wasn't more to go on.

In this business, the more information you had going in, the more likely you were to come out alive at the other end.

Once he was up to speed, MacCleary brought the envelope down to the basement furnace. As he fed the papers into the fire, he noted the latest addition to the virtually empty cellar. A plain metal box was tucked away in the shadows behind the furnace.

Smith had mentioned the box to MacCleary in passing, as if discussing the weather forecast.

The coffin had arrived at Folcroft a few months back, the day Smith had finally connected the White House line.

This was part of the ultimate fail-safe. Together with the cyanide pills, this was how CURE's secrets would remain secret. If the agency was ever compromised, Harold Smith would calmly descend the cellar stairs, climb into his specially ordered coffin and swallow his suicide pill.

Standing in the heat of the furnace, Conn noted that there was only one coffin.

In spite of the CURE director's earlier crack about their age, Smith was still planning a different kind of death for each of CURE's original agents. For Smith, this would be the way. Quiet, neat, alone. For MacCleary—the old field hand—it would be something away from Folcroft.

He tried not to think about what or when that might be.

With his hook, Conn flipped shut the cast-iron door of the furnace and turned for the stairs.

He met no one on his way outside.

When MacCleary pushed open the heavy fire door

that opened on Folcroft's employee parking lot, thin fingers of drifting snow twisted around his ankles.

Though winter was still hanging tough in the northeast, Conn smelled just a hint of spring on the breeze that blew off the sound. He held the aroma for a lingering moment before climbing behind the wheel of his dull green sedan.

The engine purred and he drove down the gravel drive and out through the main gates. The solemn stone lions watched in silence as he steered out onto the tree-lined road.

It felt good to be leaving Folcroft. It *always* felt good to leave. For Conrad MacCleary, leaving a place—any place—was always preferable to staying. He had an apartment in Rye. There wasn't anything there except four walls and an empty fridge. It felt good to leave there, too.

Someone else would have considered him a man without a country. MacCleary knew better. Sure, he might not have a real home or a family or anything remotely approaching a normal life, but the one thing he always would have was a country. More, he had the best damned country ever to grace the face of God's green earth.

"Give me your beatniks, your hippies, your big-mouth feminists yearning to burn bras," he muttered as he drove down the lonely road. "Dammit, she's *still* worth a life."

The patriotism of Conrad MacCleary was so strong a thing that no power in heaven or on Earth could have shaken it. Not even the knowledge that the life that would soon be forfeit to protect America would be his very own.

THE TWELVE-STORY APARTMENT complex stood in majestic contrast to the dingy three-story buildings of East Hudson, New Jersey. Norman Felton, Don Viaselli's man, lived in the sprawling twenty-three-room penthouse of Lamonica Towers. Since CURE's only link to Maxwell was Felton, MacCleary started there.

For three days MacCleary studied the comings and goings of Felton and his men. The first thing he realized was that this Felton was connected. Conn took care to avoid the police cars that patrolled with the regularity of a private security force outside the big building.

MacCleary spotted Felton several times. Viaselli's likely enforcer was a powerfully built man in an impeccably tailored suit. With him at all times—like an angry shadow—was Jimmy Roberts, his manservant bodyguard.

There was a handful of others Conn could tell belonged to Felton. They had the look. They dribbled in and out of Lamonica Towers at irregular intervals. Unfortunately, Conn couldn't see every entrance at all times. There was no way of knowing just how many men Felton had up there.

On the morning of the third day, Felton appeared through the front door with his bodyguard. When the two men got into a limousine and drove away, Conn decided he had waited long enough.

Conn had spent the past few days studying the habits of the doorman. The fat man vanished each day for five minutes at nine o'clock. Felton's limo was barely out in the street when the doorman checked his watch. Like clockwork, the man whirled in his blue-and-red uniform and disappeared inside the gleaming glass doors of the apartment building.

MacCleary was out of his car and across the parking lot in twenty seconds. Through the front door in twenty-two.

Keeping his left sleeve pulled low to conceal his hook, he crossed the lobby as if he belonged there.

Through a door beyond the lobby reception desk, Conn caught a glimpse of the doorman and a few other Lamonica Towers employees drinking coffee. They failed to notice MacCleary as he crossed to the stairwell entrance.

He took the stairs to the second floor, then took the elevator to the eleventh floor. Back to the stairs, he climbed up to the penthouse fire door.

He was surprised to find the door unlocked.

Conn was instantly wary of a trap. Yet there were no guards in the hallway beyond. A quick examination revealed no alarm system hooked up to the door.

Maybe reputation alone kept Norman Felton protected. In a strange way—with his connection to Don Viaselli—Felton might enjoy some of the same safety afforded the village of Sinanju by the reputation of its Master.

Still, Conn was determined not to go the way of the seven dead and missing government agents who had preceded him. He walked with care down the short corridor to the main twin doors of the penthouse.

These doors were locked. Using a set of burglary tools he pulled from his pocket, as well as the curving tip of his hook, Conn quickly picked the lock. He slipped inside.

The decor was tasteful and opulent. Smith had supplied him with a floor plan of the apartment. MacCleary steered a direct course to the back of the suite.

Pale morning sunlight filtered through the gauzy drapes of Felton's study. MacCleary hurried to the desk. Sitting in the well-oiled leather chair, he used his hook to pop the metal lock face off the top drawer. It sprang free with a soft click, dropping almost silently to the plush carpet.

Conn searched the desk quickly and methodically.

There was nothing of interest. Apparently, Felton had a daughter attending Briarcliff College. There were some personal letters from her secured in ribbon. MacCleary hadn't seen anything about a daughter in Smith's dossier.

"You're slipping up in your old age, Smitty," Conn muttered under his breath.

Other than the letters, there were a few legal documents and some uncashed dividend checks secured with a paper clip. There was also some payroll information on a Jersey City auto junkyard. If there was a connection to Maxwell in the pile of innocuous papers, Conn MacCleary couldn't see it.

"Maxwell, where the hell are you?" Conn grumbled.

There were no file cabinets in the room. Rows of tidy bookshelves were loaded with unread books. A few pictures hung on the mahogany walls. Otherwise the room was empty.

Conn did a rapid sweep between the books and behind the pictures for a hidden safe. There wasn't one.

This room was a bust. MacCleary had stepped halfway back into the living room before he knew he was in trouble.

"Find what you were after?" a flat voice asked.

Conn froze. He hadn't heard anyone come in. They

had been careful not to make a sound. Careful because they knew he was coming, knew he was already inside. It was a setup.

Norman Felton sat in the wing chair. With him was Jimmy the butler and a third man. MacCleary recognized him as Timothy O'Hara, one of Felton's lieutenants.

They weren't alone. Over in the doorway stood three more men. They lacked the culture of Felton or the comfort of Felton's two men. These were imports of some sort, not used to their surroundings. They seemed to have equal contempt for both Felton and Conrad MacCleary.

"You have picked an unfortunate time for your visit," Felton said to MacCleary. "These men are employed by an associate of mine. They're here on business." He waved a hand to the trio at the door. "Oh, and before you ask, the answer is yes, we did see you sitting out in the parking lot for the past three days. Do you think we're blind?"

"I suppose it wouldn't work if I told you I worked for building maintenance," MacCleary said. He kept his voice perfectly even. No quick moves. Not yet.

To his right a breeze off the open veranda blew the thin ceiling-to-floor drapes into the room like billowing cobwebs. In the wind the curtains enveloped one side of Conn's body before slipping back to the floor.

"Possibly," Felton said. "But since I own the building, I know all my employees. Now, I have a little problem maybe you can help me with. My friends in business and I are being harassed. It's been going on for quite some time, and we'd like it to stop. Unfortunately, so far the agents I've encountered haven't been forthcoming about who they work for.

Under persuasion some have tried to tell us but—and
here's the amazing thing—they just don't seem to
know. I've got a good feeling about you, though. I
think you're going to tell me exactly who our enemy
is.''

Conn was doing rapid calculations in his head. The
odds were definitely not in his favor. All at once, his
shoulders slumped. The fight seemed to drain from
him.

"Okay," MacCleary exhaled wearily. "What the
hell. Bastards don't care if I live or die anyway. Anything you want to know. But we should talk in private."

In his mind Conn had already decided his course
of action. His revolver was in his pocket. He had six
shots. One for each man in the room.

The three at the door were holding their ground.
Felton and the others were nearer, so they'd be first.
Conn was confident he could take out the near three.
The others would be harder, but not impossible.

Rapidly calculating his odds, Conn figured they
weren't great. Still there was a chance.

The next time the drapes blew up around him, he
was already slipping his hand into his pocket. The
move was so smooth and practiced it remained unseen. His fingertips were brushing the butt of his gun
when a new voice cut sharply across the charged air
of the room.

"Do all of you Americans rely on weapons to do
the work of your hands?"

The voice couldn't belong to any of the men Conn
had seen. It was too close. Even Felton seemed surprised by it. The Mob enforcer's head snapped
around.

When he found the source of the voice, his eyes grew dark. "You," Felton snarled contemptuously.

MacCleary followed Felton's gaze. He was shocked to find that there were now two more men in the room. Conn couldn't have missed them. They seemed to appear from out of the walls themselves. Secret panels. Had to be.

One was an Oriental, probably somewhere in his thirties. Conn quickly realized the other man wasn't a man at all.

It was just a kid. Pale as a ghost, with a mop of yellow-blond hair. Though his face was dead, his blue eyes as he peered over at MacCleary seemed to sparkle with a weird electricity. The kid had a confident grace that somehow sent a chill up Conrad Mac-Cleary's battle-tested spine.

Conn was rapidly rethinking his game plan. There was now an extra man to take out. And the presence of the creepy kid complicated things. As the drapes fell away from his stocky form, he slipped his empty hand from his pocket.

The Oriental wasn't even looking Conn's way.

"I assume this is yet another spy sent to harass our mutual employer," the Oriental said to Norman Felton.

When he turned his attention to Conn, the Oriental's eyes were blandly contemptuous. But then something strange happened. As he studied the intruder near the open balcony doors, the scorn that was as comfortable a part of his wardrobe as his black business suit melted to quiet interest.

The Oriental noted the lightness of the CURE agent's stance—the way the man with the hook seemed to balance on the balls of his feet. A little too relaxed for a beef-eating Westerner. Of course Mr. Winch was aware of the weapon even before MacCleary was reaching for it. The gun wasn't the problem. It was the stance. The pose the big man struck seemed…familiar.

Across the room Felton didn't seem to notice the change of expression on Winch's flat face.

"This one's mine," Felton said coldly.

"He was about to kill you," the Oriental said. There was icy certainty in his voice. His hooded eyes turned not to Felton, but remained locked on Conrad MacCleary.

At this Felton laughed. Even Jimmy, his main bodyguard, chuckled gruffly under his breath. The other bodyguard, O'Hara, joined in the mirth.

"Fat chance," Jimmy growled.

Still sitting, Felton aimed a neatly manicured finger to the trio of men standing at the door. The laughter dried up.

"I want them and you out of here," he ordered. "Viaselli thinks I'm working for one of his enemies. He thinks I could be behind these attacks. I'm not. I have always been loyal. Even when he took you on—" he aimed his angry chin at Mr. Winch "—I did what I was told. I cleaned up your messes, same way I cleaned up my own. Even though you made messes like none I've ever seen. Arms and heads chopped clean off. Didn't matter. I cleaned up after you, because Carmine Viaselli asked me to and my job is to protect Carmine Viaselli. But now my Don thinks I've been disloyal to him. You tell him I haven't. You tell him that I kidnapped his brother-in-law as insurance to keep me safe while I figure out what exactly is going on here. I'm keeping him until I clear up this whole mess.''

The three at the door had been keeping their cautious distance. Felton's manservant, Jimmy, had a reputation for savageness that they had no desire to put to the test. The surprise appearance of Mr. Winch, their employer's new right-hand man, had merely complicated things.

"No way," one of Viaselli's men near the door called. "We been sent to collect Bonelli, an' that's what we're gonna do. Mr. Viaselli wants his brother-in-law back."

Standing near the balcony, Conrad MacCleary was beginning to get a clearer picture of things. There was trouble in paradise. The Oriental, the men at the door. They weren't Felton's men. They all worked for Felton's boss, Don Carmine Viaselli. All pitted against one another.

Conn had been wrong these past eight years. CURE had had an effect. The men Smith had been sending in had sown the seeds of mistrust within the Viaselli criminal organization. They were turning on one another.

No one went for guns. They all stood. Staring.

The Oriental and his young charge seemed the only two in the room unruffled by the standoff.

Winch raised a dismissive hand to the men at the door. "Your mission is irrelevant," he said without turning. "This man who was about to kill you all holds the key to everything you need to know."

This time there was no laughter from Felton. A smile devoid of mirth touched the corners of his lips.

"Kill me?" he mocked. "He didn't have a prayer."

"Oh?" Winch asked. "The gun in his hand tells me a different story."

Felton's eyes darted to the man at the balcony doors.

It was true. The intruder now held a revolver in his good hand. It was Felton's own fault. He had become sloppy, distracted by all these uninvited guests. Everyone had been afraid that everyone else would draw guns and so no one had, except for the one man they should have all been watching.

"Okay," MacCleary said gruffly. "Here's how this is gonna work. You're all going to keep your hands where I can see them. You're going to go into that study and shut the door and I'm going to back calmly out of here. You're going to let me get out to my car without calling down for help. First bastard I see peek his head around a corner gets a bullet between the eyes. That clear to the whole class?"

His words were tough, but the simple fact of the matter was Conn knew he couldn't risk initiating gunfire. Whom would he shoot first? Each side seemed firmly allied against the other. To baptize this standoff in blood would give both teams a clear shared threat. If gunfire did break out, he only hoped some of them would take each other out.

It was not Felton who spoke, but the Oriental.

"I am sorry, but that is not possible," Mr. Winch said.

MacCleary's face fouled. "Who the hell are you, anyway?" he demanded.

"Someone, I believe, with whom you share a mutual acquaintance," Winch offered darkly. He folded his hands across his stomach, curling just the tips of his fingers into the cuffs of his white dress shirt.

"Your stance is good, by the way. It is wrong to use a gun, of course, but you are as right as can be expected given your limitations."

The words sounded odd, coming as they did from an unfamiliar face. But they were still familiar. And in that instant, MacCleary felt a cold knot of certainty tighten deep within his belly. And with the knowledge came fear.

Mr. Winch seemed to sense Conn's understanding. The Oriental gave a small nod of acknowledgment.

MacCleary now realized he faced something far more dangerous than a mere Mob enforcer. Felton, Viaselli, their men, the mysterious Maxwell—all spiraled away in a swirling, inconsequential sea of mediocrity. What he faced now was the best. And recent experience had taught him that he was woefully unprepared for battle.

Conn aimed his gun squarely at Winch, ignoring the others. He didn't pull the trigger. Doubted it would have mattered even if he did.

MacCleary watched for a telltale flash of movement, a rustle of fabric, *anything* that would presage attack. But Mr. Winch calmly stood his ground.

"Thank you for confirming that which I already knew," Mr. Winch said with a smile.

And when the attack came against Conrad MacCleary, it wasn't the dangerous Oriental or Felton or even any of Felton's or Viaselli's men who came after him.

Winch whispered a few low words in a foreign language. It sounded Korean, but he spoke too softly to be sure. With a nod barely perceptible to Conn, Winch did the one thing Conn hadn't expected. He sent the kid forward.

It would have been laughable under other circumstances. A room full of grown men, all of them undoubtedly armed to the teeth, and a kid was being sent to kill MacCleary.

"I don't know if you gooks have heard, but we've got child-labor laws in this country," MacCleary said. He kept his gun aimed at Winch's chest.

The kid moved in an unhurried glide. His electric-blue eyes danced as he stared blankly at MacCleary.

Near his employer, O'Hara had been watching the action with growing agitation.

"This is nuts," Timothy O'Hara growled all at once. Not waiting for orders from Felton, he stepped forward, shoving the kid roughly aside. "Get outta the way, punk."

Though O'Hara outweighed the kid by 150 pounds, the blond-headed teenager didn't fall down. He merely glided to one side, allowing O'Hara to pass.

MacCleary instantly forgot about the kid. O'Hara was charging for him. Jimmy Roberts took his lead, coming in behind. The others seemed to take up the thread. The men at the door began moving toward Conn.

For the moment even the Oriental was forgotten. Survival instincts honed from years of fieldwork took over.

MacCleary spun on Felton's men. Or tried to. As he whirled, he felt something rough snag the end of his wrist.

His hook! His damned hook was caught in the back of a couch! The off-balance moment was enough for his attackers. O'Hara was first on MacCleary. MacCleary couldn't get his balance to shoot before a strong hand had him by the wrist. His forearm struck the wall and the gun went flying.

MacCleary tore his hook from the sofa material.

Jimmy Roberts was on him. Too late to save O'Hara.

The hook buried deep in the side of O'Hara's head, just behind his ear. MacCleary tore it free and the man fell.

Conn didn't know if it was fatal. Didn't matter. The rest would be coming....

No. Not coming. Stopped. The room had frozen. Why weren't the others moving? Felton and the Oriental just stood there. Even Jimmy the bodyguard and the Viaselli soldiers looked worried. They were all watching the kid.

Conn sensed something wrong. Later no one in the room would be able to say quite what it was. A hum, a shudder of electricity. Something felt, something heard. Some invisible something that sparked the already tense air of the penthouse room, raising hair on arms and the backs of necks.

There was a Viaselli soldier standing between Conn and the boy, blocking the young man's path to MacCleary. The boy turned his electric-blue eyes on the mobster.

"The fire," the boy said softly. Conn noted that he had a vague Southern twang. "See the fire? The fire burns."

And as if some hidden switch had been thrown, the Mafia man went berserk.

Screaming, the Viaselli soldier slapped his hands flat against his own head. He beat his palms to his chest as if trying to extinguish invisible flames. Howling in pain and crying for help, he whirled in place.

At first MacCleary thought it was some kind of

seizure. But when the man spun to him, he couldn't believe his eyes.

Blisters were rapidly forming on the man's face. As MacCleary watched in terrified fascination, the erupting boils turned red, then white. They spread across the man's cheeks and down his neck. As his face became one big blister, the man screeched in horror.

There was no flame, no heat. The belief that he was on fire was enough for him to experience the effects. The skin ruptured and boiled and spit and crackled as if he were fully ablaze. As MacCleary stared in disbelief, the screaming Mafia man's eyes baked to an opaque milky white. Then he wasn't screaming anymore because he was dead. The man fell face first to the neatly vacuumed wall-to-wall carpeting.

"Sweet mother of mercy," Conrad MacCleary gasped.

He saw a shuffling movement. Numbly, Conn looked up.

The kid was coming for him. He had that same weird look on his face, this time directed at MacCleary.

Conn's eyes darted around the room.

Felton and the others melted back. All the men were shocked. Only the Oriental was unaffected. He stood rooted in place, a knowing smile on his broad, flat face.

And coming toward Conn, a look of possessed doom in his deadly eyes, was the freakish yellow-haired kid.

Hypnosis or something else entirely, it didn't matter. Conn had seen what that kid could do.

There was only one way out. Calculating every possible alternative in an instant, MacCleary came up with the only workable solution. And as soon as he had it, he acted upon it.

Conn fell back from the kid, from the Oriental. From Felton and the other mobsters.

The floor-length balcony drapes blew gauzy white into the apartment. Conn stumbled through them.

Felton and the others started to run, but it was too late. Conrad MacCleary flipped up and over the wrought-iron balcony railing and dropped from sight.

"Dammit," Felton snarled, bounding out onto the terrace.

He was just in time to see MacCleary bouncing off a third-floor balcony. Conn had tried to grab on with hook and hand. It slowed his descent enough that when he hit the landscaped evergreens they didn't tear his flesh to shreds. He struck the trees and rolled, hitting the sidewalk hard.

The uniformed doorman and a few tenants from the parking lot ran over to the body. The doorman quickly raced back inside the apartment building to phone for an ambulance.

"Witnesses," Felton growled. "Damned witnesses."

He whirled back around, face furious.

Winch was gone. So, too, was the blond-haired kid.

O'Hara lay dead on the floor. Jimmy Roberts stood over him. The two remaining Viaselli men were hovering over their own dead companion, their faces dumb with shock.

Felton shook his head, trying to shake away the shock of the past few moments. He jerked a thumb over his shoulder.

"Get someone down there to check the body for an ID before the cops get here," he ordered. "And clean this mess up." He waved to the two bodies in the room. "I don't want any evidence when they start asking questions."

As Jimmy got on the phone and started issuing orders, Felton took one last look at the burned body.

When he stepped into his study a moment later, Norman Felton's face was ghostly white.

16

"That's not to say you Catholics were always bad," the Master of Sinanju announced.

The old Korean was sitting cross-legged on a broad, flat rock in the middle of the prairie. The cold and lonely sky above his aged head was black and scattered with stars. Somewhere far off, a lone coyote howled at the waxing moon.

They had been in the desert for so long now, Remo had lost all track of time. His sunburned skin had long since gone from lobster red to a dark tan.

It was closing in on midnight. Rather than return to their motel when evening fell, as had become their custom during these weeks in exile, Chiun had proclaimed that this night they would remain out in the desert.

At the old Korean's insistence, Remo was trying to start a fire. He had been trying to start one for the past three hours. Remo didn't know what he was doing wrong. After all, he had seen it done in Westerns a million times. Something to do with rubbing sticks or banging rocks. Unfortunately, what was child's play for Gabby Hayes was proving impossible for Remo Williams. All the sticks he managed to scrape up were snapping and all the rocks were shattering in his hands.

Remo was squatting in the sand. At his toes was a growing pile of broken sticks, crushed rock and no fire.

When the Master of Sinanju brought up Catholics for the umpteenth time, Remo wasn't in the mood.

"Are we back to Catholic bashing again?" Remo grumbled as he worked. "I thought you'd reserved today for dumping on the Chinese."

The Master of Sinanju's rampant prejudices became even clearer as the days bled into weeks. By the sounds of it there weren't many members of the human race he had much use for. Even the inhabitants of Sinanju—which Remo learned was also the name of the North Korean fishing village from which Chiun hailed—weren't spared criticism. Two days ago Remo had been forced to endure a six-hour monologue on the village cobbler, with the ominous warning never to entrust him with a pair of ceremonial greeting sandals. Remo—who had never worn a pair of sandals in his life, never intended to wear a pair, thus negating the need for mending, and who had never been to Korea and had no intention of ever going there—agreed to take Chiun's warning to heart. That blessedly ended the Sinanju-cobbler harangue. But since sunup yesterday it was all about the Chinese and how they were all thieves and liars, so Remo was a little surprised when the old man started up on Catholics again.

"You just said a prayer to the founder of your cult," the Master of Sinanju explained.

Remo frowned. "No, I didn't."

"I heard you distinctly," the old Korean said. "You invoked your deity. You said 'Jesus Christ, why won't this light?'"

"Oh," Remo said, nodding understanding. "Just a figure of speech. Although I wouldn't object to a little otherworldly intervention right about now. The Lone Ranger could use his gun to start a fire. You wouldn't happen to have a .45 stashed up that skirt of yours, would you?"

"For your sake I will pretend I did not hear that," Chiun droned. His hooded eyes sought night shadows.

Remo sighed. "Back to square one." He returned to his rocks and sticks.

"There were some nice popes in the Middle Ages," Chiun resumed as Remo crushed a fresh pair of rocks. "Now, the Borgias. *There* were some popes who knew how to treat their assassins. And when there was more than one pope at a time, the babies of Sinanju ate well. But now you people have settled on one pope who seems content to follow your founding precepts. Worse even than a false religion is a false religion that actually practices what it preaches."

"Yeah," Remo said. "I can see how that'd wreck the market for professional killers." More rocks shattered in his hands. "Damn," he muttered as he threw them to the ground. "You know, this would be a hell of a lot easier if you'd just let me drive to town for some matches."

"No matches. Steer clear of those evil things, Remo," Chiun warned darkly.

Remo almost hated to ask. "What have you got against matches?" he said, sighing wearily.

"Aside from fostering a reliance on devices for doing something that you should be able to do yourself?"

"I don't fart fire, Chiun," Remo pointed out.

"Do not be gross," Chiun chided. "Matches are made of poison. The whatever-it-is they put on them that makes the fire causes a disease called necrosis. Thousands have been killed or crippled. The deadly poison at their tips has even been used for murders and suicides. Matches are wicked implements of death and destruction."

Remo's eyes narrowed. "When did this allegedly happen?" he asked suspiciously.

"Oh, just the other day," Chiun insisted, fussing at the skirts of his kimono. "I believe it was in the 1830s."

"Thought so," Remo said, nodding.

He was learning that this sort of thing was typical for the Master of Sinanju. The old Korean measured everything against the yardstick of Sinanju. Since his discipline had been around for millennia, his concept of time was skewed. Although the United States was nearly two centuries old, Chiun still considered it to be an upstart nation. Events of 140 years ago were just yesterday to him.

If he had met the Master of Sinanju a few short months ago, back when he was in his old life as a Newark patrolman, Remo would have thought the old man was senile. But he had come so far in so little time that he was finding himself accepting the words of the wizened Oriental more and more. Not that it was always easy. It seemed as if Remo could do nothing right. Earlier that morning, for instance.

Today's training had involved climbing sheer rock faces. Of course, Remo did it wrong. He used hands and toes to seek out cracks and bumps in the surface. Chiun had told him that he should make himself a part of the wall. Remo wasn't sure exactly what that meant. Besides, it wasn't necessary.

"Why should I try that hocus-pocus?" Remo had asked. "If I can find a ledge or a crack, I should use it."

"And what will you do if you encounter a completely smooth surface?" Chiun had asked.

"Find a ladder," Remo replied with certainty.

"And suppose there is not one available?"

"I'd tell Rapunzel to let down her freaking hair," Remo groused. "I don't know what I'd do, Chiun. I'd holler for help, I guess."

"And assuming there is only you?"

"There isn't just me," Remo said. "There's MacCleary and his boss and probably a dozen other guys in training like me. They'd send help."

At this, Chiun shook his aged head. "There is only you, Remo," he insisted. "There is only ever you. You must learn to rely on yourself, not others."

"You seem like an okay guy," Remo said. "For a slave-driving pain-in-the-keister. How about I call you?"

During their conversation, the harsh lines of the Master of Sinanju's face had softened ever so slightly. At Remo's words the old man's face hardened. Sniffing, he raised himself to his full height.

"Climb," Chiun commanded, his voice cold steel. Remo climbed.

But that was today and this was tonight and Remo was on his fiftieth rock combo and he still hadn't discovered fire.

"What kind of a sissy-girl desert is this?" Remo complained after another pair of rocks exploded in his hands. "That's it, I give up. These rocks are made of goddamned saltines." He threw down the stone shards in disgust, brushing the powder from his hands.

"Rock is rock," Chiun said quietly. "It is the same as it has always been. It is you that is different."

By his tone it was obvious the old man thought he was making some great point. Remo had no idea what it might be.

"What do you mean?" asked Remo.

"This," said Chiun.

And the Master of Sinanju picked up two of the bigger chunks of rock Remo had broken and discarded. Clapping the surfaces together over the pile of twigs, the old man sent off a spark that ignited the tinder.

He held the rocks out for Remo to inspect. Somehow they hadn't broken in the old Korean's weathered hands.

"You have reached a new level in your training," Chiun explained as the fire caught in the kindling.

"How'd you do that without breaking them?" Remo asked, puzzled. He took one of the rocks from Chiun. It was small in his palm. His fingers nearly wrapped completely around.

"Because I can control what I have learned."

Remo raised a dubious eyebrow. "You trying to tell me I broke rocks with my bare hands?"

"What do you think this exercise was all about?" Chiun replied. With a long stick he began turning over the small pile of brush, spreading the fire evenly.

Across the growing campfire, Remo frowned. He hadn't been aware that this was an exercise. Taking the rock tighter into his palm, he squeezed. Nothing happened. The rock remained solid, unbreakable. But that wasn't right. Just a few minutes before it had been just like all the rest, shattering from an even bigger stone in his hand.

He raised his doubtful eyes from the rock.

"You weren't thinking about it before," the Master of Sinanju said, answering his pupil's unspoken question. "You were thinking only of the fire and of your frustration. Your attention was focused on something else. Like now."

Remo wasn't sure what the old man was talking about until he looked back down. In his hand was a crushed pile of rock. Stone dust sifted from his open palm.

"Holy Christmas crap," Remo gasped, amazed. "Did you see that?" He looked up, wide-eyed.

"Your mind is unfocused," Chiun replied as he played in the fire. "We must work on that next. But that is for tomorrow. For now you need to sleep."

"Sleep? No way. Did you see what I just did? I just crushed a freaking rock with my bare hand. With my *bare hand.* That's even better than breaking boards."

"It is child's play in Sinanju."

Remo slapped the dust and shards from his hand, scooping up another rock from the ground.

"It's gotta be a trick. Show me what I did."

"No," Chiun said. "It is time for you to rest."

"I don't want to rest. I wanna break more rocks," Remo said, barely able to contain his excitement.

"You just did," Chiun pointed out.

Remo looked down at his hand. Another solid rock had been crushed while he wasn't looking.

"Hoo-wee, this is great!" Remo enthused. "You've gotta be the greatest teacher ever."

Despite his agitation that his order to sleep had been twice ignored, Chiun's face warmed at the compliment.

"Either that or I'm the greatest student ever," Remo insisted.

Chiun's face dropped. Remo felt the desert air chill.

"You have an ugly tongue, even for a white," the Master of Sinanju said. "Go to sleep."

"What?" Remo asked. "What'd I say?"

His answer was an icy stare.

"Okay, okay," he grumbled. "But this is more like what I expected from all this training. Sign me up for more of this stuff in the morning."

Remo didn't think he'd ever be able to sleep again. He felt as if he could burst out of his own skin, so astonished was he by his own growing abilities. But Chiun was adamant and so he obeyed, curling up on the ground in the glowing warmth of the blazing fire. In spite of the rush of excitement he was feeling, sleep quickly overtook him.

AN HOUR LATER, Remo awoke to the most disgusting odor he'd ever smelled in his life. Retching bile-fueled air from deep in his empty belly, he sat up.

It was just after one in the morning. A soft breeze stirred the desert dust. Chiun was still tending the fire, a thoughtful expression on his weathered face.

"Where's that stink coming from?" Remo gasped.

The old man looked up. Yellow fire danced across his hazel eyes. "You," the Master of Sinanju replied.

Remo frowned. Since the second month of his Sinanju training, he hadn't needed deodorant. He didn't know why. Just another one of the freaky changes his body had been undergoing. Chiun told him that his body was beginning to awaken, to do those things it was meant to do. But this smell was different than body odor. It was a strong stench of rotting flesh that flooded his senses and filled the air. He tasted the foul odor thick on his tongue.

"No way that's me," Remo said. "I think an animal must have died around here somewhere."

He glanced around the desert scrub for a dead buffalo. For a smell that awful, the animal had to be huge.

"*Many* animals died to make that smell," Chiun replied, still twirling his stick lazily in the fire.

"Figured," Remo said, holding his nose. Somehow the stink still penetrated. "Where'd you take me, the elephants' graveyard? There must be carcasses buried all around us."

"They are not buried. You are the one who brought them here."

"You know I didn't bring anything out here," Remo said. "You haven't allowed me any meat in months. You won't even let me out of your sight when we go into town."

"It has nothing to do with your new diet. What you are smelling is the result of more than one score years of wallowing in cow burgers, pig's feet and sheep entrails."

With a look of cautious skepticism, Remo sniffed his own forearms. The stink nearly bowled him over. Eyes watering, he looked up. "It *is* me," he said, shocked.

"I told you. Why don't you ever listen to a word I say? Sometimes I think I would be better off talking to the wall."

"No walls in the middle of the desert."

"And so I am forced to converse with you," the Master of Sinanju lamented.

A quiet moment passed.

"Chiun?" Remo asked eventually. "Why do I stink?"

The old Korean became very still. Curls of smoke from the dancing fire encircled his age-speckled head.

"It is a rite of passage called the Hour of Cleansing," Chiun explained with a knowing nod so gentle it failed to disturb his tufts of gossamer hair. "It was common for Masters of the old order. Less so for those of the new, since most begin proper diet and training not long after birth. Your body is purging a lifetime's worth of poisons. It understands better than you the changes you are going through. The pollution of beef and everything else that has clogged your body is being released."

"This is all just from eating meat?"

"It is the product of an unhealthy diet."

"Phew," Remo said, disgusted. "Remind me of this stink next time I want a steak." He tried to slow his breathing as he'd been taught. The odor still clung. "The Hour of Cleansing, huh? I suppose I can put up with it that long."

"That is just a name," Chiun informed him. "For you it will be longer."

"How much longer?"

"That depends on how many caramel-dipped cows you ate in the past year. Judging by that ring of fat around your middle I would say no more than eight years."

It actually took eight days.

During that time they remained in the desert, away from civilization. Remo's training continued.

By late afternoon of the eighth day, the Hour of Cleansing finally and blessedly passed. It was as if Remo's body had flipped a switch. The smell was there one minute, gone the next. It didn't even linger.

Relieved by the sudden wash of clear, clean desert air, Remo took in a deep breath. Somehow he felt more alive than he'd ever felt before, in tune with the plants and sand and sky and soft desert wind.

The Master of Sinanju noted his pupil's breathing with satisfaction. This white had taken the rudiments of Sinanju and embraced them like no other. That he had passed the Hour of Cleansing so soon was yet another miracle. A hint of pleasure touched the corners of the old man's vellum lips.

Remo didn't see his teacher's pleased expression. Once the smell had lifted, Chiun gave him permission to break camp.

Remo was lost in thoughtful silence as he packed their bedrolls in the back of their Jeep. As he shut the tailgate, he came to an abrupt decision. Setting his shoulders firmly, he turned to face his teacher.

"I've got something to tell you, Chiun," Remo announced reluctantly. "I was going to just do it, but I feel—I don't know—like I owe you something."

"You owe me everything," Chiun replied, frowning at his pupil's serious tone.

"Right. Okay. Sure. Anyway, all this stuff you're showing me has been great and all, but it doesn't really matter. First chance I get, I'm outta here."

Chiun frowned. "What do you mean?"

"You've been square with me, so I will be with you. I didn't ask for any of this. They shanghaied me. Screw 'em. I'm leaving the minute all your backs are turned."

Chiun's face darkened. When he spoke, his voice was filled with low doom. "You intend to run away?"

Remo's spine was straight. He nodded tightly. "You bet. First boxcar out of town, I'm on it."

Not a single wrinkle on the old man's parchment face so much as flickered. "So," he said quietly. "After all this time, after all my effort, you choose now, *now* to tell me that you were wasting my time?"

"No offense," Remo said.

"You have been selected to work for America's secret emperor, the man who will rule over all this benighted land when he chooses to ascend to the throne. And as if this great honor was not enough, you were given another one, far greater than the first. You were remanded to the care of gracious and generous-of-spirit me, who has given you the beginnings—yes, there I said it—the beginnings of Sinanju. And you wait until now to tell me that I have been wasting my time? Now? Now!"

"I wasn't going to tell anyone at all," Remo said. "But you're—" He shrugged. "I don't know, you're different, that's all. I thought it wouldn't be right to not tell you."

But Chiun was no longer listening. Bony shoulders thrust back in indignation, he turned his back on Remo. Eyes facing the desert, he crossed his arms haughtily.

"Go," the Master of Sinanju commanded.

Remo's brow lowered. "Huh?"

The old man's expression never wavered. "I cannot believe that whatever pagan god you believe in gave you those giant ears only to make you deaf. Go means go. Go."

"What do you mean?" Remo asked. "Like take off, go? Run away from the organization? Right now?"

"I have been here long enough, Remo, to see that there is no organization to this disorganized nation," Chiun sniffed. "It is a wonder you people have lasted this long, with your mad emperors, your constitutions that your own government admits do not work, your Presidents who are selected by batting their eyelashes at the dribbling masses every four years like courtesans currying favor in a Pyongyang brothel, and your would-be students who cavalierly fritter away the valuable time of their betters. There is chaos and lunacy here, Remo, but not organization. If it is your wish to run from those who brought you to this life against your will, then go. I will not stop you."

"So I got this straight, you do mean right now? This minute. In the Jeep?"

"I will survive," Chiun sniffed.

"Okay," Remo said. He climbed in behind the wheel.

"But consider," the Master of Sinanju announced before Remo could put the key in the ignition. "If you leave now, you are leaving wonderful me, glorious me. The only person who has given you anything of any use in your pathetic excuse for a life. When I found you, you were nothing. A foundling wallowing in mud and despair. I have raised you from that. By leaving now you confirm your utter hopeless worthlessness. To stay will prove to me that you are something other than just a pale piece of a pig's ear."

Remo was thoughtful for a quiet moment. "Oh, well," he said. "See you in the funny papers."

When he tried to turn the key in the ignition, he

felt a sharp slap across the back of his hand. Looking up, he saw a pair of hard hazel eyes peering accusingly at him from the passenger's seat. Chiun had the keys in his bony hand.

"What kind of cold, heartless thing are you, that you would abandon an old man in the middle of the desert?" the Master of Sinanju demanded.

Remo hadn't even heard the door open and close. He had to admit it, the tiny Korean was good.

"You're not letting me go, are you?"

"No. Take us home."

"I don't have a home anymore," Remo said bitterly.

"Tell it to someone who cares," Chiun said, tossing the keys back to his pupil.

Regretting that he'd ever said anything about his plans to the Master of Sinanju, Remo started the Jeep.

"Old buzzard," he muttered.

"Pale piece of a pig's ear," Chiun replied.

They drove out of the desert, back to civilization.

17

No light spilled through the high windows of room
36E. Night had long since claimed the Eastern Sea-
board.

Even before twilight drew its dense black shroud
across the land, the troubled gray soul of Dr. Harold
W. Smith had already been stained with shadows of
despair.

It was afternoon when the world grew as dark as a
midnight cave for the director of CURE. For the tac-
iturn Smith, the eclipse blotted out all light, all hope.

He learned of the events at Lamonica Towers
through the normal CURE network. A low-paid reporter for the local East Hudson, New Jersey, newspaper supplemented his income by passing on unusual
stories by phone to an anonymous number in Kansas
City. He assumed it was for some kind of government
agency that was analyzing crime statistics. He was
partly right. What he didn't know—could *never* be
allowed to know—was that his regular reports were
rerouted through several dummy sites until they
reached a certain lonely desk in a vine-covered building on the shore of Long Island Sound.

MacCleary had failed.

At first Smith couldn't believe it. His heart

pounded wildly when he read the news. Blood sang loud in his ears.

There were few details. The digest was concise, standard procedure for CURE's unwitting informants.

A man with a hook had jumped from a balcony in Lamonica Towers. Police had interviewed Norman Felton, the building's owner. Felton—whom the world would never know worked for the Viaselli crime syndicate—claimed that the man had attacked him in his apartment. Documents found on the jumper identified him as Frank Jackson, a patient of a private mental institution in Rye. Foul play was not suspected.

A few short lines. And the end of the line for CURE.

MacCleary couldn't be brought back to Folcroft. Not without raising too may questions.

It was all too soon.

Too soon since MacCleary had brought Remo aboard.

Too soon since his trip to Korea aboard the *Darter* to retrieve Master Chiun.

Too soon since he'd gone to Trenton State Prison in his guise as a monk.

MacCleary had been too active these past few months. Many had seen him. It had been an acceptable risk until now. MacCleary was CURE's only field agent. Everything that he'd been involved in had been necessary.

But this? This brought it all to a head.

A man with a hook jumping from a building. The news item had made it into a few papers already. How many more would it find its way into? Would it snowball from there?

How many sailors who had just seen another man with a hook would read that paper? How many prison guards would recall the monk with the hook who had visited that prisoner on death row? What was his name, Williams, wasn't it? And by the way, wasn't it odd how fast that trial was? A cop going to the chair just for killing a pusher—wasn't that strange? Maybe someone somewhere should look into that, maybe even an enterprising young reporter from an East Hudson paper who subsidized his meager pay by passing along news stories to a mysterious phone number in Kansas City.

It was improbable that it would play out quite like that. But not impossible. And therein was Smith's dilemma.

The existence of the mere *possibility* that some of those things might happen was unacceptable. Mac-Cleary could not be brought back. To spirit him from the East Hudson Hospital where he was in intensive care would raise questions.

Too many questions.

Smith's brain swam.

All the lies, the cover-ups. They had all been necessary. Necessary to preserve the most damning secret in American history. Necessary to save a country from chaos and anarchy. All absolutely necessary.

And the thing that would inevitably have to happen next was necessary, too.

Smith couldn't even think it.

At one point soon after he'd heard the news, Miss Purvish buzzed him. The East Hudson police were calling. Something about a former patient who had attempted to commit suicide in New Jersey.

Smith took the call. He didn't even know what he

was saying. The cover story came out by rote. More lies.

When he was through on the phone, he left his office, telling his secretary where he would be. With a few instructions delivered woodenly to Miss Purvish, he headed deep into the sanitarium. Up the stairs to this corner room.

He sat down in the drab vinyl chair. And there he had stayed for hours. Day bled into night. The shadowy twilight slipped away from the windowsill as fluorescent bulbs flickered and hummed to life in the corridor beyond the open door. Yet Smith stayed.

In the bed near him, the Folcroft patient who had become Conrad MacCleary's obsession in recent years continued to breathe rhythmically. The comatose young man's eyes were lightly closed.

He would never wake up. Never again open his eyes on the world.

Smith felt sick.

The chair in which he had sat all afternoon still smelled vaguely of MacCleary's aftershave. How many hours had his old comrade sat in this chair?

Smith hadn't eaten all day. His stomach was a growling pocket of churning acid.

It was well past two in the morning. For the whole time he had been there, Smith hadn't once checked his watch. His mind was still lost in swirling thought when a hand reached in from the hallway. The light switch inside the door clicked and the room was awash in garish white light.

Smith blinked away the brightness.

The prim nurse who entered seemed surprised to find someone else in the room.

"Oh, excuse me."

When she realized that it was Folcroft's director sitting alone in this room, the nurse hesitated.

"Dr. Smith," she stammered. "I didn't realize— Is something wrong with the patient?"

His vision was coming back. Blinking away the dancing spots, Smith looked over at the teenager in the bed.

"There's been no change in his condition," the Folcroft director assured her. His own voice sounded strange to him. Hollow. He cleared his throat. "I was merely checking in on him. For a friend." The last words were difficult for him to get out.

The nurse didn't notice the catch in his voice.

Smith had been balancing the patient's chart on his knee all night. He had picked it up when he came in the room. He didn't know why. It was something he had seen MacCleary do countless times. He handed the chart to the nurse.

She accepted it with a curious expression, replacing it at the foot of the bed. When she began fussing with the sheets, Smith was already leaving the hospital room.

He trudged down the hallway.

It was closing in on three in the morning. At this hour he didn't expect to meet many faces in the hall. Smith kept the sanitarium staff to a minimum at night. He caught only a few odd looks from Folcroft's civilian employees on his way out of the hospital wing.

The administrative wing was empty. He walked through deserted halls to his office suite. When he reentered his office for the first time in hours, he found a note waiting on his desk.

Dr. Smith:
The patient you were asking about showed up at about 5:00 this afternoon. The guard phoned me, but I didn't want to bother you. He and his nurse(?) are in his room. Hope this is okay. See you tomorrow.

K. Purvish

The daft woman had wasted an entire sheet of yellow legal paper for one small note. No matter how much he tried to instill in her a sense of frugality, she refused to change her spendthrift ways. And that question mark. She was always just a little too curious.

Questions. Would there be more questions? A foam-lined steel box in the basement. The questions would end when he pulled the lid tight over that airtight box.

Smith crumpled the note in one hand, throwing it to the drab carpet.

He sat there for a long time. As he contemplated the shadows, his long fingertips pressed his vest pocket.

The hard outline of his new cyanide pill was a strange and alien thing.

Finally, some rational part of his mind broke through the haze. He reached across the desk, picking up the interoffice phone. He punched the code that would connect him to the main desk.

"This is Dr. Smith. The new patient, Mr. Park, arrived back late yesterday. Please send someone to retrieve his manservant. Yes, I am aware of the hour. I need to speak with him about the patient's special-care needs."

Smith hung up the phone.

The walls seemed to be closing in around him. No. They were a million miles away.

Smith blinked. His eyes were hot. When he spoke, his voice was hoarse.

"Forgive me," he quietly implored the shadows.

Security. Everything was about security.

Leaning forward, Smith retrieved Miss Purvish's note from the floor. Smoothing it, he fed it through the special document shredder he kept at the side of his desk. It went through with a whir and was gone forever.

REMO NEVER THOUGHT he'd be relieved to be back at Folcroft Sanitarium. But after the weeks he'd spent in the wilderness, returning to civilization—even the CURE version of it—was a welcome change.

The guard at the main desk recognized Chiun as a patient who had gone on a brief sabbatical. When they returned in the afternoon, he called upstairs to relay the news.

No one seemed to care. There were no brass bands. Remo and Chiun were left alone in their basement quarters.

Remo was a little surprised when MacCleary didn't come down to see them. They had been out of touch for weeks.

Probably off on a bender somewhere. MacCleary liked his booze. At the start of his training just a few short months ago, Remo would have done anything to join him. But thanks to the Master of Sinanju, Remo's craving for liquor was almost gone. Not that he intended to become a teetotaler, but at the moment the thought of alcohol made him slightly ill. He was sure it would pass.

He took a long, hot shower.

Chiun even made him dinner. Some sort of disgusting mess made from brown rice and fish heads. It looked to Remo as if the Master of Sinanju had shopped for the ingredients from the Folcroft Dumpster.

But while the food was revolting, the portion was large compared to the subsistence meals he'd been allowed to eat in the Arizona desert. He ate greedily, drank water to his heart's content and went to sleep with a full belly.

He was awakened by a knock at the door.

There were two bedrooms in the basement quarters. Chiun used them both—one for himself, one for his luggage. He gave Remo a straw-thin sleeping mat and told his pupil to sleep out in the common room.

As the Master of Sinanju flounced out of his room to answer the door, Remo was sitting up groggily.

"Kind of early to be delivering the breakfast garbage, isn't it?"

"The desert is only a few hours away by air carriage, O garbage mouth," Chiun warned.

Not wanting to go back to desert rations, Remo stilled his tongue as the Master of Sinanju opened the door.

An elderly Folcroft security guard stood in the hall.

He spoke softly to Chiun for a few moments. Afterward the Master of Sinanju inclined his head to his pupil.

"What is it?" Remo yawned.

"Follow him," Chiun told him. He pitched his voice low. "And mind your manners."

Remo raised an eyebrow, but Chiun's mouth was sewn shut.

Remo pulled on his pants and T-shirt. Slipping his feet into a pair of sneakers, he followed the guard into the hall.

They took the stairwell to the administrative wing.

To Remo, this had become "Upstairs," the nerve center of the CURE operation. He had never been up here before. MacCleary had told him that it was off-limits for him.

From the start he had a picture in his mind of walls of computer banks whirring away as harried G-men ran from room to room with armloads of files labeled *Top Secret!* Instead he found himself walking down a colorless hall that fulfilled its intended function precisely. There was nothing there that didn't look typical for a drab sanitarium.

He noted that there were no other people.

The guard's shoes clacked on the polished floor, echoing off the walls. A few times he looked back to make sure Remo was still following. It took Remo a minute to realize why. His own canvas sneakers made not a sound on the floor.

Remo found himself straining to hear his own non-existent footfalls even as the guard ushered him into an empty office.

A brass plaque on an inner door read: Dr. Harold Smith, Director.

"Dr. Smith is expecting you," the guard said.

He went back into the hall, leaving Remo alone in the outer room.

Remo wasn't sure whether he should knock. He hesitated a moment before turning the brass knob. With the tips of two careful fingers he nudged the door open.

On the other side of the room a thin, middle-aged

man in an ash-gray suit sat behind a big oak desk. His back was to Remo. He was staring out the window at the darkness and the moon-splashed sound.

"I'm Smith," the man said without turning. "I'm your superior. Please shut the door."

At first Remo didn't know how the man knew he'd even entered the room. The floor was carpeted and the door had swung open on silent hinges. But then he saw the reflection. Owlish glasses looked back at him in the big picture window behind the desk. The image was a little too clear. Remo realized it had to be some special kind of glass.

He did as he was told, pushing the door shut. On cautious, gliding feet he approached the desk.

The office was big but sparsely furnished. Yellow light from a banker's lamp arced over the desk's smooth surface. There were two telephones on the desk, both off to one side. One was black with a series of buttons. An interoffice line. The other was blue and had a simple rotary face.

A steaming white cup sat near the phones. Smith had brewed himself some hot water from Miss Purvish's coffeepot. The drooping tea bag was on its third use.

Smith continued to gaze into the darkness. "You should know most of what you need to by now. I will get you access to weapons, clothing and money. There are phone codes that you will need to memorize for contact purposes. There is identification already prepared for Remo Cabell. The first name was retained because your profile indicated that it was one of the few things you would not surrender."

Smith spoke without passion, without inflection. It

was a simple dry recitation. Like reading a list of names from the phone book.

"Your cover will be as a freelance writer from Los Angeles," Smith droned on. "Your assignment calls for an—" he paused, his voice catching. When he finally managed to finish, the words were strained. "An *elimination*. The target is a patient in East Hudson Hospital in New Jersey. The man fell from a building yesterday. Probably was thrown. You will interrogate and then eliminate him. You need not worry about him being uncooperative. If he is alive and lucid, he'll talk to you."

Remo waited by the desk. He didn't expect his first assignment to be like this. Not that he really knew what to expect. But killing some poor schmo in a hospital bed certainly wasn't what he'd bargained for.

"Where do I meet MacCleary?" Remo asked. "He's supposed to go with me on my first assignment."

Smith's voice grew quiet. "You'll meet him at the hospital. He's your target."

Remo's breath slipped out. He stepped back a pace on the dingy carpeting. He couldn't speak.

Shoulders steeling, the seated man finally turned. The chair let off a soft squeak. Eyes of flint gray stared up at CURE's new enforcement arm.

"He has to be eliminated," Smith stated firmly. "He's near death, in pain and under drugs. There's no telling what he might say."

Remo forced out the words. "Maybe we can make a snatch," he said. "Like he did with me."

"Impossible," Smith insisted. "It's too dangerous. He was carrying identification as a patient of Folcroft. I've already been contacted by the police in East Hudson where the fall occurred. There's a direct link to us now. I told them that he was emotionally disturbed. They seemed to accept that. They have closed the case as an attempted suicide.''

Smith looked down at his cup of tea. He had brewed it but hadn't taken a single sip. It was growing cold.

''You will, if he's still alive, question him on Maxwell,'' the CURE director said. ''That is your second assignment.''

Remo was still trying to get his bearings. ''Who's Maxwell?'' he asked.

''We don't know,'' Smith admitted. ''He is an associate of Norman Felton, an agent of the Viaselli crime Family in New York. It was Felton's apartment from which MacCleary fell. Maxwell provides some new perfect murder and disposal service. The bodies disappear without a trace. We have lost several agents already, although obviously none were directly traceable to CURE. At least, not until yesterday.'' Still staring at his watery tea, he cleared his throat. ''The agents' orders were issued through the various agencies to which they were assigned. They did not know for whom they actually worked. I have pulled off all other agencies that might have an interest in this matter. You will have neither interference nor backup of any kind. With MacCleary gone, you are CURE's lone field agent.''

Remo tried to comprehend the importance of Smith's words. The moment should have been big, but it seemed so small. The late hour, the lemon-faced bureaucrat, the Spartan office. Nothing seemed large. And yet that wasn't quite true. There *was* something huge looming over all.

Remo knew he shouldn't have cared. He should have hated MacCleary. Yet he'd wound up liking him. And now he was being sent to kill him.

"This Felton," Remo said. "You said MacCleary was tossed from his apartment. Just so we're clear, I get to punch his dance card, right?"

Smith was surprised at the ice in the younger man's voice. Eyes narrowing as he studied Remo's face, the CURE director nodded.

"He is the most likely candidate to offer a lead to Maxwell," Smith said. "Beyond that he is expendable."

"Consider him expended," Remo said flatly.

Smith shifted uncomfortably in his chair. "Yes," he said slowly. "Just so you know, given the situation with MacCleary, we could already be compromised. If I learn that is the case, I will be forced to shut down this agency."

Remo almost asked what would happen to him under those circumstances. But then he thought of MacCleary. If this Smith thought nothing of eliminating Conrad MacCleary, he would think even less of taking out Remo.

The CURE director understood his unspoken question.

"Please understand," Smith said. "This organization cannot be exposed. That's why your first assignment on MacCleary is a must. It's a link to us, and we've got to break that link. If you fail, we will have to go after you. That's our only club. Also know that if you talk to anybody, we'll get you. I promise that. I will come for you myself."

There was cold certainty in the older man's tart voice. His eyes were shards of granite.

Remo's face grew sour. "You're a real sweetheart, aren't you?" he asked.

Smith ignored him. "MacCleary is in the hospital under the name Frank Jackson. Conn already briefed you on how we will contact you in case normal communications lines fail. Read the personals in the *New York Times*. We'll reach you when we have to through them. We'll sign our messages 'R-X'—for prescription, for CURE. That's it. I will have everything you need available within the hour. Good luck."

Smith took the arms of his chair and spun back around, eyes searching out glimmers of light on Long Island Sound.

Remo stood there quietly for a moment, absorbing it all. Smith only knew Remo had left the room when he looked up and saw the younger man's reflection was no longer in the one-way glass.

Alone once more, Smith released a sigh fueled with bile. He blinked his tired, bloodshot eyes.

He hadn't told Remo about the Senate committee or about the murder of Senator Bianco. There was no sense in overwhelming his new agent with more information than he needed. With any luck, by eliminating Maxwell, the threat against the United States government would dry up, as well.

Spinning back around, he took the cup from his desk. Standing wearily, Dr. Harold Smith brought the untouched tea into his private bathroom. To dump it down the sink.

18

In his mind he was falling, falling.

Warm wind whistled around his ears. His heavy overcoat flapped behind him like a cape.

The ground was a thousand miles below. He saw the curve of the Earth. Sparkling blue oceans bracketing the familiar coasts. Purple mountains rising up majestically in the west. Craggy black hills and green forests in the east. Squared-off acres of checkerboard farmland everywhere in between.

The view was so spectacular he wanted to sing. Break into a chorus of "America the Beautiful" with Kate Smith singing harmony and the goddamned Mormon Tabernacle Choir to back them up. He wanted to scream from the mountaintops the words that filled his tired old heart.

And then he wasn't falling anymore.

There was a jolt of hitting sudden ground. At the moment of impact his heart had to have skipped a beat, because the monitor beside him chirped once loudly in electronic concern before resuming its normal rhythmic beeps.

A woman in a starched white uniform stuck her head in the room. She had to have been passing by. Satisfied that there wasn't a problem, she ducked back outside.

Conrad MacCleary saw her wheel a cart filled with tiny paper pill cups down the hall. Then she was gone.

And for the dozenth time he realized the terrible truth. He was not free-falling from the sky above the nation he loved. He was in a hospital bed.

He was out of it. Couldn't pull his thoughts together. It was the drugs. The thought gave him a brief moment of terror. But even that was fleeting. In the next moment he was back in the sky, floating, falling.

Conn had been unconscious when they brought him here. He remembered going off the balcony at Felton's building, but the fall itself just wasn't there. His mind had isolated and eliminated that particular memory. He didn't remember the crowd or the ambulance ride. Didn't recall the broken arm and ribs or the emergency surgery on the compound fracture in his right leg. Didn't know a thing about the pins they'd installed in his shattered pelvis or about the kidney, spleen and gallbladder they'd had to remove. He didn't know anything about anything until the moment he regained consciousness in the private room in the intensive-care unit of East Hudson Hospital.

Painkillers that didn't quite kill the pain. They made the pain different. Forgettable if his mind wandered.

The drugs were good, but they weren't as good as booze.

A stark memory came to him late in the night. He suddenly remembered waking up briefly when they first brought him in. A nurse—a pretty young thing— was working to cut off his bloodied clothes. He had asked her to go pick him up a bottle. He remembered—God—had to be *hours* later.

For Conrad MacCleary, it was the most frightening moment of his professional life.

He had spoken to someone without realizing he was even doing it. Asked a clear question. How much more had he said? Who else had he spoken to? He was hooked to a respirator now, a tube snaking down his throat, into his lungs. But how long had he been on the machine? How long had his mind allowed his mouth to run free?

The panic came and with it the pain and then came the morphine, and the panic didn't matter so much anymore.

In his mind's eye he saw a young boy with yellow hair. Fire blazed where his hands should be. Conn had seen the kid somewhere, but he couldn't place the face.

MacCleary thought of another kid. Back at Folcroft. Lying comatose in bed for the rest of his life. The boy with fire for hands was around the same age.

Maybe he could save that kid. Hell, maybe he could save both of them.

But he was busy right now. For the moment the Germans had him. Kraut bastards had captured him somehow. They'd been torturing Conn for hours, trying to make him talk. It wouldn't do them any good. He'd escape this torture chamber and find Smith. Smith had always been the key. The brains to balance Conn's brawn. Once Conn was safe, he and Smitty could come up with a new strategy, just as they always had.

But then his mind found brief focus, and he realized he wasn't being tortured. World War II was over. It was early 1972 and he was in a hospital because he had jumped off a twelfth-story balcony.

Yes, that was right. A hospital room. That's where he was. And he wasn't alone. There was a face looking down at him. Hovering like the angel of death above his bed.

Conn knew him. Recognized him from the eyes. Hooded, hazel. Oriental eyes. He'd seen those same eyes in the penthouse of Lamonica Towers.

A flat, familiar Oriental face was looking down at him.

Another dream in a sea of dreams.

In his dream the Oriental moved. With one hand he reached for something near the bedside. The other hand reached for MacCleary's throat.

For a brief moment Conn wondered if his dream was going to strangle him. And then his unspoken question was answered. The hand latched on to his neck.

He felt the fingers press against his flesh. And in a small, rational part of his swimming brain, Conrad MacCleary realized that this wasn't part of his tortured dreams.

A gentle manipulation and the intubation tube slipped up out of his throat.

"Now I have seen everything," a singsong voice clucked disapprovingly. "Machines that breathe for you. The bottom drops out yet again on the depths of white laziness."

The Master of Sinanju's weathered face puckered in displeasure even as he slid one hand under Conn's back. Long fingers manipulated the base of MacCleary's spine.

The drugged haze began to burn away like morning mist. For a moment there was pain like nothing Conn had ever before experienced, but then the hand—the magical, wonderful hand—pressed a cluster of nerves and the pain disappeared.

MacCleary was himself again. Exhausted, more parts missing than usual. But alert.

"What are you doing here?" he asked. His tired voice was a pained rasp.

The Master of Sinanju folded his arms across his chest. "A simple thank-you would suffice," the old Korean sniffed.

"You shouldn't be here," MacCleary insisted. A thought suddenly occurred to him. "Oh, I see. Did Smitty send you?"

"The emperor told me that an accident had befallen his worthless general," Chiun admitted.

"Thank God," MacCleary said. "Please do it fast, Master Chiun. The nurse was just here. She could come back."

Chiun's face grew puzzled. "Do what fast?"

"Kill me, of course."

The old Oriental's eyes grew dull. "Forgive me, but in your delirium have you forgotten to whom you are speaking?"

MacCleary's face sagged. "What? I don't understand. You're the Master of Sinanju. You're an assassin. The best in the world. Killing is what you do."

"Killing?" Chiun asked, indignant. "Killing? Does the spring kill the winter? Does the rising tide kill the shore? When the seed dies so that the flower may grow, has the flower killed the seed? Killing. Pah! You have claimed to be an expert on Sinanju, but how limited still is your knowledge of that which we are."

MacCleary still didn't understand. "But that's what

you do,'' he insisted. ''You're professional assassins.''

Chiun nodded. ''With the emphasis on professional. I do not recall any gold passing hands.''

''Smith paid you. That's why he sent you here, right? To kill me? He *did* send you?''

The old man tipped his head. ''Indirectly,'' he admitted. ''I was out for an innocent stroll around the palace grounds and happened to pass by his window. As he spoke to my pupil about you, a word or two may have reached my blameless ears.''

''He's sending Remo?''

''That might have been said. There was so much white blathering it was hard to keep track.''

Relief formed deep in the care lines of Conrad MacCleary's ghostly pale face. ''Good,'' he breathed. ''But how did you get here first?''

''Because a bolt of lightning is faster than goose droppings. Honestly, MacCleary, I don't know where you found this one. He is lazy, he talks back to his elders. If he is late now, it is only because he chased a butterfly into the park or he lost the little note with the hospital's name on it that someone pinned to his sleeve.''

The pain was coming back. Conn's head sank deeper into his pillow. ''You think he won't come?''

''Who knows with that one?'' Chiun shrugged.

Conn felt hope slip away. ''He *has* to. If not...'' He was growing desperate. ''Master Chiun, Smith is good for it.''

Chiun shook his head firmly. ''No credit.''

''I don't have any money. I think they took my wallet.''

"It wouldn't matter anyway," Chiun said. "Paper money is merely a promise of payment."

MacCleary wanted to shake his head in frustration, but the casts and tubes prevented movement.

"If not to kill me, then why are you here?" he said in tired exasperation.

"Your Smith has ordered your death against his own wishes. I could hear the sadness in his regal voice. Like most young emperors he does not yet understand the powerful sword at his side that is Sinanju. I would prove to him that his fears are groundless. I have come to liberate you."

The light of understanding dawned weakly. MacCleary shook his head. "No," he exhaled. "I can't leave."

"White medicine is a dangerous thing," Chiun warned. "We must hie from this den of quacksalvers before they decide to open your veins in order to bleed the sickness from you."

"I can't leave here, Master Chiun," MacCleary insisted weakly. "I was carrying my Folcroft ID."

"All the more reason to spirit you away. If the emperor's enemies learn his general is vulnerable, they might see weakness and use the opportunity to move against him."

"Smith's enemies are our country's enemies, Master Chiun," MacCleary explained tiredly. "I know you don't see it like we do, but you have to trust us. I can't go back to Folcroft now. I'd be leading America's and Smith's enemies straight to him. Smith understands that. The best way for him and the nation to survive—maybe the only way—is to eliminate me. I agree with him."

The old man's frown lines deepened. This was

something unexpected. He had come to America expecting sloth and selfishness. But here was a white, ready to offer up his life in service to his king.

"You are stubborn, even for a general," he said quietly.

"Does that mean you'll kill me?"

"I do not give to charity," Chiun replied. "However, since my useless student may never find his way here—he having no doubt gotten lost in a downstairs broom cupboard where he is even now brutally assassinating the mop he has mistaken for you—I will assist you in doing what you think you must. Strictly in the interest of fostering good client relations."

Chiun had noted the open closet door when he first arrived. It was immediately next to the bathroom.

MacCleary's bloodied clothes had been thrown out. His personal effects were locked away in storage. All that remained were his shoes and one other item.

The plastic forearm of MacCleary's prosthetic had been damaged in the fall, but it was still intact. It had been removed prior to surgery and brought here afterward.

Chiun retrieved the false arm, bringing it over to the bed. The curved hook glinted in the room's pale light.

No words were spoken. None was necessary. MacCleary closed his eyes as the Master of Sinanju pressed the hollow end of the prosthetic up around the elbow nub. Chiun fastened the silver buckles around the forearm and shoulder.

In his fatigued brain, Conrad MacCleary was counting down the seconds of his own mortality. His lack of passion surprised him. He had lived life hard.

He had always figured when the time came he'd go out kicking and screaming.

In his last moments of life Conn tried to sort through recent events. A thought suddenly occurred to him.

"Chiun, do you have a son?" MacCleary asked abruptly.

The old Korean was just finishing with the shoulder straps.

"What business is that of yours?"

There was coldness to the Oriental's voice.

Conn opened his eyes. The pain was swelling. His whole body ached. For now it was dull and distant.

"I don't know. I think I might have met him," MacCleary said with a frown. "Is that possible? Maybe at that building in Jersey? The one I fell out of. There was a guy, I think. An Oriental. He had your eyes."

MacCleary heard a little slip of air.

When he looked up he would have sworn the color had drained from Chiun's face. Or maybe it was just a trick of the weak light.

"I have no son," Chiun said softly.

"Oh," MacCleary said. His head collapsed back wearily on the pillow. "I'm sorry. Maybe it's the drugs. Everything's still a little fuzzy. I'm not sure of anything right about now. I swear there was a guy, though." He tried to concentrate. To think back to the events at Felton's apartment. "There were other guys, too. And a kid. I think But the Oriental had your eyes. Same color, same everything. It was like looking at you, but younger. I don't know, maybe it was part of the dream. Hell, probably it was."

Chiun didn't respond. He straightened from the bed.

"You are ready," he announced.

MacCleary didn't notice the flatness in his voice.

Conn lifted his false arm. He turned the hook around, inspecting the sharp end. "Thanks," he grunted.

Chiun wasn't listening. He had cocked one shell-like ear to the open hallway door.

"Someone is coming," he hissed all at once.

The Korean recognized the confident footfalls. Not quite a glide, but no longer a normal man's walk. With an admonition of silence to MacCleary, the old man ducked inside the bathroom, pulling the door nearly closed behind him. He brought one hazel eye to the narrow gap.

Remo entered the hospital room a moment later, shutting the door to the hall quietly behind him.

MacCleary's face was partially bandaged. Those features that were visible were heavily bruised. Remo didn't even look at the face as he leaned over the body.

Through the slivered door Chiun saw Remo move a hand up the damp plaster cast that encircled MacCleary's chest. Good. He was looking for a cracked rib to press into the heart. The technique was sloppy, but it would get the job done. Unfortunately, the young man's heart wasn't in it. He didn't do the deed fast enough.

"Hey, buddy," came MacCleary's faint voice. "That's a hell of a way to make an identification."

Remo's hands fled the cast. As Chiun frowned, MacCleary began to babble some white nonsense to his pupil.

It was as Chiun feared. Remo had become distracted when he should have been focused on his task. This was the real reason Chiun had come to the hospital in the first place.

Remo was a sentimentalist. He liked MacCleary and so would find it difficult to kill the man. He might have done it if the silly old general who wanted death had kept his fool mouth shut. But he had to talk, and now Remo was looking at him no longer as a target but as a man. Worse, a friend.

Remo had learned too much in those early months of training. He had grasped the rudiments of Sinanju. That was partially Chiun's fault. But now he had been set loose on a world that might mistake him as truly Sinanju.

That was bad enough, but a failure in this first assignment might be—however unfairly—blamed on the House of Sinanju. As the last Master, Chiun couldn't allow that. He had hoped to get MacCleary back to Smith's castle, thus forestalling Remo's first assignment until his mind could be properly prepared. But the general was stubborn. He saw his act of suicide as noble. A final act of loyalty to his emperor and to his nation.

There was no doubt about it. These Americans were each one more lunatic than the last.

And so Chiun had done his part to help his pupil and thus Sinanju's reputation along. And when Remo arrived he hid in the next room, listening as the two fools chattered pointlessly, all the while hoping that the young man would come around and assassinate his dying friend.

For a little while Chiun was concerned that he might be discovered. Fortunately, the boy was a bit of a dullard. Remo didn't even seem curious why the hospital staff would leave the prosthetic arm and hook on a patient on whom they had performed emergency surgery and who was suspected to be suicidal. Obviously it would have been removed.

They talked for a time. When they were done, Remo turned and walked from the room.

In bed MacCleary's whole injured body tensed as he called weakly after CURE's new enforcement arm.

"Remo, you've got to do it. I can't move. I'm drugged. They took my pill. I can't do it myself. Remo. You had the right idea. Just pressure the rib cage. Remo. Remo!"

But the door slowly closed on room 411.

As the big man called vainly into the empty hallway, Chiun stepped out of the bathroom.

"I can't believe it," MacCleary gasped as the Master of Sinanju swept up to the bed. "He was supposed to do it. All the personality projections said he'd do it."

The old spy seemed crestfallen.

"Some men are more than the sum of their projections," Chiun replied evenly. "I must go now."

MacCleary was too weak to nod. Failure weighed heavy on his battered bones as he scratched his hook up across his chest cast to his neck. The defeat he felt came not from a life now at its end, but rather from distress that he might have failed in picking CURE's perfect weapon.

Chiun sensed the injured man's concern. Since it no longer mattered and since there was no one around to hear, the Master of Sinanju leaned close.

"Leave your worries about this one to the world of flesh, brave knight," Chiun confided in a whisper.

"I have seen the seeds of greatness in him. They are small and few in number now, but given time and care they can flourish. Even he does not know they are there. For what he is, you can be proud as you leave this life. For what he might become, Sinanju owes you a debt that can never be repaid."

An uncertain peace seeped across MacCleary's battered face. "Thank you, Master Chiun. I hope you're right."

With that, he buried the point of his hook deep in his own throat. Jerking his arm, he tried to tear it across, but the strength just wasn't there. Eyes wide with pain and pleading looked up at the Master of Sinanju.

Chiun's jaw tightened. "You asked a question before," the old Korean whispered. "Since you are an honorable man, bravely facing death, I will answer. It is true I once had a son. However, he no longer lives."

Chiun flicked the curve of the hook. In a twinkling it tore open Conrad MacCleary's throat, exposing a chasm of bubbling crimson. A font of red soaked the white pillowcase.

As the EKG monitor beside the bed spiked one last time before going forever flat, the old man shook his head.

"But sadly he was not the only one to share my blood."

19

That long-ago spring day had been unseasonably warm. The sun smiled bright in the cloudless blue sky, scattering sparkling diamonds on the waters of the West Korean Bay.

The air hummed. The village of Sinanju—the very world itself—was alive with joyful song.

It was a great time for the chosen few, those who by luck of birth were able to call Sinanju, the Pearl of the Orient, their home. It was the Time of Departure, the time in every generation when the old Master surrendered the mantle of protector and provider to his successor. After years of training, the pupil was finally allowed to go out into the world as Reigning Master of Sinanju.

The people had gathered to await the appearance of the new Master, who was preparing to leave the village for the first time. The old Master was there. Standing silently before the House of Many Woods. When his successor finally appeared through the door an hour after the preordained time, a chorus of happy voices rose from the village square.

"Hail, Master of Sinanju, who sustains the village and keeps the code faithfully," the people shouted as their new protector strode down the path. "Our hearts cry with joy and pain at your departure. Joy that you undertake this journey for the sake of we, the unworthy beneficiaries of your generosity. And pain that your toils take your beauteous aspect from our midst. May the spirits of your ancestors journey safe with you who graciously throttles the universe.''

The Masters who had preceded him back beyond the oldest memory, all the way back to before even the Great Wang, had all accepted the traditional words of departure with stoic countenance. But this Master was different than what the village had ever seen before. He smiled at the crowd as they sang his praises, accepted the flattery as his due. Hazel eyes turned left and right, soaking in the adulation.

Behind the new Master came the old one. Unlike his pupil, the former Master of Sinanju kept his eyes trained above the heads of those gathered, focused on some unseeable distant point. His face was stone.

''It is about time the old Master stepped aside,'' some of the villagers whispered after the two men passed by. ''Look at this new one. Such pride, such bearing. Here is a Master whose praises we will gladly sing.''

''Yes,'' more agreed. ''He is not like that old-fashioned one who went before him and stayed long past his time. This one will bring glory to Sinanju.''

''It is fortunate things worked out as they did,'' still others said. ''If the old one's son had not died in training, he would not have had to take on another pupil. Then we would not have this great new Master to feed the children and care for the old and lame of our village. How lucky we are.''

They all agreed they were very lucky the old Master's son was dead. As he walked through the village of his ancestors, the Master pretended not to hear their words.

Though his son had been dead for years, the wound was still as fresh as the day he had carried the little boy's battered body down from Mount Paektusan. Their words brought anguish to his weary heart. But he was a Master of Sinanju, and it was tradition since the time of the Great Wang himself that a Master could not raise his hand against any of the village. And so the retired Master made his ears deaf to all the hateful, petty things the people were saying.

In the village square the new Master stopped.

"I leave now on my great journey," he announced. "In Sinanju death feeds life. I will ply our art faithfully, for there is no higher calling. Death feeds life. What I embark on this day feeds the village. My labors sustain the villagers I love. Such has it been, ever shall it be."

When the cheers came, he soaked them up like desert rain.

The Master who had trained him could hear the falseness in the young man's voice. In truth he knew his pupil felt little but contempt for the village of his birth. But as Master of Sinanju his duties were clear. He would uphold the traditions as had all the Masters who had come before him.

Singing songs of praise to their new protector, the people swept the new Master up to the road that led from the village. With joyful hearts they sent him on his way. With tearful eyes they stood on the road, watching until he was a speck on the horizon and then disappeared into the muddy paddies. Certain that this new Master would restore the glory of the greatest Masters of Sinanju to the small fishing village, they returned to their homes to await the tribute from king and emperor that would fill their souls with pride and their cooking pots with food.

And they waited.

And waited.

But the tribute never came.

Their new Master, their great protector, the one who would lead the village into greater glory, never returned.

Word came through circuitous means that he had abandoned the village, seeking to ply his trade for personal glory.

The villagers heard from the missing Master only once. When first he left, he performed a service that indirectly benefited his despised village. He kept the money, but he did send a servant back with a message for his teacher and uncle, the man who had been Master before him. On a small parchment scroll were carefully inscribed the characters, "I await the day."

The retired Master slew the messenger.

The old Master was to blame. He had chosen the traitor. He had trained him. And after the betrayal, he was the one who kept the villagers' hope alive long after he should have.

Every day for years after his pupil abandoned them all to hunger and despair, the old one would come out of the House of Many Woods and pad through the village. He would climb up the craggy rocks above the bay and sit in the shade of the Horns of Welcome. Alone with thoughts that were never shared, he would watch the sea from dawn until dusk, waiting for his nephew to return. He kept the flickering light of hope burning long after he should have.

Until the years had gone on too long even for him.

One day he suddenly stopped going to the shore.

It had taken him long to admit his failure. But in the end even he realized the truth. He had chosen his pupil poorly, and so the entire village would suffer.

The one who had left as new Master, but whose title had been stripped from him, flourished in his evil. In the years following his departure from the village of his birth, he was driven by greed and hate. He amassed wealth, craved power.

He shared the same name with his hated uncle, the retired Master of Sinanju. They were not the only ones to have had this name. His uncle's father, who had also been Master, also did. And there had been others still.

Since he hated them all, all the way back to the original Master of Sinanju, he had almost changed his name. But then he heard something wonderful. It came to him through that hum of life that somehow always connects one to the place he first called home. His uncle had changed his own name, as well as that of his father. All who had shared the name throughout the history of the House of Sinanju would no longer be called the name of the hated traitor.

The sound of the name was reversed. Henceforth his uncle and the others would be called Chiun, leaving the betrayer as sole possessor of a despised name.

He reveled in the news. He had given them shame. And that shame resonated back through the ages.

Since leaving the village he had gone by many names. He was Inchu, Sun Yee, Uinch, Chuni. These days he was Mr. Winch. But those were just temporary changes as need dictated. When he formed the word of his name in his secret heart, it was always and would forevermore be Nuihc. The first true Master of Sinanju of the great new order.

In fact the aliases probably weren't even necessary. There was only one man on Earth he need fear, and his uncle had not made a move to follow him. He heard from sources within the village that the old fool sat looking out at the bay as if he actually expected Nuihc to come back to him. He had enjoyed many a laugh at the withered old idiot's expense.

Nuihc traveled the world. He found work in Russia and China, India and Italy and a dozen African nations. Wherever there was money to be made from dealing death, he was there.

The last Nuihc had heard, his uncle was still in Sinanju. No longer sitting on the shore, he spent most of his time hidden away from the villagers. An old man now, he sat in the Master's House, awaiting the end.

For Nuihc the world was just beginning. In spite of what his uncle thought in his senile old heart, all that had ended was the type of Sinanju that had been practiced for centuries in a muddy little village on the West Korean Bay. Nuihc was inheritor of the true tradition of Sinanju.

It was the most terrible secret in the history of Sinanju, never spoken of in public. The present-day art of Sinanju was founded on a lie.

The Great Wang—the Master who was the first of the current line of Masters—was an impostor. All who came after him were frauds. Oh, they all claimed to be of the pure bloodline. But they were of *a* bloodline, not *the* bloodline. Through Nuihc's veins flowed the blood of the true Masters of Sinanju. He had it on the best authority.

Nuihc's mother had married into the family of the descendants of Wang. Her blood was pure. His father had merely been a tool. The foolish brother of the Reigning Master, he was an unwitting pawn. The means by which she would get her only offspring trained in the most ancient martial art—the art that had been stolen from her family by the so-called Great Wang himself.

As a boy, Nuihc listened to her by the firelight of their tiny home. When she spoke of the great theft of their family's birthright, her voice grew cold with ancient fury.

She spoke often of that terrible day the Great Wang stole the village out from under Nuihc's family.

In that day, while there was only one Reigning Master, there were many lesser Masters of Sinanju, called night tigers. When the time came for the Reigning Master to retire, he would choose his successor from the ranks of the night tigers. But at this time the Master died unexpectedly, never having made a choice. The night tigers were fighting among themselves when Wang—Wang the Thief, Wang the Liar—stepped into their midst, claiming to have had a vision of the future of Sinanju. Using trickery, he killed the night tigers and established himself as Reigning Master. From that point on, there was only one Master and pupil per generation.

Nuihc's ancestor had been one of the night tigers slain, and a rival of Wang's. Had he not been murdered, he would have ascended to the position of Reigning Master.

Nuihc's family never forgot. The hatred burned bright down through the generations. A thousand years after, it still blazed in the eyes of Nuihc's mother as she told her son the truth of his heritage.

Nuihc liked the story. His oldest memory was of his mother telling it to him. In childhood he even shared her resentment. By then he was already being trained by his uncle. She had told her son never to repeat the story to the current false Master. As he grew older, he realized that he was only being told part of the story at home. During training, his uncle often shared another version with his pupil. In Chiun's tale, Wang was nothing but heroic.

While Nuihc doubted both versions were completely accurate, he knew that his uncle was enchanted by fables. He was blind to anything that did not show the history of his ancient discipline in the most ideal terms.

Nuihc knew his mother for what she was. A hunched old crone driven by bitterness and envy. But it was her version of the tale that he found easier to believe. The theft of his birthright made the hate so much easier.

Nuihc hated his uncle. He hated his uncle's father, and his father before him. He hated their direct lineage to Wang, the original Master of Sinanju of the modern age.

The truth was, even without his family's secret history or his mother's inspiration, it was always very easy for him to hate. Hate was such a pure thing. The hate sent him from the village and the hate kept him from going back.

It was hate that was his companion that day when fate put him on that train in Kentucky.

A chance encounter had dropped him in the path of a most remarkable boy. Somehow this child was able to use his mind to plant seeds of thought in the minds of others. When he witnessed one of the boy's mass hallucinations firsthand, Nuihc knew he had made the discovery of a lifetime.

The boy became Nuihc's pupil. He had no choice. It had only been a few years, but he was making great strides.

The pattern was established early on. Nuihc would give the boy a few lessons and then go off on business, leaving his pupil to study. If upon his return a few months later the boy had not mastered the skills he'd been taught to Nuihc's satisfaction, he would be punished severely.

It was a system that had worked magnificently. There was only a slight problem at a Swiss boarding school where Nuihc had left the boy for a brief period two years before. The child had not yet mastered the physical abilities to deal with the problem. When he learned that they had quarantined the boy after an incident at school, Nuihc had demonstrated his displeasure by killing the entire faculty and burning the four-century-old institution to the ground. After that he took a more active interest in the education of his young charge.

The boy's physical training was coming along nicely. But it was his other power—the power of his mind—for which Nuihc had the highest hopes.

A mere thought and the boy could make a man believe he was on fire. Or freezing. Or drowning.

If he convinced a man in his mind that he was suffering the ravages of some terrible disease, the victim would believe it so completely that he would actually manifest symptoms. His thoughts killed.

The potential uses of such a power were limitless.

The boy was a resource that needed to be controlled so that it could be properly harnessed. And so Nuihc taught the physical, all the while breeding fear and reverence in the boy so that when the time came the awesome power of his mental abilities could be unleashed on an unsuspecting world.

Much of the training over the past year had taken place in a secluded mountaintop hideaway in the Caribbean. But there were some things that could only be learned out in the real world. Like eliminating live targets.

Nuihc decided to seek employment. At the moment the world was in turmoil. With its social and political upheaval, the United States seemed an ideal locale. It had a rich population, a burgeoning criminal class and a government incapable of dealing with its own imminent collapse.

Nuihc went to New York City, the focus of criminal activity in America. Once there he sought out the reigning crime figure, Don Carmine Viaselli.

Others within the Viaselli crime organization were cool to the idea of bringing in outside talent. With the war in Southeast Asia still raging, many complained about having an Oriental in their midst. Several even tried to kill the new Viaselli enforcer, stirred by some nationalistic passion that made enemies out of everyone of Asian descent.

These last were perfect targets for Nuihc's pupil. The boy killed the enemies of his Master and the enemies of Carmine Viaselli. And Nuihc collected a healthy salary.

For months it had been the best of business arrangements. That had changed two days ago.

Nuihc had replayed the events in that apartment in

New Jersey over in his head a hundred times. The
white with the hook wasn't a fluke. No one came to
his knowledge on his own. He had the specific balance of someone who had been tutored by a Master
of Sinanju. And there were only two men on the face
of the planet who could have taught him.

Was it possible that his uncle had finally left the
village? Had he decided to seek revenge on his
nephew? Was he training others to do his work for
him?

This last question Nuihc had dismissed almost as
soon as his mind asked it.

Chiun wouldn't train someone from outside the village, least of all a white. He was a pathetic old dog,
clinging to a worthless bone of tradition. But the fact
remained that the white with the hook had known
proper balance. It wasn't Sinanju, but it was a hint of
something.

Nuihc had to know.

The man who had broken into Norman Felton's
apartment was his only link. If his uncle was somehow involved with Norman Felton's attacker, he
might show up at the hospital where the man was
recovering from his injuries.

Nuihc wouldn't risk going himself. His uncle's
skills had certainly dulled in old age, but he might
still sense someone watching him. Nuihc sent emissaries to keep an eye on the hospital while he waited
in his spacious apartment in the Manhattan building
of his current employer.

He had left the boy to work on his breathing in a
warehouse in Jersey City. Nuihc was alone when he
heard the heavy footfalls coming up the hallway.

He knew they were coming to him even before the two men stopped outside his door.

"Enter," he commanded before they could even knock. His voice was thin and reedy.

When the men came in, they didn't see him right away. Nuihc had to clear his throat to draw attention to himself.

They found the Oriental in a lotus position near the main living-room windows. The men seemed surprised to see that Mr. Viaselli's enforcer was sitting out in the open. Somehow their eyes had missed him. The drapes were drawn.

"We got what you wanted, Mr. Winch," one of the men said as they crossed over to Nuihc.

They were big and muscled, with greased-down hair. The stink of garlic and tomato oozed from their pores.

"Here," Nuihc ordered. He rose to his feet in a single fluid motion, waving a hand to a low table.

Nuihc sat delicately to his folded knees before the table. Huffing and puffing, the two men settled uncomfortably down beside him.

"We finished up around nine this morning," the first man said. "It took us this long to get them developed."

Each man had a big manila envelope. From each, they extracted a thick pile of photographs.

"We set up just like you told us," the man continued. "Right out front. Kinda weird you'd want that. Most guys in our line of work like to use the back."

"We are not in the same line of work," Nuihc said icily. He didn't mention that the person he was interested in wouldn't deign to use the service entrance.

"Okay, Mr. Winch," the man agreed nervously.

The two men began laying out the photos.

The pictures all showed the main entrance to East Hudson Hospital. They were taken from a car that had been parked directly across the street.

The men set out the photographs very carefully on the funny little table. They were going backward through the stacks, from the ones most recently taken to the earliest.

"We got mostly everybody who come in the front," the first man said as they set down the black-and-white photos, one on top of the other. "Right up to when we heard the guy with the hook killed himself. We figured we was done then."

"He is dead?" Nuihc asked, frowning.

The Viaselli man nodded. "Ripped his throat out with his own hook. Sick bastard."

Nuihc didn't respond. He glanced from pile to pile as the men set down the photographs. Nothing of interest so far. Just people coming and going.

At one point a man in a suit and tie caught his eye. He had wrists thicker than a man of his build ordinarily would. In the photos he seemed to have something....

But there were only two pictures of him. One as he came up the sidewalk and one of him on the stairs. They were quickly covered up. Sorting through a few more photographs, the men suddenly heard a hiss of air.

When they looked up they saw that Nuihc's eyes were open wide. The men saw a look that might have been fear dancing across the Oriental's broad face. It came as a surprise. They both knew well Mr. Winch's reputation.

"That guy showed up about a quarter to five in the

morning,'' one of the men explained, tapping the photo. "I remember we said it was weird 'cause it was almost like he knew we was there. It was like he was posing or something.''

In the photo an elderly Oriental in a long robe was shuffling up the sidewalk.

"Look at this. We were going through this bunch before we got here. It's real spooky.'' The Viaselli man laid out a few other pictures of the old geezer.

In each photograph the old man's head was turned a little more to the left. By the last one, he was staring directly down the camera lens. The Viaselli men had found this particularly disturbing when they'd had the film developed. When they put the pictures together and riffled through them from one corner, it appeared as if the man in the photos was actually turning to look at them.

"Isn't that the craziest thing you ever seen?'' the Viaselli man asked.

Nuihc didn't answer. He didn't even look up at the two men sitting at the table with him.

The silence lasted minutes. The room grew very still.

The men glanced nervously at each other.

"Um, hey, you okay, Mr. Winch?''

"Go,'' Nuihc barked.

"Oh. Okay, sure. Anything you say, Mr. Winch.''

They began reaching for the photos. A hand slapped down atop the stack depicting the old Oriental.

"Leave them,'' Nuihc ordered.

The men didn't need to be told a second time. Climbing awkwardly to their feet, they hurried from the apartment.

Once they were gone, Nuihc sat there for a long moment. He heard the elevator descend, heard the traffic sounds in the street below. Sirens howled in the distance.

This was Manhattan. The Rome of the New World. As far removed from antiquated courts and dusty thrones as one could get in this modern age.

He looked at the top photograph.

And yet there he was. Older, yes. But still the same.

Nuihc picked up the photo, holding it delicately by the corner. "So," he said softly to the empty room. "You have finally come for me, Uncle."

It was a little soon. He would have preferred to put it off another ten years or so. But it would still work. He would have to tweak his employer's plan just a little.

If he planned it just right, he would succeed. And he could finally get retribution for the injustice committed against his family a hundred generations ago.

Nuihc tipped his head to one side. With an index fingernail short but sharpened to a dagger's point, he lazily traced the outline of his old teacher's head.

"The time is come, old man," Nuihc whispered to the photo. "It is finally come."

Cut free from the rest of the photograph, Chiun's decapitated head fluttered gently to the carpet.

20

The racial situation was awful, just awful. Senator Leonard Albert O'Day wanted to make the sheer awfulness of it all absolutely clear to the gathered reporters.

"Awful, just awful. We must do all we can to address this terrible situation of race in America."

He was on the sidewalk outside 40 Rockefeller Center. Senator O'Day had just left the New York studios of NBC, where he had announced on the network's Sunday-morning news show that the racial situation in America was awful, just awful.

Senator O'Day had been using that same phrase for the past ten years. Ever since the study he had commissioned had found out that black people who lived in ghettos in America were poorer than affluent suburban white people.

The results of his study were greeted with somber faces and serious nods. Because of his work, Senator O'Day was heralded as a pioneer in the field of race relations.

Back during the sixties, one reporter who hosted an afternoon talk show in the senator's native New York noticed after a year of "awful, just awfuls" that Senator O'Day wasn't really saying anything at all about race. As a result of his very expensive, taxpayer-funded study, he just seemed to see a problem with the races that everyone knew was there, but he didn't seem to offer any solutions. The next time the senator was a guest on his show, the host decided that it was high time somebody asked him what his future plans were based on the results of his highly publicized study.

"You've said a lot about race this past year, Senator," the talk-show host stated. "After a year of talking about the issue, can you tell me what you plan for the future? The concrete policies you will try to implement in Washington to deal with this crisis you've recognized?"

"It's a terrible crime the condition these people live in," Senator O'Day said, nodding. "There are many, many Negro children born out of wedlock, which contributes to the problem. It's awful, just awful."

The senator had a lisp, a bow tie and a lock of hair that sometimes hung down over his right eye.

"I understand that," the host said. "But what would you suggest we do to remedy the situation?"

"Well," Senator O'Day said, sitting up like a fussy hen in his chair, "we must address it head-on, of course. We're the greatest nation on Earth. Isn't that marvelous?"

"Yes, but what can we *do?*" the reporter stressed.

Senator O'Day grinned his little cherub's grin and licked his darting tongue across his moistened upper lip and said a lot about money and responsibility. To sum up, he repeated once more his oft-used phrase.

After the program was through, the performance of Leonard O'Day was heralded as compassionate, understanding and bridge-building for the races. The reporter, on the other hand, was called a racist, reactionary, fascist tool of the military-industrial complex and was fired on the spot.

After that incident, no reporters dared press the senator on his specific remedies for race relations.

At the impromptu sidewalk news conference this day, the senator offered many bland "awful, just awfuls" to the press. As he did so, he glanced every so often at his pocket watch.

"Senator O'Day, it's been a week since Senator Bianco's death made you senior senator from New York," one reporter called. "What's the mood in the Senate?"

Senator O'Day licked his lips. "The sudden, unexpected death of my friend and colleague was awful, just awful. A terrible shock. We are all coping as best we can. Now, gentlemen, I really must be going."

His car was parked at the curb. A few reporters shouted more questions to him as he ducked into the back seat. Leonard O'Day was relieved when his driver shut the door.

They were pulling into traffic a minute later.

"Thank God that's over," Senator O'Day exhaled as he sank into the seat. "Drive, Rudolfo."

They headed out of the city.

Leonard wasn't completely surprised the press had brought up Senator Bianco's death. It was an open secret in political circles that the family was hiding something from the public. Some were whispering the late Senator Bianco had been murdered. Head chopped clean off on his own front steps in Georgetown, a stone's throw away from the Capitol.

Although the press was starting to dig, they hadn't found out anything yet. No surprise there. Leonard

Albert O'Day doubted there was anything there to find. Besides, the press corps couldn't find their fannies with both hands if they were given a month of Sundays and a picnic lunch.

The same couldn't be said for Leonard O'Day. New York's new senior senator knew exactly where his fanny was. It was sitting comfortably in the back seat of his black sedan as it raced along the highway to his upstate hideaway.

Leonard felt a deliciously familiar tingle.

This was a "Special Day". One of a few days out of the year that Senator O'Day carved out of his busy schedule just for himself. On Special Days, only Rudolfo was allowed to handle the driving chores. His trusted staff member was also in charge of the other details of Special Day. That thing that made Special Day so exquisitely special.

"Is it a nice one today, Rudolfo?" Leonard asked, unable to keep the excitement from his voice.

"Yes, sir, Senator," his driver answered.

Senator O'Day shuddered happily. His tingle tingled all the way up to his secluded estate. It was still tingling when Rudolfo passed right by the main house and slowed to a stop in front of the stables.

"The stables today, Rudolfo?" Leonard O'Day asked eagerly.

"You're the owner of a racehorse that's been losing at the track, sir," Rudolfo explained. "He's the jockey. Unless you can motivate him to win, you've got to fire him."

The rules seemed simple enough. Senator O'Day clapped his hands giddily. He loved games.

The senator got out of the car and rolled the barn door open just wide enough to slip through. Inside, the stable smelled like horse droppings and damp hay. Sunlight filtered in through open vents near the ceiling.

The smell of manure made him even more excited.

This was just a minor peccadillo. As he walked along the hard-packed earthen floor, Senator O'Day knew there was nothing wrong with it. Everyone needed a way to relieve the tension. Some people played with model trains, some built ships in bottles. Some, like the senior senator from New York, diddled young boys.

Rudolfo was his procurer. Leonard didn't know where his driver found the boys, nor did he care. However he came by them, he always managed to find the freshest meat. His efforts required a huge bonus at Christmas—as much a thank-you as it was hush money. But it was worth every penny.

The role-playing was always fun. Sometimes he was a sea captain; sometimes he was Scarlett O'Hara. Today it was horses, with a young jockey to discipline.

When he saw the boy, the senator was licking his lips and thinking how much fun he could have with a riding crop.

Rudolfo had outdone himself.

The young man was blond and pale, just like Leonard liked them. The thin and wiry boy stood there in the middle of the stable, alone and defenseless. Just waiting to be punished for his losing streak at the racetrack. It would have been the perfect game if not for one thing.

''Where's your jockey uniform?'' Senator Leonard O'Day pouted, jamming his loose wrists to his hips.

Some kind of uniform was mandatory, no matter

what game he happened to be playing. Without pants, of course.

The boy who wasn't wearing a jockey uniform didn't answer. He just stared at the senator. The way he looked at Leonard, the senator almost felt a twinge of guilt for his extracurricular activities. That lasted only until Leonard noticed the body in the nearest empty stable.

It was lying facedown in the hay, naked bottom aimed at the rafters. The dead boy wore a jockey uniform.

"Oh, my," Senator O'Day gasped.

In shock now, he turned to the young man.

The blond-haired boy with the electric-blue eyes was no longer standing. Somehow—impossibly—he was flying through the air directly toward New York's frightened senior senator.

And in the next instant the senator felt an explosion of pain in his hip as his right femur was shattered into his pelvis. He collapsed in a heap to the floor.

The pain blinded all rational thought.

His face landed in a pile of manure. In a flash that sometimes came just before the moment of death, the senator suddenly thought that he could maybe play a game where he was the cruel stable owner and he had to punish a derelict stable hand for not cleaning up all the horse droppings. He was going to bring it up to Rudolfo, but then he remembered he really was the stable owner and that his face was in a real-life pile of shit because his actual employees hadn't cleaned up properly. And then a toe crushed his other hip and a pair of dropped soles flattened his shoulder joints. By the time the foot that ended his life crushed his skull, the senior senator from New York was long past the ability to even feel the pain.

When the young man was through, Senator Leonard Albert O'Day looked as if he'd been mangled in the pounding pistons of some massive pneumatic device.

For a moment there passed a look of revulsion on the young man's pale face. His eyes grew moist with fear as he looked down on the body. The life he'd snuffed out. One moment a living, breathing thing. The next...

With a force of will far older than his years, he blinked away the image. His teacher insisted that emotions were for the weak. He would not be weak.

Reaching down, he removed the dead man's pocket watch.

Burying the brief hint of human emotion he'd allowed to seep to the surface, the boy turned from the body and padded back into the shadows. He left the stable through a back door. To find his Master.

21

For Dr. Harold W. Smith the wait had been going on for five agonizing days. Five days of reading the papers. Five days of checking the daily computerized reports from CURE's hundreds of unwitting employees in federal law enforcement. Five days of waiting for that one, final, fateful call on the new dedicated White House line.

Smith expected this to be the end. He assumed the connection would be made between MacCleary, Folcroft and, eventually, CURE. If not in the papers, he assumed he'd see it in the secret reports from the CIA or FBI. As soon as the President got a whiff, he would make the call.

It was the one control the nation's chief executive had over the covert agency. He could only suggest assignments; he couldn't command Smith into the field. But he could order the organization to disband.

If CURE had indeed been compromised, Smith assumed the President would hear about a rogue agency operating in Rye during his daily intelligence briefing. He would then calmly excuse himself from his meeting and—after the door was shut—run like mad to give Smith the order to disband before legitimate federal law-enforcement agencies arrived at Folcroft's gates with battering rams and tear-gas canisters.

But for the five days since Remo had been sent to deal with MacCleary and the Viaselli situation, the secluded road out beyond Folcroft's high front wall had remained quiet. Spring buds were bursting open on the maple trees that lined the lane. Cheerful squirrels cavorted in the branches. There was no sign of tanks or armed federal agents. Still, as he toiled behind his desk, he found one eye straying more and more regularly to the window. He half expected to see armed agents swarming the back lawn of Folcroft.

Remo called to check in twice during this time of high crisis. The first was after the story of the suicidal man with the hook appeared in the local papers.

Smith complimented Remo on his work at the hospital. Remo sounded violent on the phone, vowing to bring back the mysterious Maxwell's head in a bucket in five days.

Only one more call. This time asking Smith for three thousand dollars to buy an engagement ring for Norman Felton's daughter. Remo explained that he was romancing the flighty young girl to get close to her father and, hopefully, to Maxwell, the Viaselli man behind Felton.

That was it. Dead silence afterward.

Five days of waiting without knowing.

During that time, Smith did his best to put MacCleary out of his mind. Logically, he knew that it would do no good to dwell on it. Yet his mind couldn't let it go.

One of CURE's own was gone.

Remo was an add-on to the agency. It had been difficult arranging his execution, but he was replaceable if necessary. Chiun was just his temporary trainer. They weren't part of the inner circle. Mac-Cleary had been there from the start.

Conrad MacCleary. The only real friend Harold W. Smith had ever had. Dead.

"America is worth a life."

How many times had MacCleary uttered those words? One of the last great patriots, the hard-drinking agent had said it most passionately over the past eight years. It invariably came up when he was arguing the necessity for CURE to have an enforcement arm that was sanctioned to kill.

At no time had MacCleary ever thought he would be that enforcement arm's first victim. It was ironic, yes. But MacCleary loved irony, lived to find humor in the absurd.

There was no doubt that if he could, Conrad MacCleary would be sitting on the couch across the room clutching his sides and laughing that bellowing laugh of his over the circumstances of his own death. But the sofa was empty.

Unlike his deceased friend, Harold Smith found nothing humorous about death. Not MacCleary's, and certainly not the ones he was reading about this morning.

Two more United States senators were dead.

The details of Leonard Albert O'Day's death weren't complete at the moment, but they were clear enough. He had been found in the stable on his estate. His four major joints, along with his skull, had been crushed. The coroner was speculating that he had been stomped to death by one of his own horses.

Leonard O'Day had just been joined by Senator Calvin Pierce of Connecticut.

Senator Pierce's body had been found at the apartment of his mistress. The girl was dead, as well. According to the earliest reports, the bodies had been mutilated almost beyond recognition. Somehow the killer had hurled the two victims against each other with such force that their bodies became intertwined. It was a ghastly trick, obviously. The forensics experts were quietly saying that it would be almost impossible to cut the two bodies apart.

The condition of the senator's body would make the arrangements difficult for the senator's widow. Mrs. Pierce had already released a statement through her lawyer saying that, given her husband's years of public service, she expected no less than a state funeral in Washington.

As he read the reports, Smith felt a curl of ice slither like a frozen serpent up his rigid spine.

Two more senators had been murdered. Coincidence was unlikely in the extreme. Coming just a week after the murder of Senator Bianco it could only mean one thing. Some unknown force was systematically removing members of the United States Senate.

It was almost too much for the CURE director to contemplate. Smith was immersed in the latest data on Senator Pierce's death when the blue contact phone jangled to life.

Tearing his eyes from his computer monitor, he checked his watch even as he picked up the bulky receiver. Just after 2:55. It was Remo's ten-minute call-in window.

"7-4-4," Smith announced crisply.

"Hey, Chief, it's Agent K-14."

It sounded like Remo's voice. But he wasn't giving the proper code.

Smith felt his stomach knot. Remo was the only

one who should have access to this line. That was it. His worst fear had been realized. CURE had been compromised.

"I'm sorry, but you have a wrong number," Smith said woodenly. He was fishing in his vest pocket for his poison pill even as he hung up the telephone.

The phone rang ten seconds later.

"It's me, dammit, 91 or 99 or whatever the hell dippy-do dingdong number you gave me. Don't hang up."

This time Smith recognized Remo's voice. Relief washed over him. He slipped his pill back in his pocket.

"That is not quite the proper code," the CURE director scolded. "In future please do a better job committing it to memory."

"Close enough for government work," Remo said. "Listen, I don't know what you think you sent me out here to do, but I tracked down that Maxwell for you."

Smith's hand tightened on the receiver. From the start the Maxwell situation had been intertwined with the senatorial committee that was on its way to New York. Perhaps CURE had finally gotten lucky.

"Is he out of commission?" he asked, scarcely able to keep the hope from his tart voice.

"In a manner of speaking. I pulled the plug on him. Literally. Turns out he's not quite a he."

Smith frowned. "Explain."

"First I'd like to point out that you guys need better field intelligence or something," Remo said. "The short of it is this Maxwell you've been trying so hard to find isn't a guy at all. It's just a brand name on some kind of car crusher. Felton owns—*owned*—an auto junkyard in Jersey City. He's been putting bodies in cars and then using this Maxwell Steel Reducer doohickey to crush them all up together into one neat, semimushy package. So this Maxwell you were all worked up over was just a machine.''

Blinking, Smith removed his glasses. He set them to his desk with a tiny click.

"A what?" Smith asked dully.

"That's what Maxwell was," Remo repeated. "Felton was the boss."

"Impossible."

"All right, it's impossible," Remo agreed.

Smith's mind was still reeling. He hardly heard the rest of their conversation. He only knew Remo was gone when the line went dead in his hand.

Felton was dead. That was clear enough from Remo's words. But Maxwell? Just a machine?

Could it be that Conrad MacCleary was dead because Smith had sent him after the wrong target? Norman Felton was the real Viaselli Family enforcer.

All at once Smith snapped alert. He quickly hung up the silent phone. Replacing his glasses, Smith's hands flew across his computer keyboard. In just over a minute he had a trace on the line. Grabbing the contact phone, he hastily dialed the number on his computer screen.

As the phone rang, Smith checked his watch once more. It was nearly five past three. The ten-minute window on the secure line was rapidly closing.

The phone was picked up on the fourth ring.

"This better be important," Remo growled.

"We don't have much time before this line goes dead," Smith said urgently. "When did all this take place?"

"I dunno," Remo said with a sigh. "Last night sometime. Why?"

Smith looked at the green screen of his raised computer monitor. According to all the reports he had been going through, Senator O'Day had been killed in the early morning. And Senator Pierce had died some time after noon today.

"Aunt Mildred wanted me to thank you for sending roses this Easter because chocolate gives her hives," Smith said.

There was an agonizing pause on the other end of the line. Smith watched the second hand of his watch slip past the thirty-second mark. The call window was closing.

"Okay," Remo said slowly, "I'm kind of out of it on all this spy stuff. Does that mean I come back there, or we meet near the paddle boats in Central Park?"

"Cousin Lulu plants pink begonias only after the last frost," Smith replied rapidly, eyes on his watch. Fifteen seconds left.

"Cousin who?" Remo asked.

"Just come back here," Smith blurted just as the phone cut off. He prayed Remo heard.

As he replaced the phone, Smith's alert eyes darted back to his computer screen.

The two senators had been killed today. Hours after Remo had put Felton and his disposal machine out of commission. That could only mean one thing. They were killed by someone else entirely. Someone independent of anything known to CURE.

There was another enforcer working for the Viaselli crime organization. Someone who was fast, efficient, stealthy and violently cruel.

The methods used to eliminate the three senators had been unorthodox in the extreme. A pattern like that didn't develop overnight. With Felton out of the picture, Smith would have to sift through thousands of bits of information collected by CURE's network of informants to see if there was someone else who could be responsible. Unfortunately, his computers were sluggish things. It would take days or even weeks of searching to uncover a list of potential culprits.

Girding himself for a long, arduous search, the CURE director stretched his hands for his keyboard. He stopped before his fingers even brushed the keys.

Inspiration suddenly struck. Leaning forward, Smith pressed a button on his desk intercom.

"Yes, Dr. Smith?" Miss Purvish's voice asked.

"Please have an orderly go down to collect Mr. Park. I would like to see him in my office."

Clicking off the intercom, he gripped the arms of his chair, twirling around to face the big picture window. Waves of foam rolled in off the sound and attacked the shore. A warped boat dock rose and fell with each successive wave.

The Masters of Sinanju were legendary dealers of death. The old man could have encyclopedic knowledge of assassins and assassination techniques. Perhaps Master Chiun could offer some insight into the mind of this particular killer.

22

Don Carmine Viaselli placed the call from the small office off his apartment's master bedroom.

It was the private number, direct to Norman Felton. He expected either Felton or his butler to answer. They were the only ones who'd ever had access to that line before. He was surprised when a new voice answered.

"This is Viaselli," the New York Don said. "I just wanted to thank Norman for releasing my brother-in-law Tony."

"This is Carmine Viaselli, right?" asked the voice on the other end of the line.

"That's right. Who is this?"

"I'm an employee of Mr. Felton's and I'm glad you called," said the unfamiliar voice. "Mr. Felton wanted to see you tonight. Something about a Maxwell."

Don Viaselli had heard about this Maxwell from Felton. The investigations of the past few months seemed to focus around this mysterious figure. A man neither Felton nor Viaselli had ever heard of. It was because of their mistrust over Maxwell that Norman Felton had taken Viaselli's brother-in-law hostage. An insurance policy. But now Tony was free and safe, and Carmine Viaselli was being asked to personally meet with Norman Felton about Maxwell.

"Where should I meet him?" Carmine asked, knowing full well there wasn't a chance in hell he'd ever go himself.

"He has a junkyard on Route 440," the voice on the phone replied. "It's the first right off Communipaw Avenue. He'll be there."

A setup. He knew it was a trap even as the stranger gave him the time. Ten o'clock.

Viaselli hung up the phone. He sat at his desk, his hands gripping his knees through the silk of his dressing gown, knuckles clenching white.

"Bastard is setting me up," he growled at the empty room. The low sound became a bellow. "I trusted him with my life and the goddamned son of a bitch is setting me up!"

A noise came from the next room. The soft rustle of fabric.

Viaselli looked up to see a portly woman in a black dress and white apron standing in the open door. She was clutching a stack of folded linen to her ample bosom.

It was his maid. She was always popping up where she wasn't wanted. If she hadn't been with him so long, he would've sent her to Norman Felton to eliminate ages ago. As usual, she wore an apologetic look on her broad face.

"Get outta here, Maria!" Viaselli bellowed.

The woman scurried fearfully away.

Don Viaselli sank back in his chair. Felton had gone to the other side. Carmine Viaselli had made him a rich man as the Viaselli Family's main enforcer, and this was how he repaid the favor. It was the damned government. They had turned Carmine's most trusted man against him.

They were coming for him. They wouldn't stop. They wouldn't back off until they had him.

But Don Viaselli might have an edge. Mr. Winch. Felton might have blabbed to the government about the Oriental hit man, but they probably hadn't believed him. Who would? Some unstoppable gook killer who could appear and disappear at will. It was funny-farm material. But Winch was real, and he was on Don Viaselli's side. Problem was, at the moment Carmine Viaselli had no idea where his enforcer was.

"I need you back here now, Winch," he whispered to the shadows, his voice a sick murmur.

He was startled when the shadows answered.

"What do you need?" said a reedy voice.

Viaselli's head snapped up. Mr. Winch stood in shadow next to a window. His face was turned away from Don Carmine. Flat eyes watched the cars go by on 57th Street fourteen floors below.

Carmine Viaselli couldn't believe it. He had called for Winch and the hit man had appeared. Like a genie from a lamp.

"It's Felton," Viaselli said, face relaxing in lines of great relief. "He was supposed to be my white queen. My most powerful chess piece. And he's betrayed me." A smile cracked his sagging jowls. "But now I have you, thank God. You are my new white queen. I want you to find Felton and kill him before he can testify against me."

"Impossible," Mr. Winch said blandly.

Viaselli's brow dropped. "If it's money, I'll double it. I want the bastard dead, no matter what it costs."

"Then you need pay someone else, not me," Winch said. "Your Norman Felton is already dead."

Viaselli carefully took hold of the edge of his desk. "Norman's dead? How do you know?"

Still at the window, Winch turned his head. His face was bland. "Who released your brother-in-law?"

"I don't know," Viaselli admitted. "Some guy. Tony wasn't good at giving a description, but he said the guy had eyes like a dead man. That was the one thing he remembered. That and the fact the guy was whistling 'Born Free' when he let him outta that closet at Norman's apartment."

"Whoever that man is, he is the one who killed your associate. There are probably others with him. You Americans seem to view everything as a team sport. Even assassination. No, your Felton is dead, along with his men. And I would not be concerned that whoever did this thing wants to put you in jail. Whoever is responsible will be coming to kill you, not arrest you."

Viaselli's grip on the desk tightened. His heart was pounding like mad. He could feel the blood rise in his cheeks.

"You have to stop them," Don Carmine insisted.

"I could hold them off," Winch said, nodding. "For a time. But I cannot be with you forever. They will send a man, then another and eventually an army. And there will be that one time. That single, isolated, unguarded instance when they will find you alone. And they will have victory."

"This can't be happening," Don Viaselli said. "This isn't how the game is played in this country. We got laws."

At this, Mr. Winch smiled. Mr. Winch never

smiled. Now the mobster saw why. It was the most unnerving thing Don Carmine Viaselli had ever seen.

"They will not retreat," Winch warned. "Not yet. They have declared war against you and you against them. They have not suffered enough to make them consider ending it."

Viaselli was having a hard time breathing. "But what about that pervert, Leonard O'Day? Didn't you get him?"

"He and another in Connecticut have been removed. But already others vie to fill their seats. It is always the way. There is never a shortage of politicians."

Viaselli's head was spinning. He had to maintain his grip on the desk to keep from toppling onto the floor.

"I thought I could stop them. Send them a signal. This isn't how it's supposed to play out."

Mr. Winch turned fully from the window. He remained in the shadow, away from where outside eyes might be looking in.

"All is not lost," the Oriental said. "You have made a good start in this war of their making, but you have not yet done enough to insure your safety. As the head of your House, they are coming for you. Who leads theirs?"

Viaselli looked up, blinking away the cobwebs. He tried to concentrate. "The Speaker of the House, you mean?"

"No," Winch said impatiently. "He is not their leader. He does not direct the forces that have been marshaled against you. His is not the one face of all the other white faces in your nation's capital that everyone recognizes."

A dawning realization stretched across Don Viaselli's tan face. With it came a steadying calm.

"You think I should whack the President?" he asked, voice strong and even. He released the edge of his desk.

"It has been done before," Mr. Winch replied. "It would paralyze the forces of your enemies. Your power would be unquestioned. They would not dare move against you."

Viaselli's eyes twitched back and forth, studying the corners of the room. He finally looked up.

"Nice and quiet. There can't be any trail back to me."

"Of course," Mr. Winch said, his voice oily calm.

Don Carmine Viaselli nodded. The deal was struck. He turned slowly in his chair, offering Mr. Winch his back.

"Fool," Nuihc whispered under his breath, so low the word was audible only to himself.

Melting back into the shadows, he passed like a whispered thought from the office, leaving the old buffoon to his unsophisticated plots of revenge.

23

As he watched the flickering images on the TV screen in the privacy of his Folcroft quarters, a single perfect tear rolled down the cheek of the Master of Sinanju.

If he was not the Master, he would not have believed his eyes or ears. But his very soul gave witness to it.

Since he had first set sandal to soil, Chiun had thought America an ugly and barren place. A cultural wasteland whose inhabitants wallowed in the unsightly offenses of their own creation. But he was wrong. It was only mostly like that.

Here was art. Here was beauty.

There was a lesson here, even for the Master. Just because a thing seemed on the surface to be completely and utterly squalid and worthless didn't necessarily mean that there was not something worthwhile hidden somewhere in it.

In nature could not a flower grow from a dung heap? Was not a pearl formed by oyster from sand? Such was the case with this land called America. Here was a land of unrivaled ugliness, and yet...

The voices on the television abruptly stilled. In place of them a crudely drawn cartoon figure with a bald head was trying to sell a white female in heels a yellow liquid to clean her dirty floors.

Sitting cross-legged on the floor of his basement room, Chiun blinked away the tears.

The tiny Korean's joy was beyond measure.

He had begun watching America's televised art form during Remo's earliest training sessions. Broadcast daily, the short plays were things of sublime perfection. Timeless, touching studies of the human condition whose message of hope and love transcended all cultures and borders.

The best was *As the Planet Revolves*. While most of the players on the program were wonderful, the true standout was Rad Rex. The actor played the part of wise and kindly Dr. Wyatt Winston, half brother to Grace Kimberland, whose fourth husband, Royce, had recently been discovered having an affair with Patrice, the scheming matriarch of the Covington family, which was secretly planning to build a textile plant on the site of the Eden Falls School for Wayward Youth and put the displaced orphans to work as slave labor. Dr. Winston had learned about the plot from Patrice Covington's Guatemalan illegal immigrant maid, Rosa, who had been rushed to City General Hospital for emergency bladder surgery. Even though this damning secret could destroy the fortunes of amnesiac pickle magnate Roland Covington, so far Dr. Winston had remained silent.

Dr. Winston had been silent long before Chiun had gone to Arizona with Remo and he was still silent now. Two full months of silence. Every now and then City General's star surgeon would raise a knowing and disapproving eyebrow to the audience, just to let everyone know that he was waiting for the proper moment to disclose the terrible truth.

Such patience. Such acting. Such writing.

"Chiun, those are soap operas," Remo explained in those first, early weeks of training.

"They are windows into the human soul," Chiun replied as he studied the television screen. "Hush."

"Then the human soul is a smokehouse, 'cause I'm looking at a bunch of reeking hams right now."

For his insolence, Chiun touched Remo on the knee. Remo rolled around on the floor in agony for two hours. After that, Remo learned not to interrupt Chiun's dramas.

Even though Remo wasn't here to interrupt now, Chiun knew precisely where he was. Unbeknownst to Smith or Remo, Chiun had spent the past five days following his young pupil.

That was partly Conrad MacCleary's fault. In his dying moments Smith's general had placed a seed of worry in the Master of Sinanju's mind. The old man's concern had proved to be unfounded. The only people bumbling Remo encountered were other bumbling whites.

Still, Chiun didn't consider the time wasted. There was another good reason to follow his pupil. In a way Remo was a representative of the House of Sinanju. A failure on his part would reflect poorly on the House. But Remo had done his work as well as could be expected. He had completed the task he was sent out to perform without getting killed. Once Remo was done, Chiun slipped back to Folcroft with no one the wiser that he'd ever left.

He settled down in the privacy of his quarters to catch up on the wonderful daytime dramas.

On the TV an advertisement for tooth polish ended the selling moments and the program began again.

After a few more raised eyebrows from Dr. Winston and a little hinting at a devastating revelation by Beatrice Sloane, grand-niece of Mayor Simon Parkhurst and former drug-addicted homecoming queen, the program ended.

As the Planet Revolves was followed by *Search for Yesterday*. Not quite as brilliant as the show that preceded it, but it was still good.

When the program ended at 3:30, the Master of Sinanju's eyes were damp. Releasing a contented sigh, he pressed off the television with a long finger.

Closing his papery eyelids, he began replaying the best scenes in his mind. His harmony was disrupted by the sound of approaching footfalls. He hoped they would pass by, but was dismayed when they stopped outside his chambers.

There was a sharp rap at the door.

The dramas were over. Ugliness was about to intrude on his day once more. With a sigh Chiun opened his eyes.

"Enter," he called reluctantly.

Harold Smith came into the room, a pinched expression on his lemony face.

"Master Chiun, I—" He stopped dead in his tracks. "My God, what happened here?" Smith gasped.

"Where?" Chiun asked, brow dropping in confusion.

"The body," Smith replied, eyes wide with shock. "My God, there's a dead body at your feet."

Chiun turned a bland eye on the floor before him. A white-clad man lay facedown on the painted concrete.

"Oh, that." The Master of Sinanju waved. "Not to worry. I will have my pupil remove it when he gets back." He smiled. "You are looking exceptionally fit today, Emperor."

It was as if Smith didn't hear. He hurried over to the body. Crouching, he pressed his fingers to the man's throat, searching in vain for a pulse.

Chiun crinkled his nose in displeasure. This Smith hadn't even acknowledged the compliment he had just received. Chiun already suspected the man was crazy. Now he could add rude to the list of his current employer's shortcomings.

"There's no pulse," Smith said.

"No," Chiun agreed.

"This man is dead," Smith stated sickly.

"He's white. Who cares?" Chiun shrugged. "No offense," he added, lest this rude madman was the sort of lunatic who got offended by the truth.

"What happened?"

The Master of Sinanju raised his palms in confusion.

"I am not sure I understand your question, Emperor. He breathed, then he ceased breathing. Dead is dead."

"Master Chiun, you should have called me about this," Smith said. "I sent him to get you. When you didn't come to my office, I came to see why." Crouching beside the body, he looked over to the seated Oriental. "Did he say anything before he died? Perhaps clutch his heart or left arm?"

"I believe he said something," Chiun admitted. "I did not really hear, engrossed as I was in the travails of poor Lance Langdon and his alcohol-abusing wife. He got in the way, so I removed him."

Smith had been looking down at the body. Chiun's words stilled the blood in his veins. Moving only his eyes, he looked up over the tops of his rimless glasses at the placid face of the Master of Sinanju.

"Did you say 'removed'?" he asked levelly.

"No need to thank me," Chiun assured him, raising a hand to ward off praise. "The peace of mind you gain from knowing that this interrupting serf no longer stalks the halls of your castle is more than enough thanks for me."

Smith rolled the man onto his back. The body was already cold.

He didn't see it at first, so small was it. But then his eyes fell on it. A half moon sliver of a mark between the eyes just above the nose. It was the kind of mark that might be left by a puncturing fingernail.

"My God," Smith groaned again. "You killed this man."

"Perhaps a small thank-you," Chiun said modestly. "If you insist."

"Chiun, this is unacceptable," Smith spluttered. "You killed a man in cold blood. A Folcroft employee, no less."

Shaking his head in shock, Smith dropped to his backside on the floor.

Smith's pale face was more ashen than normal. As he studied his employer, the Master of Sinanju's eyes narrowed.

"Maybe your humble servant is not understanding this correctly, O Emperor," he said slowly, "but it almost sounds like you are not pleased that I did you this favor."

"Favor? This is no favor. It's another catastrophe in a week of catastrophes. Chiun, you can't go around killing people just because they disturb you while you're watching television. How on earth am I supposed to explain this?''

Chiun had assumed he was misunderstanding his employer. But he was right. The fussbudget wasn't going to thank him for disposing of this rabble at all. He was actually upset.

The Master of Sinanju's face puckered.

Some unused silverware lay on a bench near a cheap sideboard. Reaching over, Chiun scooped up a soup spoon and thrust it deep into the orderly's forehead.

''He tripped while delivering bowls of gruel,'' Chiun said thinly. Explanation delivered to this rude lunatic of an employer, who refused to give so much as a simple thank-you to his royal assassin, the old Korean rose to his feet in a single fluid motion and swept from the room. His bedroom door slammed shut.

Still seated on the floor, the CURE director cast a queasy eye across the orderly's corpse. The spoon jutted from the broad forehead like a shiny silver handle.

''What have I gotten myself into?'' Smith implored the cinder-block walls.

He pushed himself to his feet. Grabbing the body by the ankles, he began dragging it wearily across the room.

REMO COULDN'T believe it. He was actually coming back to Folcroft Sanitarium. *Voluntarily.*

MacCleary had once told him that his psychological profile said he wouldn't leave. According to their research, Conn assured Remo that he wouldn't take off. Remo was a patriot. A do-gooder who thought if he did enough good he could make the world a better place.

Remo thought MacCleary was full of shit. He fully intended to prove wrong all the faceless quacking shrinks who had figured out every little thing about him without ever bothering to go through the trouble of meeting him.

But the quacks were right. Worse, Remo didn't really care they were right. And the icing on the cake was that Remo was actually in a good mood as he drove his car up the long lane to Folcroft's front gate.

He waved to the guard at the booth. The uniformed man didn't even raise his gray head from his magazine as Remo drove up the driveway and onto the sprawling grounds.

Remo was whistling as he parked the car. Or trying to. It became easier once he dropped the cigarette he'd been puffing and ground it out with his toe.

He knew he'd get in trouble with Chiun for smoking. *If* he got caught. But he'd taken precautions.

He squirted a spritz of breath freshener into his mouth that he'd picked up at the store. As he walked to the building, he peeled a breath mint from a roll in his pocket and popped it in his mouth. Pausing at the fire exit, he covered his mouth with his hand and took a good whiff of his breath.

The perfect crime.

Ducking inside the building, he headed downstairs.

The suit he'd worn on his assignment felt confining. He didn't know why. He'd worn suits before. And it wasn't as if his police or Marine uniforms had been loungewear. But for some reason regular clothes didn't feel right anymore. For one thing the cuffs were too snug around his wrists.

He was unbuttoning his cuffs as he pushed open the door to the Master of Sinanju's basement quarters.

Chiun wasn't there.

Remo stepped into the spare bedroom, where the old Korean stored his steamer trunks.

In his infinite generosity, Chiun allowed Remo to use the small closet in the room. At the moment it was the only place Remo could really call his own.

When he went to hang up his suit in the closet, Remo found a glassy-eyed corpse propped up in the corner.

"Jesum Crow," he said, swallowing his breath mint. He jumped back as the orderly's body dumped out onto the floor.

Remo's startled heart was jumping a mile a minute. Using the breathing techniques he'd been taught, he willed it slower.

He looked down at the body. The last peeking edge of the spoon's bowl was visible in the man's dented forehead.

"Dammit," Remo muttered.

Scowling, he stuffed the body back in the closet.

He used the spoon as a hook to hang up his suit jacket. Trading his dress shoes for sneakers, he changed into a white T-shirt and tan slacks before heading upstairs.

The administrative wing was almost as abandoned as it had been that first night a week before. Despite passing a dozen offices, Remo saw only a grand total of five people.

Director Smith's secretary was sitting at her desk. She glanced up as Remo entered the room.

Miss Purvish's professional demeanor seemed to fade before his eyes. A flush came to her cheeks.

Remo was still getting used to this reaction. After a month or two of training, Chiun had told him that some women could sense a man with superior timing and body rhythms. Remo asked him why he was telling him that, since Chiun kept insisting that Remo was an untrainable klutz with a radish for a brain. Chiun said that, given the yardstick of other whites to go by, having a whole radish in his head could make Remo king of the western hemisphere. Women would sense his radish, so watch out. The old man had been right.

"Oh, hello," Miss Purvish said with a too wide smile. "You're Mr. Park's nurse, aren't you?"

She licked her lips. She wasn't unattractive, but she wore too much makeup. Remo thought they could make ten bucks on the weekends if they stuck a rubber ball on the end of her nose and rented her out for kids' parties.

"I prefer the term 'physical-needs specialist.'"

Her leering smile told him the physical needs she'd like him to specialize in.

"Dr. Smith told me to send you right in."

As he passed her desk, she followed him with her eyes.

Before he was within ten feet of the door, Remo heard an ungodly shriek from within Smith's office.

"Perfidy!" cried a muffled singsong voice.

The door flew open and the Master of Sinanju swirled out into the outer office like a cloud of purple doom. A hand of parchment-covered bone stabbed Remo's chest.

"You have been inhaling tobacco smoke," the aged Korean accused angrily.

"Howdy-do to you, too," Remo said, peeved.

Miss Purvish was frozen in her chair. Her hands were locked to the edge of her desk and her jaw hung open as she stared wide-eyed at the ancient Oriental in the purple-and-gold kimono who had just raged from her employer's office.

Smith sprang through the door a heartbeat after Chiun. Out of breath, his eyes darted to his shocked secretary.

"Er, you've met Mr. Park," Smith explained hastily to her. "The patient is a stickler for issues of health." He turned to Chiun. "I agree, Mr. Park, that your nurse should have more consideration for your concerns. Let's discuss the issue in the privacy of my office, shall we?"

Smith's bloodless lips formed a parody of a reasonable smile as he ushered the two men into his office.

"What's he doing here?" Remo asked after Smith had closed and locked the door on the young woman's baffled face.

"You dare?" Chiun snapped. "You dare question why I, a loyal servant, would be where I belong, at my emperor's side? You who would stick tubes of burning leaves between your blubbery lips? Oh, and after all the hard work I put in trying to get your lungs and body to begin doing some of what they are supposed to do. This is how you repay me?"

"If I recall, I was the one putting in the hard work all those months," Remo droned.

Chiun's voice grew low with menace. "If you think you had it difficult before, just you wait."

"Would you both please keep your voices down?" Smith said tightly.

"I'm sorry—" Remo was going to say more, but stopped. "What do I call you, by the way?"

"Either Doctor Smith or Director Smith will suffice."

Remo clearly wasn't pleased with the choices. "Don't have a first name, huh? Okay, *Smitty.*"

Smith let the nickname slide. The only other man who'd ever called him that was Conrad MacCleary. Rather than pick that particular scab, he opted to ignore it. Besides, if he called attention to it, this Remo might make it a habit.

"I'm sure you want to know why I called you back here," the CURE director said. "Other than your apparent inability to remember the simplest of phone codes."

"Does it have something to do with the corpse-in-the-box I found rigged up downstairs?" Remo asked. "That was hilarious, by the way."

"No," Smith said, shooting a glance at the Master of Sinanju. "That is an issue that will have to be dealt with separately. I need clarification of the details of your assignment. Norman Felton is dead, correct?"

"He's toast," Remo said. "I pushed the button myself. He got crushed into a bite-sized cube."

"Do my ears hear true? You used a *machine* to assassinate?" Chiun gasped. His voice flirted with heretofore undiscovered octaves of horror.

"That is irrelevant, Master Chiun," Smith admonished. "Remo, you removed Felton last night. This morning two United States senators were murdered."

This got Remo's attention. "Murdered? I heard about it on the radio. They didn't say anything about murders."

"The details have not yet been released to the public. It is my belief that they were targeted for assassination by the Viaselli crime syndicate."

He quickly filled Remo in on the details of the senatorial committee on organized crime that was making its way across the country. He finished up with the decapitation death of Senator Dale Bianco.

"I didn't hear about him," Remo said once he was through.

"It happened while you and Chiun were away," Smith said. "That was why I sent MacCleary into the field. There is a pattern to these deaths. It clearly points to someone out to throw the Senate committee, perhaps the nation, into chaos. The latest pair of executions took place after you eliminated Felton, who you claim was the true Viaselli Family enforcer."

"He was," Remo insisted.

"Then someone else is responsible for these new deaths. Perhaps even some of the others, with Felton using his device to destroy the evidence. I have consulted with Master Chiun. Unfortunately, he couldn't place the modus operandi to anyone who travels in the same, er, circles as he."

Neither Remo nor Smith noticed the flat expression that settled on the Master of Sinanju's wrinkled face.

Smith continued. "Remo, I need you to find out who is responsible, and I need you to stop them."

"I thought I was supposed to get back to training," Remo said, glancing at the Master of Sinanju. "Not that I was looking forward to it or anything."

"You may come back to Folcroft to resume your training after this situation is resolved."

"I urge you to reconsider, Emperor Smith," the Master of Sinanju interjected. "It is sheer dumb luck that he survived this long. You are taking a grave risk if you send him back out to blunder around some more.''

Remo scowled. ''You know that bullshit's rude enough when you say it just to me, but it's about a billion times more insulting when you say it *about* me when I'm standing right next to you in the goddamned room.''

''Silence,'' Chiun hissed. ''This is for your own good.''

There was something beneath the admonition. Something Remo hadn't ever detected in the old man's voice before. If he didn't know any better, he'd swear it was worry.

''Remo has handled the situation well thus far, Master Chiun,'' Smith said. ''I'm not sure what your objections are.''

''I object because he is nowhere near ready,'' Chiun replied. ''As soon as he is out of my sight for five seconds, he forgets all that I have taught him. He reeks of alcohol, cigarettes and loose women. Smell him. Go ahead. Smell.''

With a bony hand he propelled Remo forward. Remo had to grab the edge of Smith's desk to keep from falling.

''Knock it off, will you?'' Remo groused. ''I needed a drink 'cause I was in a crappy mood. And did you ever stop to think that maybe, just maybe, I needed the cigarettes because you've gotten me so wound up I needed to relax?''

''So it is my fault?'' Chiun said, his eyes saucering wide. ''Me? *I* am to blame? Blameless me is to blame for your failings? Me? Me?'' He wheeled on Smith. ''Do you see what you have given me? Do you see the impossible task you've asked me to perform?''

Smith took in a breath to respond, but the old Korean had already wheeled back to Remo.

"And I suppose I am to blame for the harlot? Don't deny it. The emperor and I were both nearly overpowered by that cloud of vile white musk that trailed you in here."

Smith's blank face indicated his utter lack of ability to smell anything but stale, recirculated office air.

"Actually, Master Chiun—" the CURE director began.

Chiun interrupted with an upraised hand. "I know you are bothered by it, Emperor Smith. Who wouldn't be? I am afraid you will have to take shallow breaths until you get someone to clean the odor of carnality from the carpets." He crossed his arms and stared at Remo. "Well?"

"She was just pleasure in the line of business," Remo said, annoyed. "I told you about Felton's daughter when I checked in," he said to Smith. "I used her to get to him."

"Remo told me his intentions, Master Chiun," Smith said. "I understand what he had to do."

"Do you?" Chiun challenged. "Then it must be some cabalistic white thing, because I am at a loss." He waggled a stern finger in Remo's face. "You are not taking time off from your training to care for the baby."

"There's not gonna be a baby," Remo exhaled.

"There is *always* a baby with you people," Chiun said darkly. "My teacher always said every time a bell rings another white female has been impregnated."

Remo folded his arms. "So you come from a long line of racists, do you?" he asked.

"And there is another thing," Chiun said to Smith. "That tongue. It is a vicious thing incapable of showing proper gratitude or respect. If you send him out with that tongue, he will insult the wrong warlord or khan and the next thing you know you will have hordes of Visigoths swarming over your palace walls. I have seen it happen a hundred times."

Smith shook his head firmly. "Remo has proved competent enough, Master Chiun. If you are having a personality conflict, that is something that the two of you will have to work out on your own. For now we have a grave crisis to deal with. Remo, use the cover documents you were already issued. The phone codes are still in effect. I'll refresh your memory on proper procedure before you leave."

The Master of Sinanju crossed his arms. "I am going with him," he insisted.

"Huh?" Remo asked flatly.

"He has taken the glory that is Sinanju and squandered it all on dissolute living," Chiun argued to Smith, ignoring Remo. "I have wasted months on him, but it is like throwing pearls before swine. No matter how flawless the pearls, the swine will always prefer wallowing in mud. If you insist on sending him back out so soon, I insist on accompanying him, lest his incompetence bring disgrace to me as a teacher."

Leaning back in his chair, Smith considered the old man's words. "I would ordinarily resist such a suggestion."

"Good," Remo said, the first strains of worry in his voice. "Resist away."

"These circumstances, however, are dire," Smith continued. "War has been declared against a branch of the United States government. At the moment there is only the three of us to stop the other side from winning.''

Remo glanced at the Master of Sinanju. The old man raised a superior eyebrow.

"Oh, goody," Remo muttered, shoulders sagging.

"They were acting cautiously at the outset, but they have raised the stakes," Smith pressed. "We have no time to waste. Start with the Viaselli Family itself. Use any means necessary to stop them and end this madness. If you try to call me and get no answer, assume Folcroft has been compromised. The Mac-Cleary matter is quiet for now, but that doesn't mean it will remain so. If I am gone, do not return here. Continue in your mission without me."

"Can do," Remo said.

"We live to bring glory to your throne, O Emperor," Chiun said, offering a deep bow.

Orders given, Smith focused his attention back on his computer. The two men turned and headed for the door, Remo with a deep scowl on his face.

Behind them, a thought suddenly occurred to Smith. He raised his eyes from his monitor.

"Oh," Smith called after them, "there is one matter you will need to attend to before you go."

24

They had to wait until nightfall when most of the sanitarium employees had gone home for the day.

Only when the administrative wing was completely empty of non-CURE personnel did the rear delivery door open. Harold Smith's gaunt face appeared for a moment. He glanced around, checking to see that the coast was clear.

Smith ducked back inside and Remo and Chiun appeared a moment later. Remo hauled a heavy bundle through the door. The door closed behind them.

"You and those damned soap operas," Remo complained as he dragged the orderly's corpse across the loading dock and down the side stairs. "I knew this was gonna happen one of these days. I just thought it'd be me."

"The night is young," Chiun replied thinly.

The Master of Sinanju was wearing a blue business suit instead of a kimono. Smith had managed to track down one in Chiun's size in less than an hour. The old man fussed at the sleeves, which at his request were a little too large, allowing for freedom of movement.

As Chiun fretted about his suit, Remo struggled with the dead orderly. The corpse was too big for him to carry. He had to drag it down the damp lawn to the boat dock.

"You know you're the one responsible for Mr. Spoonhead here," Remo griped. "You could grab a leg."

"It is bad enough I have to train garbage. I will not stoop to carting it around," Chiun sniffed.

"You're not much of a people person, are you?" Remo grumbled.

The dock jutted far into the sound. A single light on a post at the far end usually illuminated the warped wood. Smith had doused the light from inside the building.

Remo dumped the body in a pile of rotting leaves.

There was a boat upended on some cinder blocks at the edge of the woods near the dock. Remo struggled to haul it up the dock. He dropped it into the water with a splash.

"That was heavier than it looked," he grunted. Though the night was cool, he was hot from his exertions. Thanks to his months of training, he hadn't broken a sweat.

"What do you expect?" Chiun said. "You are still straining muscles like a typical American."

"How the hell'd you expect me to get it in the water, balance it on my pinkie?"

The Master of Sinanju shook his aged head. A dispirited sigh escaped the old man's papery lips.

Without a word Chiun bent at the waist. One bony hand reached for the boat. The next minute it was back out of the water and above the dock. The boat flipped up and around until it was standing directly upright.

Remo couldn't believe it. The prow was balanced on the tip of the old man's right pinkie. Although gusts of wind howled in across the sound, the boat remained rock still, as if the Korean and boat were one fused unit.

"I do not expect you to understand, smoker of tobacco," Chiun said blandly as he balanced the boat in the air. "I tried to teach you. I tried to show you men could be more than beasts of burden. If you still think strength comes from mere muscle alone, have Smith hire you another trainer. One who will tell you to hold heavy weights above your head to make your muscles big and fat. Perhaps when the day comes, your swollen American muscles will even slow down the bullet that will inevitably kill you."

Chiun let the boat back down into the water. Although it dropped fast, it landed without a splash.

The old Korean was still trying to get through this skull of granite. A demonstration every now and again was necessary for the dimmer students. This simple trick would impress this numskulled white who smoked cigarettes even after all the time and effort the Master had invested.

Chiun stood on the dock, awaiting the accolades.

Remo looked from the boat to Chiun.

"If you could do that, why didn't you help schlepp it out here in the first place?" he complained.

When he saw the look on Chiun's face, Remo shrugged.

"Hard to be impressed when I've already seen you dodge bullets, rip up floorboards with your bare hands and scale mountains without breaking a sweat."

Leaving Chiun, Remo went to retrieve the orderly's body. He dumped it in the boat, then hauled over the cinder blocks the boat had been resting on. He laid them carefully up the middle of the boat before climbing down inside, all the time worried about capsizing the heavily laden craft.

He was concerned that the added weight of the Master of Sinanju might prove too much, but the boat didn't seem to recognize an additional burden when the old man climbed down from the dock. Chiun sat in the front.

Remo stuck out the oars that had been stored inside the boat and began rowing.

When they stopped three miles out, he was surprised that his arms weren't as limp as wet noodles. He credited it as much to the hours of rope climbing in the Arizona desert as to the special breathing techniques he'd been taught.

Remo weighed the body down with the cinder blocks. Before he could roll it over, Chiun used his long fingernails to slash open the orderly's belly and lungs.

"Yuck," Remo griped. "What'd you do that for?"

"Emperor Smith did not want this vulgar interrupter of beauty to return," the old man explained. "I have removed the gas and air that bloats all you whites. When you have grown your nails to their proper length, you will be able to do this menial work yourself, without dragging me along."

"You've got a hell of a nerve," Remo said. "I'm only out here hauling bodies around because of you, and you don't even lift a finger except to show off."

"I helped," Chiun said. "Who here didn't see me help?"

"Yeah, some help. Just don't expect me to do this for you ever again."

"Why would I expect anything more from you than sloth and ingratitude?" Chiun asked.

Remo ditched the body over the side. "And I'm not growing Fu Manchu fingernails," he concluded.

"Die as you wish," Chiun said. "But when you do, don't come crying to me."

It took forever to row back to shore. Remo dragged the boat up out of the water and left it upside down on the lawn.

They found Remo's car in the Folcroft parking lot. On the way to Jersey City, Chiun fell into a thoughtful silence. Off Route 440, they turned onto a gravel road. It was ten o'clock.

"The junkyard's up ahead," Remo explained as they bounced along the dark road. "Viaselli called when I was back at Felton's apartment. I told him Felton wanted to meet him here tonight. He should be here soon. We can find out everything we need to from him."

In the passenger's seat, face illuminated weirdly by the green dashboard lights, the old Korean eyed his pupil.

"You told someone who knows he is under attack by forces unknown to him to meet an employee who may now be an enemy in the dead of night in an unfamiliar location?"

"Yeah, but don't sweat it. Felton was holding this Viaselli's brother-in-law as a sort of insurance policy. I let him go with a pat on the head and a big wet kiss from Felton, so everything should be hunky-dory now."

"My apologies, Remo," Chiun droned. "Here all this time I thought you were dumb and you are actually very clever."

Remo smiled. "Thanks."

"No, thank you. It is an honor merely to be in the presence of a brilliant tactician such as you."

Remo's smile melted. "Okay," he sighed. "What's wrong with— Hey, what are you doing on the floor?"

The question was barely out before a blaze of gunfire erupted from the path before them.

The windshield shattered in a hail of bullets. Remo would have been cut to ribbons if a strong hand hadn't reached up and yanked him to safety below the dashboard.

"Remember this next time you try to think," the Master of Sinanju whispered through the gunfire. "Never should an assassin attempt to be anything other than an assassin."

The car was still rolling forward. At Chiun's urging the two men popped their respective doors. Chiun sprang out one side, Remo the other.

Remo hit the ground hard. His shoulder took the brunt of the fall as he rolled across the edge of the dirt road. He landed behind a pile of scrap metal. The metal cubes had been cars that were compressed into solid blocks by Norman Felton's car crusher. They were stacked ten cubes high.

Remo's car continued on without them, passing through the fence into the junkyard. The gunfire stopped abruptly.

Remo's shoulder ached. He'd felt something tear as he rolled from the car. Behind the stack of crushed autos he scrambled to his feet. Fingers pressing gingerly into the joint, he tested his injured shoulder.

It still worked well enough. He sank back into the shadows and waited. It didn't take long. Less than thirty seconds passed before a rifle barrel peeked around the stack of cubed cars. A huge shadow lumbered into view.

Remo couldn't believe the size of the man. He weighed four hundred pounds if he weighed an ounce. A ring of fat encircled his neck like a flesh-colored inner tube. He wheezed rotten breath as he waddled through the darkened alley formed by piled scrap iron.

Remo did as he'd been trained, allowing instinct to take over. When the gunman was close enough, Remo reached out with one hand and grabbed the gun barrel. He yanked.

A startled yelp.

The big man at the other end of the gun was knocked off balance. Before he could right himself, Remo was on him.

One hand grabbed the man's wrist, snapping it. The other hand shot forward, cracking the gunman's temple. Eyes rolling back in his head, the big man fell to the ground.

Remo crouched back against the scrap metal, waiting for the next attacker. None came. After two solid minutes of utter silence, he began to think something was wrong.

He peeked cautiously up over the metal barricade.

There was no one in sight. Remo wondered briefly if the others had fled. But then he saw something move.

It was a single figure, small in silhouette. With a confident glide, it came through the gates of the junkyard.

"Criminy," breathed Remo Williams, even as the Master of Sinanju emerged full from the darkness.

The old Oriental had a pair of dripping bundles clutched in each hand. The bundles had eyes.

As Remo scurried out of hiding, the tiny Korean tossed the four heads to the oily dirt at Remo's feet.

"And what moonbeam were you chasing while I did all of your work for you?" the Master of Sinanju demanded.

"I got one," Remo said defensively.

The old Korean gave him a baleful look. As Remo clammed up, Chiun swept by. With one hand he hauled up the fat man that Remo had knocked unconscious, propping him against the crushed cars. With a few sharp slaps across his blubbery face, he woke the slumbering behemoth.

The Viaselli Family soldier blinked away the cobwebs. When he saw Chiun, a strange look crept across his face. His great sagging jowls drew up in a smile.

"It's you," he breathed.

Remo frowned. "You know this guy?" he asked.

"Silence," Chiun admonished. He had seen something deep in the eyes of the hit man. He leaned in close. "Speak, fat one," he whispered sharply.

"Your time is past, old man," the man said. He spoke in a voice that seemed too precise, not at all like that of a Mafia killer. "He knows you're here. He knows you wouldn't work for anything less than the ruler of any country. Your arrogance wouldn't allow it. He's going to kill your charge and send you back home in disgrace, where you'll die alone and shamed in the eyes of your ancestors."

There was a glazed look on the man's face. Remo figured he'd cracked him too hard in the head.

"What does he mean 'your charge'?" Remo asked. "Chiun, what's this guy talking about?"

"It is nothing," Chiun spat. "The one who pulls this fat one's strings has made an error in judgment. It would not be the first time. He thinks that the Master works for the puppet President of this land. He knows not of Harold the First, the true leader."

"Puppet President?" Remo said. The light dawned. "Is he saying they're going to kill the President?"

"Yes," Chiun replied, his tone flat.

Remo looked hard into the eyes of the weirdly

smiling Mafia man. There was the passion of a zealot in those eyes. He was telling the truth.

"This is big," Remo said. "We better call Upstairs."

"I agree," Chiun said. "When the day comes to eliminate the pretender and install Emperor Smith to his rightful place on the throne of America, it will be *my* doing, no one else's."

He leaned his lips to the hit man's hairy ear. "You may await your wicked master in death," he whispered, so quietly that Remo failed to hear.

A sharpened talon pierced the heart. The Viaselli soldier clutched his chest and collapsed to the ground.

"You ever meet someone you *didn't* kill?" Remo asked, skipping back to avoid the settling corpse.

"Do not tempt me," the Master of Sinanju menaced. He was staring down at the twitching body.

"Maybe we should have asked him more questions," Remo complained. "Like where, when and how, for instance. Did he seem doped up or something to you?"

Chiun's face was grave. "During the Second Idiocy of the Barbarian Nations, the Japanese trained men for suicide missions. Through certain techniques they were convinced they could bring glory to themselves and to their emperor."

"You're talking kamikazes, right?" Remo asked. "What do they have to do with this?"

"The Japanese method was crude. It was stolen from Sinanju by the first Emperor, Jimmu Tenno, 2600 years ago."

Remo frowned deeply. "Yeah? Well, I think Jimmy What's-his-name is off the hook. This guy's not Japanese. He's just some Mafia slug from Jersey."

Chiun said nothing. Remo could see that the old man was troubled.

"Look, I wouldn't sweat it," Remo said. "Two thousand years is a long time. Jimmy's long dead by now. Besides, I've seen you in action. Who in their right mind would want to mess with you?"

At this, Chiun turned a hazel eye to his pupil. "Someone who wishes to test the Master," he intoned quietly.

And though Remo pressed him to elaborate, the wizened Korean would say nothing more.

SMITH HAD QUIZZED Remo on the phone codes and gave him another ten-minute window to call in at eleven o'clock. Remo made the call from the junkyard's office trailer. Over the scrambled line he quickly explained the situation.

"Is Master Chiun certain?" Smith asked urgently.

Remo glanced out the window. The old Korean stood out in the yard surrounded by a pile of heads.

"You're kidding, right?" Remo asked. "Hell, I almost confessed. It sounds like the real deal to me."

"I will alert the Secret Service and the local authorities in Washington," Smith said.

"I don't think they'll cut it. Chiun's convinced that this is some sort of special attack that only he can stop. Don't ask me how he knows, but he says he's certain."

Up the coast in his darkened office in Folcroft sanitarium, the worry lines formed deep on Dr. Harold W. Smith's face. Smith had already lost one President on his watch. Granted, CURE was barely operational in those days, but it had eaten at him for the past decade. He could not bring himself to lose another so soon.

"This could be even more problematic," Smith said. "The remains of Senators Pierce and O'Day are to be flown to Washington for a public viewing at the Capitol tomorrow. It's going to be a big affair. Every major political figure in the nation is likely to attend."

"Get them to cancel it," Remo said.

"On what grounds?" Smith asked. "A possible assassination attempt? These days every public function attended by political figures comes at great risk for those attending. And we don't know for certain that's where the attack will come, if an attack even comes at all."

"Then let it go on. Just convince the President to skip it," Remo argued.

"The two deceased senators were members of the opposing political party," Smith explained. "I doubt he would risk not attending. However, I will convey my concerns."

"Viaselli's the one behind all this," Remo said, exhaling angry frustration. "It sounds like he's snapped his twig. Lemme go after him."

"He owns property around New York and around the nation," Smith explained. "He could be anywhere. By the time you find him, it might be too late to derail his plan."

"So we go with Chiun's option," Remo said. "Send us both down to protect the President."

Smith's hand was tight on the blue contact phone. "It would be a terrible risk to send you to Washington," he said.

It was only a few months since Remo had been brought aboard. Even with the plastic surgery, this could be too great a gamble. And MacCleary had handled the recruitment. If Smith lost Remo now, he might be losing the only enforcement arm CURE would ever have. To make matters worse, this conversation had been far too specific. If the CURE line had been tapped, the agency could already be lost.

All of this and more did Smith consider in the briefest of moments. He made an abrupt decision.

"Go," Smith ordered. "Get a flight to Washington National Airport. I'll have documents waiting for you when you arrive. Try to stop whatever this is. With luck you may be able to save him."

"And if we don't?" Remo asked.

"Have you seen the vice President?" Smith asked.

"We've got to save the president," Remo said.

"One thing, however," the CURE director said before his field operative could hang up. "If there is a hint that you might be compromised, let the assassins succeed." The words were difficult to get out. "Better to lose another chief executive than allow CURE to be exposed."

"Gotcha," Remo's voice said. He broke the connection.

The CURE director hung up the phone. With a world-weary sigh he swiveled in his chair.

Long Island Sound sparkled cold and black under the midnight moon. In the quiet of his heart as he watched the waves roll to shore, Harold Smith said a silent prayer for the nation he loved and for the souls of all the men who would lead it.

25

Eight months ago Alphonso "Rail" Ravello wouldn't have believed it was possible. Eight months ago he was a Viaselli foot soldier, loyal only to his Family. Back then he wouldn't have dreamed of swearing allegiance to anyone but his beloved Don, let alone someone like Mr. Winch.

"Goddamned Chink," Alphonso growled when he first heard about the little Oriental who had wormed his way into the Viaselli organization. "He ain't tough. Gimme a crack at him. Kid in my neighborhood got shot down by some Vietcong. Gimme five minutes with that Winch and I'll show him what's what for shootin' down our boys."

Everyone was whispering about this Mr. Winch. They said he was unkillable. That he could disappear at will. They claimed he killed three men in the lobby of the Royal Plaza, fourteen floors down from where Don Carmine Viaselli ruled like a feudal lord over his personal fiefdom of Manhattan.

No matter what he thought of the rest, Rail Ravello absolutely did not believe that last one. Don Carmine would never let someone get away with whacking his own soldiers in his own building. If that part of the story was true, this Winch would have been put on ice so fast it would have made his head spin.

When he found out he was being loaned to the creepy little Oriental who had somehow gotten in good with his Don, Alphonso almost refused. But then he thought of what might happen to someone who refused a direct order of his beloved Don Carmine, the boss of all bosses. With reluctance Alphonso Ravello accepted the assignment.

He soon found that he wasn't the only one from the Viaselli organization who had drawn Mr. Winch duty. That first day a handful of others stood with him on the sticky concrete floor of that lost little warehouse in the swamps of New Jersey. Mosquitoes buzzed the humid air.

Alphonso wasn't nicknamed Rail because of some unique method of execution he'd developed for the Viaselli crime Family. No matter how much he ate he stayed skinny as a rail. One of his less creative companions had mentioned this when they were teenagers. The name had stuck.

Next to Rail stood Lou "Fatso" Fettuci, who was as fat as Alphonso was skinny. Down the line was five-foot-tall Anthony "Tiny Tony" Meloni. The rest of the men seemed pretty average compared to these three.

Mr. Winch personally greeted all of them. With him was that freaky little kid with the weird blue eyes.

Winch blabbed on and on about loyalty and discipline. How he was going to teach them to be better soldiers for their Don. At first it all sounded like some sort of orientation for freshman killers.

At the beginning of his conditioning, Alphonso thought Mr. Winch was nuts. He decided to just go along to get along. Humor the Chinaman who was so stupid he actually thought he could teach a goodfella something about loyalty.

The sessions wound up being more intense than Alphonso had bargained on. They went on for hours. In small, dark rooms. Isolated from the rest. With little sleep or food.

In the end Mr. Winch managed to show something new to Alphonso about loyalty after all. Alphonso's lifelong loyalty to Don Carmine Viaselli had crumbled like the walls of Jericho. The same was true for the others. Their greatest desire was to serve the will of their new master.

Alphonso was crestfallen when Mr. Winch selected Fatso Fettuci and a few others to go off on the first mission. It had something to do with delivering a message at a junkyard in Jersey. Alphonso Ravello had wanted to be first. He wanted desperately to prove his worth to Mr. Winch.

Deep disappointment turned to hope the moment he was summoned to the McNulty Funeral Home in Enfield, Connecticut.

Rail parked down the street. As he approached, he saw that the entire building was bathed in darkness. He crept around back just as he had been instructed.

Mr. Winch met him at the back door.

The Korean was alone. It seemed strange. It was the first time since Alphonso had first met the Oriental that the blond-haired kid wasn't with him.

Inside, the cool air held that strange funeral-parlor mix of flowers and embalming fluids. In hushed tones in the darkened back hallway of that small Connecticut funeral home, Mr. Winch gave Alphonso "Rail" Ravello his destiny.

Alphonso couldn't have been more proud when Mr.

Winch selected him for the special assignment. Unlike Fatso, who was a mere messenger, Rail was going to go down in history.

"Booth, Oswald, Ray," Mr. Winch had said. "Why are their names different from your name? What makes people remember them, while you will die forgotten?"

"They're famous," Alphonso replied.

"They are not famous, they are infamous. Infamy is a coveted thing. Composers and playwrights work a lifetime at their craft to become famous enough to be remembered. Most never achieve that level of success. They die forgotten. But a single moment, one small act of infamy, properly directed, and an otherwise ordinary man becomes a legend that none will ever forget. Just ask Brutus."

This was the only thing Ravello didn't understand. What did the fat guy from *Popeye* have to do with whacking someone?

Mr. Winch brought Rail into the viewing room. An ornate mahogany coffin with gold handles was nearly engulfed by expensive bouquets of flowers. Both gleaming lids were up. Alphonso saw that the silk-lined box was empty.

Mr. Winch noted the confused look on Alphonso's face.

"I have taken care of the previous occupant," the Oriental had said. "Get in."

At first Alphonso didn't quite know what he meant. But when Mr. Winch explained just exactly what was expected of him, a sense of calm confidence descended on Rail Ravello.

"I can do this thing," Alphonso said as he climbed inside the box. His long legs made it a tight fit.

"Of course you can," Mr. Winch replied. He passed several items to the skinny man. Everything he would need.

"I can do *anything*," Alphonso insisted as he tucked the items alongside his thin frame.

"Anything I tell you," Mr. Winch cautioned as he closed the lid and sealed it tight.

Catches inside could be sprung when the time came.

Eight months ago Alphonso might have been afraid of being sealed inside a box like this. But somehow his mind was different now. Those talks with Mr. Winch had done it. When Mr. Winch talked, he made things like this make sense. Even the constant ticking in his ear didn't bother him.

And so Alphonso "Rail" Ravello stayed in the coffin. He didn't make a sound at midnight when the uniformed men came to collect it. He remained silent in the car to the airport, where he was loaded onto an Army transport. He didn't say a word when the plane landed and the coffin was taken off and brought to another waiting car.

It was daylight now.

Alphonso was hot in the box. He pulled the air down deep into the pit of his stomach, just as Mr. Winch had taught him. The breathing helped him retain his calm for the drive in the hearse from the airport.

There wasn't a problem that anyone was going to look inside. As long as he didn't make noise and kept from moving, Alphonso would be all set.

One of the items Mr. Winch had given him back in Connecticut was a pinhole periscope. It stuck out into one of the gold handles. The other handles had crystal tips. The one with the periscope was made of one-way glass.

Inside the box Alphonso had an eyepiece that he could wiggle around to see outside. It was through the periscope that he saw the familiar white dome appear in the side window of the hearse. The dome loomed close, then disappeared as the building beneath it swallowed the somber black car.

They stopped in some kind of underground garage.

More jostling as the coffin was brought to an elevator. Upstairs it was met by a group of soldiers. With somber faces they carried the box into a round open chamber.

Through his periscope, Alphonso could see another closed coffin resting across from his.

The soldiers stood at attention, the doors were opened to the public and a line of sad-faced mourners began to pass respectfully by the matching coffins.

Unbeknownst to any of them, curled up inside the coffin of Senator Calvin Pierce was Alphonso ''Rail'' Ravello. At his bent knee was a semiautomatic handgun.

Sweating in his solitude, he watched for the face of the President of the United States to pass down the line. And awaited his chance to write himself into future history.

26

Deputy Director Bernard Tell of the Central Intelligence Agency spotted the two men as they came toward him through the busy terminal of Washington National Airport.

Tell got up from his seat and walked toward them. As they were passing by, he stepped partly into the path of the younger of the two, bumping lightly into him. At the same time Deputy Director Tell let the manila envelope he'd had stashed under his suit jacket fall to the floor.

"Oh, I beg your pardon, sir," Tell said. "Here, you dropped your envelope." He retrieved the envelope from the floor and tried to hand it over.

"No, I didn't," Remo Williams said.

Remo and the Master of Sinanju started to walk off. Deputy Director Tell chased after them.

"I'm certain you *did* drop this, sir," he insisted tightly as he dogged them to the door.

Remo stopped. "Oh, I get it. Give it here."

Deputy Director Tell didn't allow the world to see the relief he felt inside. He didn't even know why he'd been hauled out for so insignificant a drop. There were plenty of junior agents at the CIA who could have handled this.

Tell started to leave. He was horrified when the young man grabbed him by the arm.

"Wait a sec," Remo said.

He tore open the envelope and pulled out the papers. As soon as they were exposed to light the white edges began to turn pink, then red. The reaction to the light was to show whether they'd been read before. This was one of the many security details he'd had drilled into him by MacCleary and his band of spy school rejects.

Remo released Tell's arm. "I guess you get to live."

Deputy Director Bernard Tell beat a hasty retreat.

As the CIA man went one way, Remo and Chiun headed out the door and into sunlight.

"Upstairs rented us a car," Remo said as he sorted through the documents. "That's a relief. That Smith doesn't exactly look like a big spender. I figured we'd be hoofing it to the Capitol."

Outside, Remo asked a passing stewardess where the car rental agency was. While telling him, the woman continuously licked her lips and batted her eyelashes provocatively. When she was through, Remo gave her a buck for Chap Stick and Visine. She, in turn, gave him her apartment keys and told him he could follow her in his rental. Remo waited for her to get in her car, then tossed her keys down a storm drain and hightailed it for the rental office.

"Did you get a load of that?" he asked as he and the Master of Sinanju hurried along. "And did you see the way the stewardesses were fawning all over me on the plane?"

"No," Chiun replied dully. "From my vantage I

could not see past the udders thrust in your drooling face.''

''That's what I'm talking about. And they're not the only ones. There was a receptionist at Mac-Cleary's hospital who reacted to me the same way. It's bizarre. I mean, you told me that women might find me more attractive with all this training, but I figured you were full of it.''

Chiun's eyes narrowed at the unfamiliar expression. ''I am full of many things. Love and niceness and brilliance and beauty, to name just a few. To which of these are you referring?''

''None of the above. You know, full of it. Shit, crap. Like that. But you were spot-on with the women one. I can't wait till this assignment is over and I can take this sucker out for a real road test.''

The Master of Sinanju made a disgusted face. ''I don't know which is worse,'' the old man said. ''That you are a pervert, that you insult me or that, even after all this time wasted in training, you fail completely to observe the most obvious things in your surroundings.''

''Hmm?'' Remo questioned absently. He was back to looking over the papers that Smith had supplied.

So engrossed was he in the stack of papers he hadn't noticed the man who was about to attack them.

The man was barely taller than the Master of Sinanju, just a little over five feet in height. He had spotted Remo and Chiun in the terminal and had trailed them outside. Hurrying to circle around, he waited between an airport bus and an empty guard booth, a pistol in his hand.

Chiun glanced at his pupil. Remo was oblivious.

''By the looks of it, I'm some kind of special Secret

Service agent and you're a security adviser,'' Remo said. Leafing through papers, he passed Chiun a badge with the seal of the United States Department of Treasury.

Ten yards.

The fool was going to get himself killed. He didn't see the little man at all.

Five yards.

That was it. Chiun would let him die. Remo couldn't be the Destroyer of legend. Chiun had come here with a fool's hope. Free of this burdensome white, the Master of Sinanju could return to his village. Twice in his life he'd had his chance to take a student and failed. His nephew could have the world. Chiun would return to Sinanju in disgrace.

Two yards. The little man was well hidden. The gun was raised. Finger tensed on the trigger. Remo, still preoccupied.

Idiot. Chiun would have to save the dullard's life.

It had nothing to do with the pupil. Nothing at all. It had everything to do with honor. He had made a pledge to his emperor, who, while crazed, had retained the services of Sinanju. The pupil didn't matter. Oh, there were some nice things about him. But mostly not. Chiun would save the loutish pupil from his own stupidity this one time and put off his dumb death to another blockheaded day.

One yard.

The Master of Sinanju began to sweep forward, about to intervene, when something unexpected happened.

Remo came up beside the short man. Unaware of the attacker's presence, he was still going through his documents, in a world all his own.

Then all at once, without any telltale signs signaling a blow, Remo's hand flashed out.

One instant both hands were clutching papers, the next all of the papers were in one hand and Remo's free hand was buried up to the knuckles in the forehead of his tiny would-be attacker. They came back out so fast they didn't have time to be smeared with brain matter.

"Hey, boy, howdy," Remo said. He jumped back, shocked, as the attacker dropped to the pavement.

The gun clattered away. Remo wheeled on Chiun.

"Did you get a load of that? That little guy had a gun. Damn, I didn't even *see* him. He had a gun and he was gonna shoot me and I *knew* it. I just knew it without even thinking about it."

"Of course not," Chiun sniffed. "If you thought about it, you wouldn't have known it and you would be dead."

"Sweet Gazoo," Remo said, looking in awe at the body.

"Beginner's luck," Chiun said.

"Holy freaking crap," Remo said.

"Oh, shut your mouth and get rid of the body," Chiun grumbled, fussing with the cuff of his business suit. "People are starting to stare."

Fresh concern. Remo glanced sharply around.

There was no one in the vicinity. No one had seen what he had done except for Chiun, who didn't seem impressed.

Remo came to his senses. He quickly dumped the body of Anthony "Tiny Tony" Meloni into the empty guard's shack.

"We better get out of here," he said, shutting the door.

Flushed with victory, Remo headed off to the car rental office.

Chiun looked once in the window of the guard shack.

The assassin had been short.

A short man. Not a thin man, as Chiun had expected. A betrayal of tradition, calculated to insult.

Turning from the booth, he padded after his pupil, a hard look on his weathered face.

WHEN THE PHONE RANG, the President of the United States was in the middle of getting dressed for a very public wake.

At first the ringing startled him. It wasn't the usual sharp ring of his nightstand phone. That ring he was accustomed to. This was more a muted jangle.

Only on the second ring did he realize it was coming from his bottom bureau drawer. Although he had used it to call out once, he had never heard the phone ring before.

The President sat on the edge of the bed in his black suit trousers. His shirt was unbuttoned over a crisp white T-shirt. His coat was on a rack by the door. A somber striped tie was laid out at the foot of his bed near the quilt with the presidential seal.

He rolled open the drawer and brought the dialless red phone to his ear.

"What is it?" the President asked worriedly.

"We have a problem, sir," Harold Smith announced tartly. "I believe your life is in danger."

The chief executive's shoulders relaxed. "I'm the President of the United States, Dr. Smith," he said. "Have you looked at a paper the past couple of years? My life's in danger every day and twice on Sunday.

You'll have to get a hell of a lot more specific than that.''

As he spoke, he picked up his tie one-handed, pulling it around his neck. He had to thread it past the phone.

"I believe the threat comes as a direct result of this agency's involvement in New York," Smith said. "You were the one, sir, who pressed the cleanup of organized crime there prior to the arrival of the Senate committee."

The President stopped fussing with his necktie. "Yes," he said questioningly.

"There have apparently been consequences as a result of that action. It is likely that Senators Bianco, O'Day and Pierce were murdered because of our stepped-up campaign. A warning to us to back off. There are indications that this private war is not over. According to my sources, you have now been targeted for assassination by the Viaselli crime syndicate."

This Smith was a cold bastard. Not even news of a potential assassination seemed to ruffle his feathers.

"Do you know when or where they might strike?" the President asked.

"No, sir, I don't. In matters like these, public events have the greatest chance for success. Were I the assassin, I would choose today's viewing at the Capitol. A public place, impossible to completely monitor with a large crowd of civilians. It would be easy for a professional to blend in with the rest of the mourners and await your arrival."

"But you don't know for sure?"

"As I indicated, no, sir, I do not," Smith said.

The President sat up straight at the edge of the bed. "In that case, I'm going, Dr. Smith. You can't tell me when they'll attack, or if they will at all. The press would eat me alive if I didn't go, not to mention the opposition.''

There was a little impatient sigh at the other end of the line. ''I expected as much,'' Smith said. ''In anticipation, I have sent that special person to protect you. He will arrive shortly, along with his trainer.''

''Is that wise?'' the President asked.

''Possibly not. But I had to weigh the risk to this agency against the harm that might befall the nation if an assassination against a sitting President were to succeed again. This agency was founded to prevent the nation from either becoming a police state or falling into chaos. Either scenario would be that much closer to reality were another President killed so soon after the last.''

The President paused. It was easy to think of himself as just another man. But this Smith was right. The nation had mourned enough in the past decade. In a time rife with turbulence, another assassination might be the thing to finally plunge the nation over the edge.

''I suppose you're right,'' the President said reluctantly. ''When can I expect them?''

''They will be there shortly. I have arranged for them to be part of your personal security detachment. There is no guarantee the attempt will be today—if there is one at all. They will remain with you until we have determined that the crisis has passed.''

''Very well,'' said the President. ''Is that all?''

''There is one more thing,'' Smith said.

''Yes?''

''Good luck, sir.''

The dedicated phone went dead in the hand of the President of the United States.

THEIR FALSE Treasury Department IDs got Remo and Chiun through the gates and gained them entry to the White House.

Remo was more impressed with the building than with the President. When the chief executive hustled downstairs, CURE's enforcement arm was like a tourist, looking up at the high ceilings, at portraits and statues.

Remo and Chiun were standing with the rest of the Secret Service detachment. The President seemed to single out the two men with a glance before moving on.

They were outside and piling into cars a minute later. Remo and Chiun were in the back seat of the third sedan behind the presidential limousine. Two regular treasury agents sat in the front.

Once the President was settled into his car, the stream of vehicles and motorcycles began crawling down the drive and out the gate onto Pennsylvania Avenue. The limo followed. Behind it came the rest of the motorcade.

"It looked like he noticed us back there," Remo whispered as their car started off.

"Of course he did," Chiun sniffed. He was tugging at his cuff once more. "Even these ridiculous Western garments cannot conceal the brilliance that is Sinanju."

Chiun was watching official Washington through tempered glass. As seats of power went, he had seen worse. The place seemed well planned, with wide-open spaces between clean buildings and tidy monuments. From what he's seen of this America, he'd give it a hundred years before the place was in ruins, overrun by hordes of Canadian invaders.

"Maybe," Remo said. "Or maybe Smith let him know we were coming. I guess if we've got a presidential audience we should be on our toes, huh?"

Chiun's entire face puckered. "Do not presume to urge the Master to caution, ghost-skin. If there comes a point I am not on my toes, it will only be because clumsy you is standing on them."

Remo sank back in his seat, the very soul of confidence. "No need to worry about me. I realized back at the airport that I was right before. I'm a great student."

"You should aspire to be adequate," Chiun said as the Washington Monument slipped behind the car. "And even then prepare yourself for bitter disappointment."

"Tell that to that guy I zapped," Remo said. He thrust his hand at an imaginary air target. "Zing, bap, boom and he's gone. With moves like that, we've got nothing to worry about. I'm gonna save the day today."

"If there is credit to be had, it is mine," Chiun said, "for the real greatness lies in my instruction. It is not impressive when a man is taught to sing. I, on the other hand, have taught a pig to sing. Even a few sour notes amid the usual grunts and oinks are miraculous."

"I'm not a pig," said Remo.

"Tell that to someone who hasn't seen you eat."

"Anyway, teaching, learning. Wherever it comes from, this is great stuff. You should bottle it. I guess I'm prepared for anything that comes along, huh?"

Chiun's troubled thoughts were on the description Smith had given him of the superhuman deaths delivered to the three United States senators. Deaths with a Sinanju signature.

"First fat, then thin."

"What?" asked Remo.

Chiun looked up. Remo was sitting across from him, a questioning look on his youthful face.

"Mind your own business," Chiun grumbled.

The boy had learned so much in so little time. Even now his breathing was right, his heart and lungs strong. He was centered in himself as he had been taught.

It was wrong. He was not of the village. Worse, he was a white. Yet the spark of something was there. He was everything Chiun could have hoped for in a pupil and nothing he had ever expected.

And then there was the "right" student.

First fat, then thin. That was the order when one Master of Sinanju issued a challenge to another. The man at the junkyard had been fat. Thin should have been next. But the man at the airport had been short.

This was what Nuihc thought of his teacher. Chiun was small. A message of disrespect to an unworthy Master who had outlived his time.

The Capitol Building had risen up from the trees. The presidential motorcade sped up to it. A somber line of mourners snaked along sidewalks and clogged roads.

"What are you so quiet for all of a sudden?" Remo asked abruptly as they drove around to the entrance.

Chiun turned his level gaze on his pupil. "Be careful, Remo," he warned darkly. And in the quiet of his heart the old Korean was surprised by the depth of his concern.

27

Dr. Harold W. Smith placed the small black-and-white television on the edge of his oak desk.

The TV had been a gift with the purchase of his station wagon. The times required that he have an office television. The enticement of a free TV was the reason Smith had chosen that particular automobile dealership.

A piece of aluminum foil from the Folcroft cafeteria was wrapped around the tops of both silver rabbit ears. Smith fiddled with the antenna to clear up the staticky image.

When the picture cleared, Smith saw the familiar interior of the Capitol rotunda. A pair of gilded coffins sat in the center of the floor. A slow-moving line of men and women trudged between them.

The image chilled Smith. It was too familiar. Too reminiscent of a time not long enough ago.

As the network anchorman droned on over the black-and-white image, Smith sat down in his leather chair.

Near the blue contact phone sat a silver spoon and a small bowl of prune-whip yogurt. Both were untouched. Smith had asked Miss Purvish to bring him the food from downstairs but found when it arrived that he had no appetite.

Under ordinary circumstances he would have let appropriate police and security agencies deal with the threat to the President. But these were not ordinary times for America. The bedrock on which she had been founded had turned to quicksand. It was far worse than it had been when Smith was selected to head up CURE nearly a decade before. The once-great nation seemed to be faltering. Even something as straightforward as television news was rife with subtext.

Smith generally avoided Walter Cronkite. The man was not a reporter in the old sense. His broadcast tended to editorialize on the news rather than recite the facts.

Smith switched the channel to ABC, where the voice of coanchor Harry Reasoner was commenting on the day's events.

The ABC anchor had just announced the arrival of the President at the Capitol when the picture abruptly cut out. A flash of hissing static was followed by a test pattern. This lasted only a few seconds before ABC's two anchormen appeared on-screen, assuring viewers that the technical difficulties from Washington would be fixed quickly.

Smith allowed himself a flicker of hope.

He had turned on the TV to watch for Remo or Master Chiun. Damage control for CURE would depend on what played out at the Capitol today. This was the first real stroke of good fortune in a dismal affair.

Leaning forward, Smith switched to CBS, then to NBC. As he had suspected, the networks were using a single camera feed from the Capitol Building. There was a total blackout from within the building itself.

On NBC they were playing tape of the arrival of the President's motorcade, already a few minutes old. The footage focused on the chief executive himself, not on his entourage. Smith didn't see Remo or Chiun anywhere.

Perhaps things weren't as bleak as they had seemed. America was overdue for a change in luck.

With a flutter of cautious optimism, Harold W. Smith reached for his bowl of yogurt.

"WHERE DID YOU disappear to?" Remo asked as the Master of Sinanju padded up beside him.

They were inside the Capitol. Chiun had vanished as soon as the motorcade stopped at the steps outside.

"My emperor has made clear his desire to remain anonymous until the time of his ascendance to the throne," the Oriental said. "I have seen to our anonymity."

Remo wasn't sure what the old man meant. He wondered if it had anything to do with the group of agitated newspeople who seemed to be arguing at the periphery of the crowd and pointing up at the lone camera in the gallery.

As men worked around the camera, Remo returned his attention to the floor of the rotunda.

The President had not invoked privilege, insisting that he join the line like the rest of the mourners. He moved along with a small group of congressmen. Two Secret Service agents pretending to be civilians remained near the chief executive. The rest had fanned out throughout the rotunda.

Remo's entire body was coiled with nervous energy. He and Chiun stood away from the line. The younger man's eyes were skipping carefully from mourner to mourner.

If a killer was there, Remo couldn't see him. Neither his police instincts nor his crash-course CURE training in how to spot a criminal seemed to be working very well. As far as he could tell, the only one who looked like he had something to hide was the President of the United States.

"You really think they'll strike here?" Remo whispered.

"Yes," Chiun replied.

"You seem pretty damned sure."

Chiun didn't turn. "I am the Master of Sinanju."

"Right. Any last-minute pointers?"

Chiun nodded, tufts of white hair bobbing above his ears. "Actually, there is something that might be useful to you," he said, face etched in stone, "since, after all, it is you who is going to stop the actual attack."

Remo blinked. "Me? I thought we were partners here."

Chiun gave him a withering look.

"Knock that off," Remo said. "You were supposed to help. That's why Upstairs sent you down here."

"Stop whining, "Chiun said. "I intend to help by keeping you alive long enough to die another day." He took a deep breath, as if reaching some great internal decision. "You are not of Sinanju. I do not fault you for this, for you could no more alter the circumstances of your own birth than you could control the pasty paleness of your skin. As an outsider, you ordinarily would not be privy to the tales of my ancestors. For what I am about to tell you, know that I am breaking a long-standing tradition.''

Despite the insults, Remo felt a sense of momentousness emanating from the tiny figure beside him. As if some great line had been crossed, some hidden chamber door opened. There was an importance to the moment that Remo couldn't seem to quite understand. Yet he felt it to his marrow.

''I'm honored,'' Remo said after a pause. He almost said the words ''Little Father.'' He didn't know why. As an orphan, he had never had a true father.

Chiun glanced around, as if checking to make certain the ghosts of his disapproving ancestors weren't hovering nearby.

''Once upon a time—'' the old Korean began.

The mood broke.

''You've got to be kidding me,'' Remo interrupted.

''Listen, idiot,'' Chiun snapped. ''It is important. Once upon a time there was a Master of Sinanju named Bang…''

THEY WERE IN the village of Sinanju. Gulls played in the misty updrafts above the rocky shore.

''Now Bang was a Master of the early order,'' the Master of Sinanju intoned, ''before the New Age of the Sun Source.''

As he began the tale of his ancestor, he kept a sad eye on one seagull as it floated and fell in the cold air.

It was plain that youth had begun to flee for the Reigning Master of the House of Sinanju. His once black hair was now the gray of old pewter. Streaks of white cascaded from the leading edge of his widening bald spot.

In the village they whispered that it was the death of his son, Song, that had aged this Master before his time. The strength and speed were still there, but the vitality had been sapped from him that day he carried his first pupil back from Mount Paektusan. The villagers hoped that this new pupil, the son of the Master's brother, would return life to the hollowed-out shell of the Master, for the people relied on the rapidly aging fool for their very sustenance.

The pupil who would one day cause his teacher great shame sat cross-legged at the Master's feet.

The eyes of the little boy were similar to his uncle's, yet there was a quiet cunning deep within them. Even at the tender age of eight, there was a hint—ever so slight—of the twisted path the student would one day take. On some level the Master saw it. Always knew it to be there. But grief and urgency and history suppressed his better judgment.

"Now in the time of Bang there was not one Master and one pupil, as is the case now. While Bang was head of the village and could alone claim the title Master of Sinanju, he had many students, called night tigers. So feared were these night tigers of Sinanju throughout the world that Bang rarely found it necessary to venture from the village. When men came from far-off shores to hire the skills of Sinanju, Bang simply dispatched an underling to handle the duties. Some of these night tigers were not fully trained and on occasion lost their lives to sword or stone, but that mattered not to Bang. If one died in the line of duty, he simply sent another. And so Bang spent nearly his entire Masterhood in Sinanju, content to grow old in pursuit of a leisurely life.

"Now Bang had a son called Shik whose wife had

given him a son. Bang was greatly joyed with this child, and loved his grandson with all his heart. He doted on the boy, carrying him on his shoulders when he walked through the village and holding his tiny hand as they skipped stones across the waters of the West Korean Bay. All seemed perfect for Master Bang and he fully expected to remain rooted in the village of his birth, watching his beloved grandson grow to manhood and one day succeed him as Master of Sinanju. But the gods find ways to frustrate those who plan their future with certainty.

"In this time which, although not official, could be considered Bang's retirement, a Chinese warlord did choose to challenge Sinanju. This warlord had raised a mighty army, which was encamped around his mountain stronghold. When neighbors hired one of Bang's night tigers to send against the warlord, the warlord's army slew Bang's young student. Another night tiger was sent off, only to meet the same fate. And so it was that several were dispatched and all were killed, for they had been trained to fight men, not armies.

"Although the House was young, Sinanju was already feared and respected. Even in his dotage, Bang eventually realized that Sinanju's reputation was at stake. Only the Master himself could hope to defeat the Chinese warlord. The day he left Sinanju, his grandson came with him to the shore road at the edge of the village and waved to the old man until he vanished from sight. And Bang did go to China, and there he did meet with success, which is what the world always expects from the Master of Sinanju.

"While Bang was away plying his art, emissaries of a Babylonian prince who wished to hire the services of Sinanju arrived in the village. Since the Master was away, the men were given lodging and told to await his return. Unbeknownst to all, the visitors had brought with them a great fever. Before anyone knew what was happening, the strangers had died, one by one. The disease quickly spread to the people of Sinanju and many in the village succumbed. Sadly, the final victim was the grandson of the Master of Sinanju.

"When Bang returned from China, he found the village in ruins. Those homes where sickness had claimed many victims had been burned to the ground. Curls of black smoke brushed the sky like twisting serpents. The streets were thick with the stench of death. Some of the villagers were there to meet him upon his return. Bang anxiously searched the crowd for only one face. But the moment he saw his son, Shik, Bang knew the terrible truth. His precious grandson had been sent home to the sea. Here is his last resting place."

The Master of Sinanju paused in his tale. With a slender hand he gestured to the black water of the West Korean Bay. Frothy foam licked the shore.

His nephew seemed unmoved by the story, as was usual for the stone-faced boy. This cold child was never affected by even the most heartrending tales. He looked out blankly across the waves before returning his gaze to his uncle.

The old man continued.

"Bang grieved the loss of his young grandson. He blamed himself for the child's death. If he had only gone to China immediately after the death of the first night tiger, as he should have, he would have been back in time to recognize the sickness in the Babylonian emissaries. Had he not gone at all, the same would have been true. After the death of his grandson, Master Bang was racked with grief and guilt. So anguished was he that he made a grave misjudgment.

"In a mud hut at the edge of Sinanju lived a crazed old shaman. The man claimed to be an Immortal of the Gods, one of time and not of time. In his youth he had studied the arts of dark magic in China and Egypt. Now in his old age, his days were spent communicating with the dead and dispensing potions of love. It was to this shaman's door that Bang came, weeping at his great loss.

"Now the shaman was a wicked man. It was well known that his own son, who was a lesser night tiger, coveted the title of Master of Sinanju. For years in the firelight of their squalid home had both men—the shaman and his son—plotted the death of Bang. This was known to Bang, yet in his grief he did not care. He pleaded with the shaman to use all the powers of his black magic to restore his grandson to life. When the wicked shaman agreed, hope touched Bang's grieving breast. Bang returned to the House of Many Woods, which was home to the Reigning Master. And there he waited.

"For days Bang was given reports of the shaman's progress. The magician toured the village burning incense and sprinkling sacred herbs. He followed the path down to the shore where the boy's body had been thrown into the bay. He sat on the stones and chanted at the cold sea. When night fell, he remained. When the morning sun rose, it found him unmoving. After a week of chanting and meditation, the shaman returned to the village in triumph. With an entourage that grew larger as he passed through the village, he went to the House of Many Woods and knocked on the door.

"When Bang answered, there was great hope on his aged face. 'You have succeeded?' Master Bang asked. And the words of the shaman filled his heart with joy. 'I have, Master of Sinanju. The body of your son's son was asleep. With my arts have I awakened him.'

"And the shaman did clap his hands. A basket was brought forward, carried by the shaman's evil son. Tightly woven from the reeds of the bay, it was large enough to hold a child. With great reverence was it placed on the Master's knees. When the hands of the shaman's son retreated, Master Bang felt the basket on his lap move. Something within it did indeed live. Elated, Master Bang tore off the lid of the basket. But sadly the movement came not from a child.

"From deep in the basket snapped a coiling asp, which the shaman had discovered on his travels to Egypt. Before Bang could move, white fangs sank deep in the Master's hand. Another asp struck out and bit Bang on the throat.

"In a younger day, not distracted by grief, having not just returned from a long and arduous trip, Bang might have sensed the snakes. He might have had speed to avoid them. He might even have had strength to fight the poison. But, woe to Bang, it was all too much. For the anguished old Master, the end came quickly. Lying down in the dust before his home, Bang breathed his last.

"Once the Master was dead, the shaman did turn to the crowd and in a loud voice did he lay claim to the title of Master of Sinanju for his own son. But, lo, before either man could enter the Master's house, a figure of dark menace did explode from the shadowy door. Too late had Shik arrived on the scene to save his father. But with hands made blinding fast by fury he did slay the wicked shaman and the treacherous night tiger—which was not a shameful thing for him to do, for this was before the time when Masters swore an oath not to raise a hand against other villagers. And he did curse the family of the shaman and he banished them to the mud hut at the edge of the village, where to this day they continue to mix their potions and work their spells, some say in the hope of finally bringing to fruition the plot that failed the first shaman all those years ago.''

By the time the Master of Sinanju finished the story of Bang, the sun was setting brilliant orange, burning fire across the bloodred bay.

''Do you know who it was that killed Bang, the true Master of Sinanju?'' he asked his pupil.

''Yes, Master,'' Nuihc replied.

The Reigning Master of Sinanju nodded. ''All was not lost on that long ago day. In fact it was a beginning. A year later Shik's wife bore him another son. The boy became a Master in his own right and it was he who fathered the Great Wang, founder of the modern line of Masters of Sinanju. Shik's banishment of the shaman's descendents was lifted by a succeeding Master.'' The old man's harsh countenance grew soft. ''The past is what it is and cannot be changed. Remember, young Nuihc, the sins of his fathers do not transfer to the son. Every man has it in him to be more than what the world thinks he is supposed to be.''

Even at such a young age, the words spoke to the

soul of the youth who sat at the feet of his foolish Master.

"I understand, Uncle," replied Nuihc, speaking truthfully. And he smiled. For in his heart he understood all too well.

NUIHC PROWLED the steps of the U.S. Capitol Building like a ghostly shadow.

No one noticed the Oriental in the neat black suit who—despite the vast morning crowd—somehow always seemed to be in those spots where no one else was.

Nuihc felt the confidence of victory coursing through his veins. His uncle's slavish devotion to the legends of Sinanju would be his downfall.

The legend of Bang. His uncle only saw its significance as it related to Nuihc. He never realized that he himself—Chiun, the last Master of Sinanju of the New Age—had, in his dying years, *become* Bang.

Chiun was the foolish old Master from that tale. He would assume that Nuihc was copying Bang's death. The threat to the President therefore would come from the basket. So devoted was he to history that he would never expect it to be improved upon. The true threat was not from within. While his uncle wasted time on a diversion, the President would march into the lion's jaws. By the time Chiun realized what was happening, the President would be dead and Nuihc would be gone. With his failure the feeble old Master would return home forever. A pathetic, hollow disgrace.

Nuihc smiled at the thought. And in his head he counted down the seconds to the final humiliation of his hated uncle.

"WELL?" the Master of Sinanju said once he had finished relating the tale of Bang to his American pupil. "Do you see why I have told you the story of my ancestor?"

Remo thought deeply. "I'm not sure. Guy's name was Bang." A thought popped into his head. "You think they're gonna try to blow up the Capitol?"

Chiun's eyes were flat. "Make this easier for me, Remo," he said aridly. "Just how stupid *aren't* you?"

"That's not it? Too bad. By the looks of it, most of Congress is here today. Okay, I give up. The guy had a basket and pulled a switcheroo. Stuck a snake inside instead of what Bang expec—" His voice broke off. "Oh."

With a sinking feeling Remo turned his gaze to the twin coffins in the middle of the rotunda.

The President was nearly to the gleaming coffins, inching along with his fellow politicians. And as the line of men reached the base of Senator Pierce's coffin, Remo saw the lid begin to lift quietly open.

For an instant it was like an image from some Saturday-afternoon Vincent Price horror movie. All similarities to Hollywood fiction ended when the gun barrel poked into view.

The world seemed to trip into slow motion.

Remo was twenty yards away. Too far to save the President's life. He had to try. He started at a sprint.

Confusion already gripped the line of mourners. A woman's scream. Men stumbling, falling to get out of the way.

The President was in the line of fire. Startled, locked in place with nowhere to go. No one to save him.

A flash of yellow. An explosion from the coffin.

A blue blur to Remo's right. Simultaneous with the gunshot.

The President buckling, dead. A clean chest shot. No way he could survive. No way Remo could stop the gunman before he fired even more rounds into the chief executive.

But in the moment that should have been precursor to yet another period of national mourning, Remo Williams witnessed an actual, honest-to-God miracle.

The blue flash that had passed by him as he ran somehow caught up with the first yellow flash. It was as if a hiccup in time itself had formed around the United States Capitol.

Remo's eyes had an impossible time reconciling the image. The President wasn't buckling over from a bullet wound. He was being grabbed around the waist by the blue blur, which Remo now knew to be the Master of Sinanju.

Time caught up to Remo's slow-motion vision.

Chiun flung America's chief executive from the path of the impotent ball of hurtling lead. The President landed in a crush of converging Secret Service agents.

"See to the boom-shooter!" Chiun commanded back over his shoulder.

The Secret Service shielded the President's body and began hurrying him to the planned exit. With sharp slaps and harsh words, Chiun redirected them deep into the bowels of the Capitol Building.

For the gunman in the coffin there was no longer any pretense of stealth.

Alphonso "Rail" Ravello had missed the President, missed his chance to be remembered with history's great assassins. Roaring with rage and shame, Ravello flung the upper coffin lid wide and began firing wildly into the scattering crowd.

People ran screaming in every direction.

A congressman was hit in the shoulder and spun like a top, sliding to a blood-streaked stop on the polished floor. A woman who had come from Maryland with her two small children was struck in the leg as she tried to flee. Men dragged her to safety.

Ravello killed another man who was running toward him. At least he thought he did.

He shot the man, but for some reason the man didn't fall. He kept running, a look of doom in his deep-set eyes.

Enraged, Ravello fired again. And missed once more.

As Alphonso Ravello fired again and again, the figure kept charging. Somehow he seemed to be everywhere and nowhere. Skittering left and right as he ran. By the time the specter arrived at the side of the coffin, Ravello had only one bullet left. But it didn't matter, because his gun was no longer in his hands. He sat there, dazed in his coffin, hands empty, looking up into those deep, dead eyes.

Alphonso Ravello shook his head in incomprehension.

"I missed the President," he lamented. "I *can't* miss. I was supposed to be remembered forever."

"And I was supposed to be Sky King," Remo Williams commiserated coldly. "That's the biz, sweetheart."

Planting the barrel of the gun far back in the gunman's mouth, Remo pulled the trigger. A stew of brain and blood splattered the inside satin lid of the coffin.

Remo tossed the gun into the coffin and slammed the lid.

He regretted using a weapon. Guns always used to make him feel safer. Now for some reason they just felt wrong.

Remo was turning, searching for the Master of Sinanju, when he noticed something out of the corner of his eye.

Twelve feet away across the floor of the rotunda, the second coffin lid was squeaking slowly open.

"Geez, Louise," Remo groused.

Marching over, he planted his fist through the opening lid. In training he had practiced this stroke with Chiun on birch trees on the grounds of Folcroft. The coffin wood surrendered even easier than a birch trunk.

The lid slammed down, and Remo's hand buried deep in something soft and squishy. There was a fatal sigh and a sickly gurgle from within. Remo pulled his hand free.

"And don't come out till I tell you," he snapped.

That was that. He had stopped the attempted assassination. Now it was just a matter of going back to New York and taking out the man responsible for this madness.

Flushed with success, Remo was turning when he felt something beside him. A sudden displacement of air.

This was something he had worked on in training—to sense an opponent. But he was years away from mastering the technique, years away from proficiency in anything but the rudiments of the perfection that was Sinanju. He had seen but a hint of dawn, was blind still to the hidden sun.

And then his own limitations no longer mattered.

The air moved and so did Remo. Up and over the coffin in a flash of brilliant white light that enveloped his brain before coalescing into a single dot of pure energy. It sparked once, then collapsed to black oblivion.

When Remo hit the cold floor, he did not move.

THE FIRST THING Nuihc saw was the coffins.

Something was wrong. He knew it when the Secret Service had not hustled out the President by their pre-ordained route.

He saw the hole in the right coffin. It curved in the half-moon shape of a human hand.

Screaming, tripping, crying, the crowd had streamed out the exits. The rotunda was empty.

Nuihc was alone.

No. Not alone. He hadn't seen him. Only saw him now because he chose to be seen.

A grave miscalculation. He was old, but not weak. It had been years since he'd seen him. He assumed that his powers would have begun to ebb. An understandable mistake. A deadly one in their line of work.

Chiun stood between the coffins. His eyes were slivers of haunting accusation. The Reigning Master of Sinanju made not a move to his former pupil.

For what seemed an eternity they faced each other, Master and student. Old and young.

Chiun's gaze never wavered. Nuihc tried to offer only malice to his former teacher. But for the younger Sinanju Master, there was suddenly something else.

Another, alien emotion buried beneath the arrogant surface.

Without a word Nuihc turned to go.

Chiun's mouth thinned. The aged Korean's entire being was a compressed fist of fury. As his traitorous pupil offered his back, Chiun raised one sandaled foot, dropping it hard to the marble floor. And when the thunder came, the very dome of the Capitol Building trembled with fear.

"Hold, wicked one!" the Master of Sinanju commanded.

Nuihc froze. When he turned, the emotion he had hidden a moment before had bubbled to the surface. A look of fear flashed through his hazel eyes.

"You are not supposed to be here," Nuihc said. Blood pounded in his ears. "The world has passed you by, old man. Why are you here and not in your precious Sinanju?"

"You dare ask?" Chiun demanded. "You? You would ask me why I am about my business of feeding and clothing my village? The village you abandoned in your arrogance?"

"Then you are about your business and I am about mine," Nuihc said. "Leave me to mine."

"And what business is that, traitor?" Chiun's tufts of white hair swirled angrily around his bald scalp. "Here, child of evil. Here is your handiwork." He waved a bony hand at the coffins. "I should embowel you and hurl your worthless carcass into these boxes, a feast for the bugs and worms."

Another flash of fear.

"You would not kill me," Nuihc challenged. "You are forbidden to harm one of the village."

"The village of Sinanju ceased being yours the day

you turned your back on your obligations. And do not think I do not know all you are doing, pitiful, transparent creature that you are. You knew I had come to these shores. Did you think I did not know your lackeys brought you pictures of me from the hospital? Since Sinanju gravitates to greatness, you assumed I worked for the leader of this nation. You thought killing my charge would shame me into retreating to Sinanju. Once more you prove yourself the fool. The man you failed to kill this day is but a public face. I work for the power behind the throne. True Sinanju seeks out strength, not celebrity. How typical of you, worthless one. Pitiful student that you were, you followed only the dictates of your true masters. The masters of avarice, envy and pride. You never understood that there are forces driving this world that go far beyond what the eye sees or the ear hears."

And at Chiun's words, Nuihc did something that surprised even the Master of Sinanju. He smiled.

"Yes," Nuihc said, his voice suddenly low and cold. "There are forces that were unknown to me in Sinanju."

There was a sudden confidence in his nephew's voice. As if he hid some powerful, terrible secret. Whatever it was suddenly brought quiet assuredness to the younger Oriental.

Chiun's leathery face was impassive.

"The time of my seclusion has passed," he intoned. "I am back in the world, duck droppings. Know you fear."

Their meeting was done. Nuihc nodded.

"I await the day, old man," the younger man spat.

And with that he was gone. Out the doors through which the crowd had swarmed minutes before.

There were still the sounds of confusion outside. Sirens were approaching. The Capitol police would be back inside soon, along with the D.C. police.

Once he was certain Nuihc had left, the Master of Sinanju hurried over to the spot where Remo had landed.

He found his pupil where he'd thrown him in order to protect him from Nuihc. Remo was unconscious behind Senator O'Day's coffin. For an instant, Chiun feared his pupil was dead, but the heartbeat was there.

Chiun didn't know why he should care. But in spite of himself, his relief was great.

It was Nuihc's fault. Nuihc, who had been given everything and cast it all away. Here was this foreigner who was more of a pupil than Nuihc ever was. A white—worse, an American—who accepted the wisdom of Chiun's ancestors as if the blood of Wang coursed through his pale veins.

Nuihc. Nuihc was to blame. If he hadn't been such a bad pupil, Chiun never would have felt such relief when he found this Remo person with the nasty tongue was still alive.

Remo's eyes fluttered open. "What happened?"

"You did what you vowed you would do," Chiun replied gently. "You saved the day."

"Really?"

Chiun's face soured. "Of course not, idiot. I did." He kicked Remo to get him to his feet. "Now, let's get out of here before someone sees us and thinks I am with you."

28

Don Carmine Viaselli was watching television when he first heard about the attempt on the life of the President of the United States. When he heard that Alphonso Ravello was the gunman, he coughed seltzer and lemon onto his carpet.

"What the hell?" he spluttered at the TV.

The answer to his question came not from the network news anchor, but from his own living room.

"It is an unfortunate cost of doing business," came the thin voice from beside his sofa.

Viaselli whipped around.

Nuihc stood at silent attention. His hooded eyes watched the TV. He didn't even look at Don Viaselli.

"What was Ravello doing there?" Viaselli demanded. His face was caved in. He was finding it hard to breathe. "You were supposed to do it quiet, not use one of my guys."

"It was necessary," Nuihc said.

With shaking hands Don Viaselli put down his drink.

"Ravello was a loaner to you. He was one of mine. Everybody and his brother knows it. Goddamn it, you throw him out into the middle of all this, and everybody knows I'm connected."

"That is true," Nuihc said, nodding. "The man who hired me will be pleased with this outcome."

"The man who hired you?" Viaselli asked. "*I'm* the man who hired you! I've paid you a fortune this past year."

"As has he," Nuihc replied. "A tidy sum for which I should thank you both. Unfortunately, you could not be told about my other employer, since the arrangement I made with him involved your being directly tied to the assassination attempt on your President."

"What!" Viaselli exclaimed.

A few rooms away there came a pounding at the apartment door. The sound of shattering wood was followed by the panicked shout of a maid. Don Viaselli wheeled on the sound.

"The cost of doing business," Nuihc was saying. As the voices closed in, he was already fading back into the shadows.

"You son of a bitch!" Viaselli screamed.

The Mafia Don jumped for an end-table drawer.

When the FBI agents burst into the living room ten seconds later they found a wide-eyed Carmine Viaselli screaming in Italian and shooting at shadows.

They didn't bother to ask the New York Don what he thought he was shooting at. Instead, they returned fire.

And in the ensuing, brief gun battle, merry little bits of Don Carmine Viaselli splattered against the tidy walls of the apartment like hurled tomatoes.

THE VISITOR WAS politely ushered back to the private office on the first floor of the Neighborhood Improvement Association building in Little Italy.

The building was old and solid enough to withstand a mortar blast from the street. The wallpaper was purple and fuzzy. The crazy floral pattern was interwoven with vines that looked like coiling serpents. An aroma of tomato sauce clung to the old wood paneling.

In the office a thin man who looked older than his sixty years sat behind a broad desk. At his elbow a brown paper bag stained with grease sat on a newspaper. The grease had melted into the front page, bleeding across the banner headline announcing the attempt on the President's life.

When the door was closed and his visitor stood before the desk, Pietro Scubisci smiled a row of yellow teeth.

"You done good work," Scubisci said. "Me and my Family been waiting for a chance. But that Carmine, he's stubborn, you know? I been in this game longer than him. He's just a kid, but I have to play second fiddle. That kind of thing eats at you after a while."

He pulled an ancient ledger out of his top drawer and began carefully writing out a check.

"You don't know what that's like, do you?" Scubisci asked as he wrote. "Always coming in second. Always having to smile and nod when in your heart you know you're better. Sometimes you gotta make your own changes. A push here and there to see things finally go your way."

He tore the check out and slid it across the desk.

"A good year's work, I'd say," Pietro Scubisci said. "You thinned out Carmine's soldiers. Can't believe he let you do that. Musta felt safe with you around, you know? The Viaselli Family's dead. I try to take over from Carmine, we woulda had a war.

This way it's bloodless.'' He smiled. ''Well, my blood's where it's supposed to be, anyhow.''

On the opposite side of the desk, Nuihc said nothing. He picked up the check without looking at it, slipping it into the pocket of his suit coat.

''I added a little to what we agreed on,'' Pietro Scubisci said, clicking his pen and setting it neatly into a drawer along with the ledger. ''You earned it. I just got off the phone with a friend in the police. They said Carmine tried to shoot it out with the Feds. They'll be sponging brains off the ceiling for a month. Don't know how you worked that, but good job.

''Now we cool off for a while. That was Carmine's problem. No patience. I sat behind him long enough to develop plenty of patience. A Senate committee coming to town and he goes all to pieces. Let 'em come now. We'll be quiet while they're here. They find nothing, they go back to Washington. They go, we're back in business.''

He looked up with rheumy eyes for a hint of agreement from his guest. Without a word Nuihc turned for the door.

''Hey,'' called Don Pietro Scubisci, the new head of the New York Mafia. ''You innerested in a full-time job?''

But the Oriental hit man was already gone.

29

"So it would seem Alphonso Ravello was the second Viaselli Family enforcer," Smith explained.

The CURE director had come down to Chiun's quarters to meet with Remo. He wasn't comfortable with using his office. While Miss Purvish seemed to have accepted the cover story of Remo and Chiun as Folcroft nurse and patient, she remained too inquisitive. Smith was thinking it was time to replace her. He was leaning toward Miss Hazlitt or the Mikulka woman, both of whom seemed competent in the job.

"The FBI found three watches smuggled into the Capitol inside the coffin with Ravello," Smith continued. "He had apparently gathered them as souvenirs from the three senators he murdered. His record indicated that he was a low-level functionary in the Viaselli organization. But obviously he was operating under everyone's radar, for clearly the data gathered on him was incorrect. It took a particular sort of genius to come up with such a diabolical assassination plot."

"You say genius, I say lunatic," Remo said. He was sitting cross-legged on the floor. It wasn't as easy as Chiun made it look, but his knees were starting to get the hang of it.

"In the white world the two are indistinguishable,"

the Master of Sinanju mumbled in Korean. The old Oriental was across the common room, busying himself at the small stove, seemingly uninterested in Smith's words.

Chiun wasn't about to tell Smith the truth about who had been the mastermind behind the presidential assassination plot. Internal Sinanju matters were not open to prying eyes.

"Excuse me, Master Chiun?" Smith asked.

"Nothing, Emperor Smith," Chiun replied. "Words of praise from an unworthy. Please continue."

"What about the other coffin?" Remo asked.

"Just another minor Viaselli Family player. Our records indicate he was mostly a numbers runner."

"And we all know what a bang-up job your records did finding out about the maniac-in-a-box," Remo said.

"Yes," Smith said unhappily. "I will have to look into our method of gathering data. In any case, apparently Carmine Viaselli had been growing increasingly paranoid of late. Possibly a result of the agents I had placed in the field over the past few months. His maid even heard him make a threat against the President. She said that he was talking out loud a great deal lately. Having whole conversations with an empty room."

"So in a way you're the one who drove him to it," Remo observed. "Maybe if you'd left him alone instead of dogging him like you were doing, he wouldn't have snapped and sent that Ravioli guy after the President at all."

Smith fidgeted in his hard-backed chair. Leaning

forward, he pitched his voice low enough that he assumed the Master of Sinanju could not hear.

"Remo, it was suggested from on high for CURE to clean up the Viaselli organization before the Senate got here and, if possible, to remove its enforcer."

"Ever been to Nuremberg, Smith?" Remo asked dully.

"As a matter of fact, yes," the CURE director replied. He forged ahead. "As for the Viaselli matter, it worked out better than I could have hoped, considering the difficulty we encountered. Not only have we put an end to the enforcement branch of the criminal empire, which was our original mission, but Carmine Viaselli is dead and his organization is in ruins. And we've accomplished this without our being implicated. All in all, a job well done."

"And only one of us had to die to get us over the finish line. Rah-rah, team."

Smith's jaw tightened. "Remo, Conrad MacCleary died in the line of duty. I would rather it had been me, but that isn't the hand we were dealt. And the sacrifice he made was one that many patriots have made before him. America is worth a life. He believed that to his core. What's more, he was my friend and he will be sorely missed."

Remo thought he heard a crack in the older man's voice. He was surprised. From what he'd seen, the only friends Smith had were his spreadsheets and filing cabinets.

"The President sends his thanks," Smith continued. "And to you, Master Chiun."

The Master of Sinanju had just padded over from the kitchen area with a bone-china cup of steaming tea. He sank to the floor, balancing cup and saucer on one knee.

"Watch out for that one, Emperor Smith," he warned. "If you will accept the council of a lowly servant, I suggest you seize power now. That shifty-eyed puppet President is up to no good. Say the word and I will present you his perspiring head. For a nominal fee, of course. After all, we haven't yet signed a proper contract."

"No, thank you," Smith said, coughing uncomfortably. "That won't be necessary. However, we do need to discuss a more long-term contract for Remo's training, if you wish to stay on." He quickly changed the subject. "About your living conditions. You may stay at Folcroft for the time being, on one condition. Obviously, we cannot allow another situation like the one involving the orderly."

"Obviously," Chiun agreed, sipping tea.

"Good," Smith said. "Then we're in agreement."

"Why would we not be?" Chiun asked, baffled that they should even need to discuss the matter.

"No reason," Smith said, relieved. "No reason. Good."

Remo shook his head. "He's not agreeing that he won't kill anyone else who gets in the way of his TV, Smith," he said with a sigh. "He's agreeing that he can't allow it to happen. As in, TV gets interrupted, orderly assumes room temperature. Isn't that right, Chiun?"

"Of course," the Master of Sinanju said. He rolled his eyes at his dense pupil who insisted on stating the obvious.

"I see," Smith said slowly. "On second thought perhaps it would be wiser to relocate the two of you from the premises. I will compile a list of hotels. Excuse me.'' He headed for the door.

''Four stars or better!'' Remo hollered as the CURE director left the room. Once they were alone, he turned to the Master of Sinanju. ''Okay, care to tell me what or who knocked me out like a light down in D.C.?''

''No,'' Chiun said blandly. ''Would you care to tell me why you embarrassed me in front of Smith's puppet ruler with that shoddy performance?''

''Nope,'' Remo said. He folded his arms and inhaled deeply. ''Guess that makes us even.''

At this Chiun cackled. ''Even? Heh-heh-heh. *You* even with *me?* That makes us even. Heh-heh-heh. Even.''

Remo felt his good mood dissipate. ''Okay, jolly joker, how long till we *are* even?''

Chiun placed cup and saucer on the floor. He tipped his head in serious concentration.

''For an exceptional Master, trained from birth, thirty to forty years. For you, there are not numbers high enough to measure without inventing new ones.'' He shook his head, cackling once more as he rose to his feet. ''That makes us even. You and I. Heh-heh-heh.''

''If you think I'm putting up with abuse from you for thirty years, you're crazy,'' Remo mumbled as the Master of Sinanju disappeared, still chuckling, inside his room.

''You should be so lucky,'' a squeaky voice called back.

EPILOGUE

He brought the boy to the Caribbean, to the French-Dutch island of Saint Martin. There was a safe place there, a ruined castle on a craggy black rock called Devil's Mountain.

The castle had been built by a merchant from Holland two hundred years before.

The natives were superstitious. When they saw the young boy with the blond hair and the pale blue eyes, they assumed the ghost of the merchant had returned to haunt his castle.

They called the boy the Dutchman.

Nuihc didn't care what name they gave him. The boy didn't deserve a name. He was nothing more than a tool. An instrument that would be used to further his own ambitions.

The fallen Master of Sinanju stood on the stone balcony. Behind him, doors opened on the great hall. Yellow fire leaped high in the six-foot fireplace.

After events in America, Nuihc realized this would take longer than he had anticipated. His uncle was as strong as ever. Even stronger, perhaps, than he was before.

Training Nuihc hadn't restored the vitality that Chiun had lost after the death of his son. But for some reason, all these years later, on a distant shore, a spark had been ignited in the old man's eyes. Nuihc didn't know what had put it there, but he saw it clearly in Washington.

It was plain to him now that his uncle, like the traditions of Sinanju, would not be easy to kill.

As Nuihc looked up at the warm night sky, he heard a soft sobbing behind him.

Time.

It took time to bleed a man's soul. But revenge had been brewing in his family for thousands of years.

Nuihc had the time.

More sobbing.

He glanced over his shoulder.

The Dutchman sat crying on the floor of the great hall. His face was slick with sweat, reflecting yellow firelight. Above him was a beautiful native girl of about fifteen. She had caught the boy's eye during a trip into town. The secret smile they had exchanged wasn't lost on Nuihc.

The girl was chained to the hearth. A rag was stuffed deep in her throat. Firelight glinted in her terrified eyes.

The boy wept at her feet.

He was obviously having trouble with the evening's exercises. The boy required instruction.

"Soon," Nuihc vowed to the stars.

Turning his back on the warm night, he disappeared inside the castle.

*   *   *   *   *

Don't miss the exciting conclusion of
THE MASTER'S LINE.
Look for FATHER TO SON, on sale
October 2002.

James Axler
Outlanders®

DRAGONEYE

Deep inside the moon two ancient beings live on—the sole survivors of two mighty races whose battle to rule earth and mankind is poised to end after millennia of struggle and subterfuge. Now, in a final conflict, they are prepared to unleash a blood sacrifice of truly monstrous proportions, a heaven-shaking Armageddon that will obliterate earth and its solar system. At last Kane, Grant and Brigid Baptiste will confront the true architects of mankind: their creators…and now, ultimately, their destroyers.

In the Outlands, the shocking truth is humanity's last hope.

DEATH LANDS®

Amazon Gate

Available in
September 2002
at your favorite retail outlet.

Adventure and suspense in the midst of a new reality

JAMES AXLER

DEATH LANDS

Amazon Gate

In the radiation-blasted heart of the Northwest, Ryan and his companions form a tenuous alliance with a society of women warriors in what may be the stunning culmination of their quest. After years of searching, they have found the gateway belonging to the pre-dark cabal known as the Illuminated Ones—and perhaps their one chance to reclaim the future from the jaws of madness. But they must confront its deadly guardians: what is left of the constitutional government of the United States of America.

Stony Man is deployed against an armed invastion on American soil....

DEFENSIVE ACTION

A conspiracy to cripple a sophisticated antimissle system—and the United States itself—is under way, fueled by the twisted ideology of a domestic militia group. Their campaign against the government has gone global, their terrorist agenda refinanced and expanded by a cabal of America's enemies: North Korea, Russia and China. Crisscrossing the North American continent, Stony Man enters a desperate race against time to halt this act of attrition...before America pays the price in blood.

Available in August 2002 at your favorite retail outlet.
